LAST PLACE SEEN

ALESSANDRA HARRIS

Last Place Seen
Red Adept Publishing, LLC
104 Bugenfield Court
Garner, NC 27529
https://RedAdeptPublishing.com/

This is a work of fiction. Names, characters, places, and incidents either are the product of the author's imagination or are used fictitiously, and any resemblance to locales, events, business establishments, or actual persons—living or dead—is entirely coincidental.

---

1. http://StreetlightGraphics.com

For everyone who is caged, that they may find freedom

CHAPTER ONE

A familiar ache gripped Tiana's chest. Hand over her heart, she focused on the evening news reporting an Amber Alert for a missing ten-year-old. The small flat-screen television displayed a picture of an adorable brown-skinned girl with her hair in two braids, lighting up the screen with her smile.

Tiana leaned over and ruffled Marcus's curls while he stacked jumbo-sized red, green, and blue Legos. Jay bent forward on the worn gray sofa and turned up the volume. His elbow on his knee, he rested his chin on his fist and focused on the TV.

A reporter stood outside a big-box store. "The girl was separated from her mother at this Walmart in San Jose this afternoon and has not been seen since." Tiana wiped the sweat from her face. Though the oscillating fan provided a brief rush of relief every few seconds, the sweltering apartment's temperature hovered in the nineties.

Marcus pointed a chubby index finger at the TV. "Store, Dada."

Jay turned to Tiana. "Marcus and I were right there at that Walmart this afternoon. I heard them calling the girl's name over the intercom. Crazy."

She gasped. "Really? You didn't even mention you went to Walmart today. What did you get?" They didn't have an extra dollar to spend. She hoped he hadn't bought something else for Marcus. Their cramped two-bedroom apartment already overflowed with toys, board books, and toddler furniture.

Jay shrugged his broad shoulders. His navy tank top stuck to his body with the sweat that also glistened off his muscular golden-

1

brown shoulders. "I was supposed to meet Travis there to check out camping gear. Marcus and I looked at tents and stuff, but Travis didn't show. So I bought Marcus some fruit snacks, and we bounced. Didn't think twice about it."

Tiana arched her eyebrows. "You're planning a camping trip?" It sounded like an accusation. If anyone deserved a getaway, Tiana did. She put in sixty-hour workweeks and barely covered the bills-—not to mention her mama duties. She would have loved to escape to somewhere fun like Cabo San Lucas or even just Southern California for a weekend with her best friend, Ava. But she couldn't afford to take time off work, let alone the expense of travel and lodging.

"I wouldn't say 'planning.'" Jay locked his round brown eyes with Tiana's. "Travis has talked about us going camping for a weekend in Gilroy. I guess he and a group of guys go every summer. I hadn't committed to nothing yet. Just made a quick stop at Walmart before I took Marcus to the park with the water area. He loved it." Jay swiped his hand across his short black fade. "Running through the cold water felt so good. Marcus and I didn't mind wet clothes on the drive home."

Tiana started to say that Jay's only focus should be finding a job but held her tongue. She only had so much energy and wouldn't waste any stating the obvious. "That sounds nice. My mom's offered to pay for swimming lessons for Marcus at their athletic club. Maybe now is a good time to take her up on that offer." She turned to her two-year-old. "You wanna swim, Marky?"

Their trip to the pool at the beginning of June had started out enjoyable enough but quickly soured after they'd dunked Marcus's head underwater. He'd become so hysterical that they had to leave the pool altogether to calm him down. She regretted not acclimating him to the water as a baby, but her whole life had turned upside down the year before his birth. Single-handedly raising a newborn and staying afloat financially, physically, and emotionally had consumed her.

Marcus shook his curly-topped head. "No swim."

Jay chuckled. "I don't think we're quite ready for the pool yet. Buddy, let's clean up your toys and put on your pajamas before Mama comes in to put you to bed."

"No bed, Dada." Marcus continued stacking the plastic blocks.

Tiana kissed Marcus's chubby cheek. "'No' is your favorite word, huh?"

Marcus rubbed his eyes with both fists. "No."

"Cleanup time." Jay joined them on the floor. He tossed the Legos into Marcus's toy bin along with the other toys cluttering the alphabet rug in the small living room. They usually pushed the coffee table against the wall to free up space between the couch and TV stand. The open front door on the opposite side of the living room allowed a stubborn breeze to enter, but it wasn't enough for relief.

Tiana smiled as she stood, grateful Jay would assume the bad-guy role and get Marcus dressed for bed. To keep it as cool as possible, they had the lights off, and the waning sunlight left the apartment dim. The smell of the chicken-and-garlic-butter pasta dinner Jay had cooked hung in the air. Tiana trudged the twenty feet into the kitchen to wash the dishes.

She'd been in the apartment for almost two and a half years and still missed the dishwasher they'd had at their old house. This was the first time she'd lived in a home without the appliance, and in the middle of a heat wave, she couldn't decide which she wanted more, AC or a dishwasher. She followed that train of thought to a washer and dryer.

More and more frequently, she regretted her decision not to follow in her dad's footsteps and attend law school after she graduated from Stanford, which had been the family plan for most of her life. Instead, she'd opted to follow her passion and take an internship at a social media startup and had learned the hard way that passion didn't pay the bills. And especially not attorney fees.

Though Jay had set the fan above the stove on high while cooking, the vent didn't work well, and the kitchen felt like a deep fryer. As she scrubbed a pan, her mind drifted to the missing girl. Something about her seemed familiar. For decades, African-Americans only made up about two percent of San Jose, and even with over a million residents, there wasn't exactly a tight-knit Black community. Tiana didn't expect to know the girl or her family, but she would mention their last name to her parents, who had a lot of connections throughout the San Francisco Bay Area, and see if it rang a bell.

She startled when her husband wrapped his arms around her belly. "I didn't hear you sneak up on me."

Jay kissed her neck. "You look so serious. Everything okay?"

Tiana faced her husband and pecked his lips. "I was thinking about that poor little girl. Do you think someone kidnapped her?"

"I hope not." Jay clenched his jaw, and a dark shadow of fear narrowed his eyes. "Losing a child is a parent's worst nightmare."

"Yeah." She sighed and returned to her chore, dunking her hands in the warm soapy water to find more dishes as if bobbing for apples. "I'm almost done, so let me know when Marcus has his pj's on."

Jay cared for Marcus during the day, so Tiana shared a special one-on-one time bedtime ritual with Marcus every evening. Regardless of how drained she felt at times, she was grateful to have her family back together. Life would be easier once Jay found work—sooner rather than later, she hoped. Either way, Tiana needed to spend extra time loving on Marcus tonight. She cherished the child she still had. The memory of the one she'd lost would always haunt her.

CHAPTER TWO

Secondhand anxiety raced through Jay. Ending up at the same store at the same time as the girl who'd gone missing left him on edge. *What if that'd been Marcus?* He forced the thought away and tightened his grip on the laundry basket full of clean, lavender-scented clothes he carried back from the laundry room. He glanced to the sky above the dilapidated apartment complex. Smoke from the fire up north sullied the sunset, the burnt-orange sun descending for the evening like an employee clocking out after a long shift. The unrelenting heat remained. Though it was almost nine p.m., his weather app showed the temperature had only dropped to the low nineties.

Stepping back into their apartment felt like entering a sauna. Jay wanted to strip off his tank top and wrap a clean towel around his neck to catch the steady drip of sweat. He closed the screen door behind him but left the main door wide open.

Tiana's hushed voice as she read to Marcus traveled through the thin walls. He imagined the missing girl's parents returning home without their child, trapped in a nightmare, unable to wake up. That feeling was all too familiar to Jay. He'd been forced to miss nearly the first year and a half of Marcus's life—his son's first cry, first words, first steps, first hugs. He couldn't change the past, but he made every effort to make up for the lost time.

Jay shoved the coffee table in front of the couch and plopped the laundry basket down beside it. His phone vibrated in the back pocket of his shorts—probably Travis explaining why he hadn't shown. He pulled it out. Jay would tell him the camping trip was off. Tiana

5

clearly disagreed with the idea of him going away. Guilt nagged at him for wanting a weekend to himself. It was selfish, given how much Tiana did for them. Still, he couldn't pretend a weekend away hadn't appealed to him. Caring for a toddler nonstop left him craving adult interaction.

Instead of a message from Travis, a red notification alerted him to an email sent from the company where he'd interviewed last week. He sucked in a breath, opened the email, and read it aloud. "Thank you for your time. Unfortunately, we've decided to go in a different direction."

Dammit. Another no. Finding a job ranked highest on his list of priorities. Not contributing financially had an expiration date. He hated how hard Tiana had to work to support their household. Based on the way men eyed her when they went out together, plenty of them would have been more than happy to pick up Jay's slack. She was five-eight with long legs, a tight waist, an ample chest, and a beautiful face. Men shamelessly gawked at her even when Jay was there. He hated to think what they did in his absence.

Phone still in hand, Jay dialed Travis. After several rings, an automated message played. *What's up with that dude?* It wasn't like him to not show and ignore Jay's call.

He mentally traced back to his most recent interaction with Travis. They'd met a couple days before at the dive bar on two-dollar Tuesday like usual. Each had had a couple cheap beers as they cemented their plans to meet at Walmart. Jay hadn't actually planned to buy camping gear. Two-dollar beers were all he could afford—barely. *Did I piss him off somehow?* Jay scrolled through his texts. Travis had sent him one that morning to remind him to meet at three-thirty at Walmart. Then Jay had texted him when he'd arrived at the store. *Something must have come up.*

Tiana joined Jay in the living room and slumped on the couch next to him. The heat had painted her russet-brown cheeks red. She tucked her short, curly brown hair behind her ears. "Operation put-crabby-toddler-to-bed partially complete. He's fighting it. I don't blame him. This heat is irritating me too."

"Yeah, it is too hot to sleep." Jay squeezed Tiana's warm shoulder. Heat wave or not, he refused to complain. With a beautiful wife, a healthy son, a roof over their heads, and his freedom, Jay counted his blessings every day. "I had no idea south San Jose could get this hot. I want to stick my head in the freezer for half an hour."

"Why d'you think the rent is so much cheaper down here?" She huffed. "The further south, the higher the temperature in the Bay Area."

Born and raised forty minutes away in a rough neighborhood in Menlo Park, Jay had grown up before the tech behemoths like Facebook had invaded the town. What began as ideas in garages and on college campuses had morphed into companies gobbling up office space, jacking up the cost of living, and forcing Black and brown people out of town. On the eastern edge of San Mateo County, Menlo Park had become unrecognizable to Jay, completely unaffordable.

"Summer used to be my favorite season, but it gets hotter and hotter every year. Throw in the wildfires, and I'm completely over it. Let's move on to fall and pumpkin-spiced lattes already." Tiana wiped sweat that trickled down the side of her face away with the back of her hand.

Jay laughed. "You don't even drink those."

She chuckled. "I know, but it sounded good."

"A kiss also sounds good." He leaned toward her and pressed his lips against her full ones. Then he leaned back against the couch and took in his wife. Eyeliner defined her large almond-shaped eyes, and her nose sloped to a round end. Somehow, he found himself more in love with her every day.

For some unfathomable reason, she had stuck with him for six years, and they'd been married for five. She stayed even after the hell of the last three years and after he'd plead guilty to manslaughter. Jay daydreamed of ways he would make it all up to her. An all-inclusive trip to the Caribbean where they could lie out on the beach, sipping tropical drinks. Brand-new car to replace her beat-up old Honda. New place with every home appliance of her dreams. But none of that would happen until someone decided to take a chance on him and give him a job.

While Tiana scrolled on her phone, Jay plucked clothes out of the laundry basket and folded them. He hated feeling stuck at the dirt bottom of Silicon Valley. Even his salary at the last job he'd held for seven years hadn't caught up with the soaring costs of living in the area. He'd worked his way up from teller to junior home-loan consultant at Wells Fargo. For someone like him, who hadn't graduated college, making six figures was a dream come true. With a down payment from her parents, his job had even helped them purchase their first home four years before.

He shook his head. It hurt too much to think about how perfect life had been before they had to sell the house to pay restitution and attorneys.

"Dada!" Marcus screamed from down the hall.

Tiana started to push herself up, but Jay hopped to his feet. "Relax. I'll go."

She mouthed, *Thank you*, pure exhaustion etched on her heart-shaped face.

Jay walked the short hall crowded with framed family photographs and opened Marcus's door. "Hey, buddy. It's night-night time." A fan pushed the hot air around the small room that had a dresser, crib, and other toddler stuff crammed into it.

"No night-night, Dada," Marcus whined from a horizontal position, giving away his fatigue.

Jay leaned down into the crib and smoothed Marcus's curls. "Want me to tell you more story?"

Marcus kicked his feet with excitement. "Story, Dada."

Jay sat on a wooden stool in front of the short bookshelf and treasure-chest bin full of toys. He enjoyed the made-up, never-ending story he'd started when he'd come home six months before. It followed the life of a little boy, Kenny, who was a little older than Marcus. One night, Kenny had fallen asleep then awoke in a magical kingdom. As Jay's imagination worked overtime, he painted a picture of flying creatures, sorcerers, and a royal family. The perfect world vastly differed than the one he grew up in.

Family life had been utterly chaotic with Jay's dad, Walter, a real-life villain who continued to outdo himself with his cruelty toward Jay, his mother, and his younger brother, Xavier. Jay didn't want to give his dad any more credit but blamed the man for the ruinous state of his life.

Walter would be utterly disgusted if he knew Jay stayed home with Marcus. He always called anything to do with raising Jay and Xavier "women's work." Walter had expected Jay's mom to take care of everything related to them and demanded she put on a happy face while doing it, chauvinistic to a T.

Jay hated his father with absolute fury. He would never forgive Walter for what he had made Jay do.

When Marcus stopped egging Jay's story on with his exclamations, Jay stood and peered over the crib. In spite of pink cheeks and a hairline wet with sweat, Marcus had finally fallen asleep.

"Night, son. I love you," Jay whispered. Even though Jay needed a paying job, he appreciated the time he spent raising his son. *You'll get back on your feet. Promise yourself.* He nodded. He would stop at nothing to improve life for Tiana and Marcus.

CHAPTER THREE

Tiana patted the space next to her when Jay returned to the living room. He placed two beers on the coffee table, sat next to her, and wrapped his arms around her. "Why don't you put the news back on? Maybe there's an update that they found that girl. Once an Amber Alert goes out, it's cool how quick the community responds to find a missing kid."

She broke the hug and wiped sweat from her forehead. She couldn't wait for the heat wave to pass. "Good idea." She turned on the TV, hoping someone had found the girl. Tiana had texted her mom earlier, but her mom had said she didn't know the girl's family. She said the family lived in Oakland and were just shopping in San Jose.

Jay grabbed the beers off the coffee table and handed one to her. He kicked his feet up and pressed the cold can against his cheek. "I'm exhausted. Who knew a toddler could have so much energy? Guess he needs a little brother or sister to keep him company, huh?" He glanced sideways at her.

She shook her head. "You're kidding, right?" She'd been so tired and couldn't imagine ever having the energy to have another baby. More importantly, a lot would have to change in order for them to even broach the subject of another child.

"Yeah, I'm kidding. But not gonna lie—we made a good-looking little boy." His eyes lit up with pride.

She couldn't deny that. "He is adorable." Having another child wasn't off the table indefinitely. But she needed to make sure they could provide for their family before expanding it.

"Oh, look. It's your pops." Jay pointed to the screen.

"What's he up to now?" She leaned forward, chugging her cold beer.

Dressed in a black-pinstripe suit, her dad stood on the steps of a police station, surrounded by microphones. With his salt-and-pepper hair cut short and mustache perfectly trimmed, he looked well prepared for the press conference. "What happened in this case is not a tragedy. It's a crime." He projected authority and confidence that whoever had done wrong would be served justice.

Her dad had an impeccable record as a district attorney. He always gave an inexhaustible amount of time and attention to his cases.

"We are going to make sure that justice prevails."

The news anchor appeared on the screen. "That was Martin Moore, Alameda County District Attorney, at a press conference held this afternoon. Many remember Moore from the high-profile case in 2010, when he successfully prosecuted the man who attempted to bomb a historical Black church in Vallejo. Since then, he's worked on cases ranging from hate crimes to criminal gangs. Moore spoke about the ongoing trial of three college students charged with the brutal beating and murder of another student at Merritt College. They have also been charged with committing a hate crime. Next, we turn to the wildfire raging in Yountville, a small town less than twenty miles from Napa."

Tiana switched the channel to an entertainment gossip show. She'd had enough of lawyers and the criminal justice system to last a lifetime. "Dad's at it again."

"That's what hotshot attorneys do." Jay drained his beer then set it on the coffee table next to Tiana's. "Want another one?"

"Sure." She yawned.

He stood. "I'll wade through the heat to get one."

He returned and handed her another beer. "Cheers." He held his beer up. "To our family?" His wide and uncertain brown eyes peered into Tiana's.

She tapped her beer against his. "To our *perfect* family." She stroked his brown cheek then pecked his lips. "How did the job search go today?" She'd wanted to ask all evening but didn't want him to think she'd been obsessing over it, even though she had been.

"I filled out a bunch of applications online. Knew this wasn't going to be easy." He sighed. "Didn't think it'd be this hard."

What an understatement. She wanted nothing more than for them to move on and leave their recent troubles behind. It would take patience. Change seemed to happen at a snail's pace these days, if at all. She sipped her beer. "I know. I think it's harder to find a job in the summer."

"I've been doing research. It might be good if I do an apprenticeship program. Something like clean technology. Clean-energy jobs are supposedly the future. New decade, new career... We'll see."

Tiana would support any plan that would lead to him getting a legit paycheck. "That sounds promising. Have you looked into if you'd be able to get work if you did that? I mean, if those professions hire—"

"I need to dig a little deeper to find that out." Jay traced her lips with his index finger. "I'm sorry." His eyes pleaded with her.

"I know." She turned away and focused on the celebrities on television. They all looked so beautiful and put together. In contrast, Tiana's life had completely unraveled. She couldn't remember the last time she could afford to buy a new outfit, get her nails done, or enjoy a spa day. She hadn't realized how privileged she'd been until everything had been taken from her.

After gulping down her beer, she rose from the couch. She needed to get some sleep since she had to walk through her office doors by eight the next morning.

Loud banging on their front door caused her to jump.

Jay stood. "I'll see who it is."

Tiana braced herself. Only one agency pounded on doors late at night like that. She didn't wonder who but why.

CHAPTER FOUR

Jay cracked the door open. Two uniformed police officers stood on his welcome mat. Decades apart in age, they wore matching grimaces on their faces.

"What's the problem, officers?" Jay's voice came out unnaturally high.

The older officer, a gray-haired man with deep wrinkles in his face, stepped forward. "Are you Jaylen Williams?"

Damn, they got the right spot. "Yeah—yes, I am. How can I help you?"

"We need to question you about the disappearance of a girl." The officer held up the same picture that the news had featured earlier of the girl who'd been at Walmart.

"I don't know how I can help, but come on in." Jay took a step backward and opened the door wider.

"Uh-uh." The officer shook his head. "You're coming with us."

The other officer, a blond-haired fellow with freckles, couldn't have been more than twenty-five. He rested his hand on the gun holster on his hip. "We're not asking you to come with us. We're telling you. It will be as hard as you make it."

Tiana appeared and stood in front of Jay, forcing him to stumble backward. "Excuse me, but what does my husband have to do with any of this?"

"I'd stay out of this." The young cop glared at her.

The older officer ignored her and took another step toward Jay. "Let's go."

Jay squeezed Tiana's hand. "Please, Ti, just go inside. I don't want us to have no problems. I'll be back." His voice had grown gruff. He wiped the sweat from his cheek, his hand grazing the stubble on his five-o'clock shadow.

Tiana bit her lip, her eyes filling with tears. "I'll call my mom to watch Marcus and meet you at the police station."

The blond cop held up his hand. "Don't follow us out." He motioned for Jay to walk.

Now it was her turn to ignore them. She walked behind the police officers, who had Jay sandwiched between them. They gripped Jay's forearms, forcing him through the apartment complex.

A low orange glow barely lined the sky as the sun took its last breath of the day. Jay hung his head and ignored the stares of the neighbors peering out from their open windows and doors while the cops forced him toward the parking lot. The evening breeze that had barely entered their apartment rustled the trees in the crowded complex. He ducked into the squad car waiting at the curb. Tiana put her hand up to say goodbye. Jay couldn't help but remember the last time this had happened.

Muggy, stale air suffocated him in the cramped back seat. Competing thoughts fought for his attention. The winner simply repeated, *Not again.* Thick plastic separated him from the older police officer. Jay seethed in anger as the man nonchalantly pulled away from Jay's apartment as if on a Sunday afternoon drive. He itched to bang on the plastic. He wanted to scream. *Why the hell do you want to talk to me about that girl?* But he wouldn't dare. As a Black man in America, any action that law enforcement considered aggressive could end with him losing his life, and Jay had too much to live for. "Can you tell me what this is about, officer?"

The officer eyed Jay in the rearview mirror. "We're the ones who ask the questions, not you."

His bad luck had struck again. He'd just happened to be at the same Walmart as the girl. Luckily, Marcus had been with him the entire day. Jay's life was predictably boring. He'd done nothing out of the ordinary and absolutely nothing illegal. He would just explain that he hadn't even seen the girl at Walmart, and they would let him go home. *Probably won't be that easy.* The color of his skin made him a suspect.

The officer parked the squad car in the lot outside the San Jose Police Department. Jay eyed the nondescript concrete building surrounded by trees and shrubbery intent on swallowing it whole. The cop opened Jay's door and yanked his forearm until he stood. "You'd think once you got out, you wouldn't want to come back here. But you people can't seem to stay out of trouble."

Jay gulped the air to calm his rage. Instead of relief, a hint of smoke from the wildfire burning in Yountville filled his lungs. The officer stuck close to his side as they walked toward a back door. The harsh shrubs pricked Jay's arms. He couldn't have the whole damn thing over with soon enough. They barely fit through the narrow, dimly lit hallway. After passing several closed doors, the officer stopped in front of one and unlocked then opened it, revealing a small room with nothing but a table, two folding chairs, and a jarring fluorescent light. "Sit and wait," he commanded as if Jay was a dog.

Jay kicked the metal chair slightly then dropped into it, purposefully positioning his back to the one-way mirror. He'd seen a lot of those mirrors when he'd been in rooms like that before. The torture had come from looking at his reflection and knowing he'd messed up. He didn't have that guilt now. *But will it matter?* The police and district attorneys locked up countless people for crimes they didn't commit. They went to prison for life or were sentenced to death for something they never did. He had to do everything in his power to get home.

CHAPTER FIVE

There was a knock on the door, and Tiana rose then opened it. "Thank you so much for coming, Mom. I'm going straight to the police station. I hope I won't be long."

Worry lines creased her mother's forehead. She'd already removed her makeup for the night, so brown sunspots that foundation usually covered spotted her tawny-brown skin. She'd pulled her honey-blond weave back into a low ponytail. "Now, hold on one minute. Sit down and tell me everything before you leave. I want all the details."

Tiana shrugged. "There's not much to tell you." She led her mom to the sofa. "Two officers showed up at the door. They said they needed to talk to Jay about that girl who disappeared at Walmart."

Her mom raised her palms. "Why? What does she have to do with him?"

"Nothing. That's why I need to hurry down there. He's probably ready to be picked up." Tiana doubted it. The police always seemed to keep people as long as possible, like they get paid hourly or something. But she didn't want her mom to think she would be out all night.

"I hope you're right." Her mom placed her hand on Tiana's knee. "I really wouldn't be able to watch you go through—"

"Come on, Mom." She rose to leave. Her eyelids were heavy. "Of course Jay hasn't done anything. Marcus keeps him completely busy all day. Even if he wanted to, Jay has no ability to kidnap another kid. And where would he keep her? The closet? It's not even a walk-in."

Her mom cracked a half smile. "Not funny."

"I'll be back. Thank you again." Though exhausted, Tiana was filled with gratitude that her mom had come over. She wouldn't have to wake Marcus and take him with her.

Regardless of the difficulties she had faced in life, her mom had always been there. She'd had Tiana when she was eighteen. They'd grown up together and sometimes seemed more like sisters than parent and daughter. The past three years had tested Tiana beyond belief, but every time she questioned whether she had the strength to continue, her mom had been right there to keep her pushing forward.

Tiana stepped outside. The air had cooled substantially, finally granting reprieve from the heat. She rushed through the worn-down complex, past the laundry room, and to the crowded carport. Once in her car, she caught her breath then pulled away. The route to the police station was all too familiar.

Jay definitely had not kidnapped the girl. A laugh escaped her. She couldn't believe the absurdity of the situation. Jay no longer had the resources to buy her gifts or roses, as he had in the past. Instead, his undivided attention, love, and loyalty made up for it. They'd struggled hard since he'd come back home. No doubt about it. But they loved harder.

Like the headlight beams focused on the road ahead, Tiana fixated on one thought: *When will they let Jay go home?* She had another long day of work tomorrow. She imagined collapsing into bed and falling into a deep sleep. But that would have to wait. She hoped the police would obtain answers to whatever questions they had and let her husband go home with her. After eighteen months without him, she couldn't endure another separation.

CHAPTER SIX

Jay straightened in his chair when the door opened. A slender white man with a receding gray comb-over entered the room. He pushed up his thick brown glasses then placed a black iPad on the table. Holding up his badge, he slipped into the chair opposite Jay. "Jaylen Williams, I'm Detective Peter Long." He glanced at his wristwatch. "It's late, and my intention is to ask you some questions and, if possible, get you home tonight."

Jay crossed his arms. "If possible?" He couldn't mask his irritation. "Look, man, I haven't done nothing wrong. I regularly see my PO. I've stayed within the fifty-mile radius. I'm not getting in no trouble. I'll tell you straight up, I don't know that little girl. Period."

The detective didn't acknowledge Jay's comments and powered on the iPad then held it up to display the picture of the girl from the news. "Have you ever seen this girl? Now, before you answer, know that we have information that directly links you to her. Again, have you ever seen this girl before? Her name is Zoe Miller."

A hard lump formed in Jay's throat. The dude clearly thought he could intimidate him. But Jay'd never be dumb enough to confess to something he didn't do. "Nah, I haven't."

Detective Long swiped to a different picture of the same girl. "Have you seen this girl?"

Jay didn't have to think. "No."

Detective Long showed Jay another picture then another and another. The parents must have loved taking pictures of their daughter. Jay's folks never bothered even to order his or Xavier's yearly school portraits. Though the girl's outfits changed in each picture, the brown doe eyes and infectious smile remained the same. Jay almost wished he did know something about the girl if it would help bring her back to her family. After the last picture, Detective Long repeated the same question. "Have you ever seen this girl?"

"No. Why would I have?" Jay demanded.

Detective Long rested the iPad on the table. He took out a notepad. Leaning forward in his chair, he looked eager for answers. "Tell me what you did today. I want every detail. Even the boring stuff."

Jay exhaled. "I woke up early, like six thirty. My wife and I ate breakfast with our toddler before she left for work. My son and I watched a few cartoons. We walked to the park by our house. Stayed about thirty-five minutes. We normally stay an hour, but it'd gotten hotter by the minute. I didn't want my son to overheat. Plus, the smoke from the fire's drifting here. I didn't want him outside too long." Jay paused, trying to remember every face he'd encountered. It'd only been the usual stay-at-home-mom playgroup doing some type of awkward workout routine while their kids sat in strollers.

"What'd you do next?" Detective Long held his pen suspended above the notebook as if just itching to write down Jay's next words.

"We headed home and watched a little more TV." He hoped this chronology wouldn't make it to Tiana's attention. She always lectured him about letting Marcus have too much screen time. "After lunch, I put my son down for a nap for about an hour. He woke up. We read a few books. Then we went to Walmart. After—"

"Why?" Detective Long arched an eyebrow.

"To meet my boy Travis and check out camping gear." Jay had once been advised by his lawyer not to say anything other than answer the question asked. So that was exactly what he did.

"So where'd you meet Travis? In the parking lot? Out front?"

Jay shrugged. "He actually didn't make it."

Detective Long continued scribbling on his paper. "Did you look for Travis in the store?"

"Yeah. I couldn't find him, so after about twenty minutes, I left with my son." Jay added the last part to remind the detective Marcus had been with him the whole time. While at Walmart, Jay hadn't spoken to anyone other than Marcus. He definitely hadn't seen any other Black kids. With such a small population of African-Americans in Silicon Valley, he would have noticed her and definitely spoken to her parents out of courtesy.

"Did you call your friend Travis to see where he was?" Detective Long asked.

"Nah, I sent him a text saying I was at the store."

Detective Long looked up from his notepad. "Did he respond?"

"Nope."

Detective Long bridged his fingers and leaned forward. "Did Travis call or text you after you left to tell you why he didn't show up?"

"No. Now that you mention it, I still haven't heard from him." Jay tried to sound nonchalant about it.

"Is that how Travis usually is? You two make plans and he doesn't show up?"

An alarm bell rang in Jay's mind as Long honed in on his friendship with Travis. Jay needed to set the record straight. "We don't usually make plans. We show up to play ball around the same time at the park. Sometimes, we get a beer. But we don't really hang out with each other."

"But you were planning to spend a weekend camping together, correct? Travis is"— Detective Long hooked his fingers together—"'your boy,' right?"

Jay could have kicked himself for calling Travis that. He shook his head. "Not really."

"Come on, now, Jaylen. Would you spend the weekend camping with someone you don't know?" Detective Long's eyes narrowed like an eagle tracking its prey.

Fortunately for Jay, he had nothing to hide. "Travis had kicked around the idea of a camping trip a few times. After everything I've been through the past few years, I thought a weekend away might do me good. Gilroy's within the radius I can travel while on parole. Based on your questions, I'm glad it didn't happen."

Detective Long picked up the iPad again. He flipped through it and held up a photo of Jay inside the Walmart. "We tracked you down by your credit card purchase this afternoon. You were at Walmart at the same time as Zoe Miller. That's the last location she was seen. I don't believe in coincidences. Now, do you remember seeing Zoe at the store? Did you have any contact with her at all?"

Jay stared directly into Detective Long's eyes without wavering. "Absolutely not. I've told you everything I know. If you have more questions, I need to call my lawyer."

With a smirk, Detective Long placed the iPad on the table. "All right. That'll be all for now. But don't even think this is close to the end."

Jay stood, his shaking knees trying to betray the false confidence he projected.

Detective Long opened the door. "Follow me to the front. You can call yourself a ride."

Relief washed over Jay like a cold wave crashing over a hot body on a scorching day at the beach, but he had his own question: *What the hell happened with Travis today?*

CHAPTER SEVEN

Tiana drove to the police station without hitting traffic. With the exception of a few streets with nightclubs and bars, the majority of downtown San Jose became a ghost town at nightfall. After pulling in to SJPD's parking lot, her eyelids won the fight, and she closed them.

Raising Marcus alone while working full-time for a year and a half had nearly broken her. With an infant waking up every two to three hours to nurse, Tiana didn't know how she had physically met the demands of both work and motherhood. Sometimes, after she'd picked up Marcus from daycare and they'd eaten dinner, she ignored Jay's evening call. She couldn't help but blame him for leaving her to care for a newborn alone.

A car horn blared in the parking lot and startled her. She mustered enough energy to make it into the police station and left the car. Climbing the concrete steps, she hoped it wouldn't be long before Jay came out. She opened the door, stopped in her tracks, and did a double take. Her dad sat on one of the metal benches. *Damn! How'd Dad already find out they wanted to question Jay?* She walked toward him. "Dad? I'm sure it's nothing."

Her dad jumped at the sound of her voice. "Tiana?" He turned his bloodshot eyes, dark bags clinging underneath them, her way. He must've had a hell of a day. The harsh fluorescent lighting cast an unfavorable glow on every line in his face, making him appear years older than forty-five. "What are you doing here?"

"I'm waiting for Jay. That's why you're here, too, isn't it? Did Mom tell you they brought him in for questioning about the missing girl?" That had to have been how he found out.

His gaze wandered, as if he was deep in contemplation. He straightened and focused on Tiana. "What the hell does Jay have to do with Zoe?" Her father's tone held the familiar edge he used when referring to his son-in-law, and his use of the missing girl's name was strangely intimate.

"Martin Moore." A police officer stood at the open door that led back to the station.

Rising, her dad murmured, "We'll talk later." He hurried to the officer, shook his hand, then followed him back.

Tiana couldn't figure out why the police would want to talk to her dad so soon after the girl had gone missing. She doubted he could possibly have any information about Jay or the girl. *Has a suspect even been identified?*

She hurried to the reception window then tapped on the glass.

A policewoman turned on the microphone. "How can I help you?"

Tiana smiled and tried to sound as proper as possible. "The police brought my husband, Jaylen Williams, in for questioning this evening. I'm checking to see if he is ready to be picked up."

"Have a seat. I'll see what I can find out." The policewoman shut off the microphone and picked up her phone.

Instead of sitting, Tiana paced the station. A handful of others occupied the gray metal benches bolted to the ground. She took out her phone and called her mom. "You didn't have to tell Dad." All her politeness had vanished.

"What? Tiana, what have you found out?"

She rolled her eyes. "Nothing yet. But why'd you tell Dad?"

"Honey, Dad worked late today and hadn't come home yet when I received your call. As soon as you and I spoke, I tried to get ahold of him. He didn't answer. We still haven't talked."

A chill ran down Tiana's spine. "Dad's here. The police just called him back."

"I'm sure there's a perfectly good reason. You know Dad's always working."

The door opened again, and Jay walked through it. "Jay just came out. I'll see you soon." She shoved her phone into her purse.

Jay's eyes searched the station before locking with Tiana's. He gave a half smile and hurried toward her. "Let's go, Ti."

She wanted to ask a million questions, but only one meant anything. "They're letting you go?"

Jay cast his gaze to the linoleum floor. "Yeah. I'm sorry 'bout this. You got work early tomorrow. I don't wanna stay here a second longer."

Tiana reached for his hand, and Jay laced his fingers through hers. They walked out together. He definitely hadn't done anything. *Wrong place, wrong time.*

Jay opened the passenger door for her. She sank into the seat and rested her head against the window. When Jay had settled into the driver's seat, she peered into his eyes. "What was that all about?"

Jay spoke in a low voice. "Since I have a felony conviction on my record, they wanted to talk to me."

Tiana shuddered at the word *felony*. It'd been almost two years since he'd pleaded guilty, but she couldn't get used to it. "I figured that was all. I hate how they can drag you out of the house whenever they want as a condition of your parole. It's not fair."

Jay backed out of the parking spot. "Something was weird." He glanced at Tiana, a haunted look in his eyes. "She didn't look exactly like the picture on television. In the other pictures they showed, the missing girl looked like..."

Goose bumps lined her arm. "Like what?"

Jay shivered. "Never mind. I just wanna get home." He turned out of the parking lot, and they drove down the street in silence.

Though Tiana wanted to press the issue, something told her to leave it alone, at least for the time being.

CHAPTER EIGHT

When they walked into the apartment, the TV was playing on a volume so low that Jay couldn't make out the words. His mother-in-law stood from the couch and focused on him, her almond-shaped eyes identical to Tiana's. "I'm so relieved to see you both."

Tiana hugged her mom. "Thanks again for coming over."

Jay forced himself to smile at Wanda. Inside, he wanted to throw a punch at Detective Long. But he appreciated Wanda always being a call away when Tiana needed her. He'd never had that type of relationship with his own mom. "I'm sorry to drag you out of the house so late for nothing." He itched to take a shower and wash off the police station.

Tiana yawned. "Did you ever hear from Dad?"

Wanda waved her hand dismissively. "No, he hasn't called me back."

Jay arched an eyebrow. "You didn't have to involve Martin. It's not serious at all."

Tiana shook her head. "Mom didn't tell Dad. He was already at the police station when I arrived to get you. I'm not sure why."

"I'm sure there's a perfectly good reason why Dad's there. He's a prosecutor, after all." The expression on Wanda's face betrayed her unease.

"The missing girl is from Oakland." Jay yawned and stretched his arms. "So that's his jurisdiction even if she disappeared in San

Jose." Jay had already worried Wanda. He didn't want her up all night thinking about Martin too.

Tiana pecked her mom's cheek. "We're both exhausted. Ask Dad to call me when he comes home. Drive safe."

"Will do." Her mom grabbed her purse and slid the strap over her shoulder. "I'll see you two later. Kiss my grandbaby." She walked to the door, put her hand on the doorknob, then paused. "Stay out of trouble, Jay."

"Yep." He skulked to the kitchen. After the nightmare of a night, he needed a beer. He opened the fridge and cursed under his breath. *No beer. No money. No job. No chance.*

Tiana rubbed his back. "Sorry. I drank the last beer when I was waiting for my mom. I'll get more tomorrow."

Jay loved how his wife always knew his thoughts without his having to say a word. He turned and wrapped his arms around her. "As long I got you, I don't need another beer for the rest of my life. Get ready for bed. I'll be in soon."

"I want to put the news on a few minutes and see if they found that girl. If they have, we can put the whole thing far, far behind us." Tiana tugged on his hand.

After all the pictures Detective Long had forced him to look at, Jay didn't want to see that little girl's face ever again. Adrenaline still pumped through his muscles after Long's rapid-fire questioning. But he couldn't say that to her. She might grow suspicious that he had something to do with the girl's disappearance. Instead, he followed his wife to the couch.

Tiana snuggled next to Jay and switched on the eleven-o'clock news. As if on cue, it led with the story of the missing girl, Zoe Miller. A Black lady named Josephine Miller who looked around Wanda's age spoke to the camera, her voice quivering and tears leaking from her eyes. "We need Zoe back. She's just a little girl. Only ten. Please... bring my baby..." Overwhelmed by emotion, she buried her face in the shoulder of the man next to her.

"Home," the man said. He looked similar to Josephine, maybe a few years older. "We'll do anything. Just help us bring Zoe home to her family."

Jay leaned forward, focusing on the pair. *Something isn't right.* Zoe bore no resemblance to either of them at all. Jay shook his head. *Not my problem.* He turned to Tiana. "I'm so sorry 'bout everything that happened tonight. There's no way I would have thought stopping by Walmart would lead to police questioning. No matter how hard I try to put the past behind me, it won't let me go." His shoulders slumped in defeat.

She kissed his cheek. "I'm just happy you're home safe. We both know too many people that look like us that don't get to go back home. If they would have booked you and set a bail, I wouldn't be able to pay it this time." She let out a loud yawn before covering her mouth. "I guess I should go shower. Don't stay out here too long, okay? You need sleep too."

Though not racing quite as quickly as earlier, Jay's heart still pounded in his ears. Sleep wouldn't come easily, per usual. "Okay, I'll be in." He smiled, and Tiana pressed her full lips against his. Life tasted sweet again.

After their bedroom door clicked shut down the hall, Jay pulled out his phone and paused. He didn't exactly want to contact Travis in case the dude was up to something shady. But Jay would feel better if Travis explained why he didn't show at Walmart. He sent a quick text. Detective Long had been way too interested in their friendship. Travis's disappearing act didn't help.

In hindsight, Jay barely knew anything about Travis. Jay'd never been to his house, though Travis said he lived a couple blocks away from the park. Jay'd never met Travis's family, though Travis said he had a son around Marcus's age.

His phone rang. *That was fast.* Jay picked up the phone to answer. One look at the number, however, and he let it go to voicemail. A minute later, a voicemail alert appeared. *She just won't give up.* He started to delete it, but something inside him wanted to hear Janet's voice. Against his better judgment, he pressed play.

Jay, it's me. I know you've told me to stop calling. But I can't. I love you and always will. Please. Call me. I miss you.

The memory of Janet's scream pierced Jay's mind. He could still hear it. He dropped the phone and clutched both sides of his head, squeezing his eyes shut. A puddle of dark-red blood grew larger and darker. He stood from the couch and shook his arms. He grabbed the phone and deleted the voicemail and call from his phone's history with trembling fingers. He would never make the same mistake and let Janet in again. He paid the price every day for what she'd made him do.

CHAPTER NINE

After showering, Tiana sat on her bed and opened the location app she and Jay used to share their locations with each other. After clicking on his name, she scrolled through his history for the day. The app had tracked his trip to the park and afternoon Walmart visit. He'd come straight home from there, and nothing seemed out of the ordinary.

She closed the app and scolded herself. Jay absolutely hadn't kidnapped a girl. But she'd learned the hard way that Jay could hide secrets. Serious ones. Like the details of his relationships with Walter and Janet. Though she'd never caught him in an outright lie, he had a tendency to omit the truth. *But don't we all.*

Knowing Jay would probably be up all night, stewing, she headed back to the living room to try to convince him to join her in bed. She froze in the hallway at the sight of her husband stooped over the couch. Though his back faced her, she could tell another flashback had forced him to his feet. Every fiber in her wanted to run over and love on him to make the hurt go away. But she'd learned it was best to give him space. She retreated a few steps into the hallway to wait.

Family pictures spanning decades lined the walls on either side of her. Her mom had nailed most of them up when she'd helped Tiana downsize from their first house. Selling their home had completely devastated her. With affordable housing nearly impossible to find in Silicon Valley, she'd gotten lucky to find the run-down low-income apartment. The property owner turned a blind eye as units reached triple and quadruple the maximum occupancy. Both her parents had begged her to move in with them, but Tiana had refused. She'd insisted on having her own place with a nursery for her baby, who had been due in three months.

No longer a child, she had absolutely refused to crawl back to her parents' house. Deep down, she'd known if she moved in with her parents, she wouldn't have moved back out when Jay finished his sentence.

She imagined the heartbreak of the missing girl's parents as they returned home to a place filled with family pictures but not their daughter.

She tiptoed down the hall and peeked into Marcus's room. He slept soundly in his crib. The humming fan helped cool the small space. She wouldn't even entertain the thought of what she would do if Marcus disappeared. She already lived with the memory of a baby haunting her and knew she wouldn't survive if someone took her son away.

After crossing the hall, Tiana entered her and Jay's bedroom and flopped onto their bed again. Before placing her phone on the side table for the night, she dialed her mom. "Sorry to call so late, Mom. Is Dad home yet?"

"You can call me any time, honey. You know that." Her mom's tone changed from motherly to concerned. "And no. Still no word from your father. I'm worried. Even if he's caught up with something, he always calls or, at bare minimum, responds to my text if he's going to be home late. I know he's okay because you saw him. But it doesn't make sense."

Tiana wished she had the answer. "I don't know what to think. I'm exhausted. Send me a text when he comes home. That way, when I get up in the morning, I'll see it and won't worry. I love you."

"Love you too. Sleep well."

Tiana shared her mom's concern, so she next dialed her dad. His voicemail picked up, and she left him a quick message asking him to call her back. He couldn't possibly be at the police station so late.

Tiana trudged back to the living room to find Jay resting on the couch. The flashback had passed, and they both needed sleep after the night's drama. "You all right?"

Jay's cheeks flushed. "I'm fine.

"Tonight's been horrible. Let's both go to bed." She grabbed her husband's hand and tugged to get him up.

Jay stood and stretched his arms. "I could use a good and long night's sleep."

Tiana forced a smile. With Jay's police interrogation, the heat, and her father's mysterious behavior, a good night's sleep would most likely be the last thing she would get.

CHAPTER TEN

After tossing and turning in bed for over an hour, Jay'd had enough. He removed his arm from around Tiana's warm belly. Her even breathing signaled that she'd finally fallen asleep. He inched away then snuck out of bed. The stress knot in his stomach had only grown larger the more he mulled over the night's events. He couldn't stand how the police could just show up at his house and force him to go with them whenever they wanted. He hated having to document his every move with his parole officer.

His criminal record had him bound in a tight corner, but he still needed to do what he could. Tonight, that meant getting answers about Travis. He threw on a pair of jeans and a dark-blue T-shirt. He eased the door shut then crept down the hall.

In the pitch-black living room, he paced in the space between the television and couch. Tiana always passive-aggressively complained about their small apartment, but compared to the four-by-nine cell he'd barely managed to survive in for eighteen months, shared with a man who didn't like to shower, it felt like a mansion. When he'd heard the grind of the metal bar locking him in on his first night of imprisonment, he'd become convinced he'd die from claustrophobia. Toilet, sink, two lockers, bunks stacked on top of each other. He had to ensure no one could ever try to send him back there. He picked up his keys and left the apartment.

Shadows filled the silent apartment complex. Jay readied himself in case someone materialized from a dark corner. He couldn't face any neighbors. He hated how the police paraded him out like a criminal even though he'd done absolutely nothing wrong. He hoped no one had recorded it on their phone.

He sped through the narrow streets, dodging the parked cars, then turned the corner and drove under the overpass lined with tents filled with homeless people, an all-too-common sight in the Bay Area.

After a five-minute drive, Jay parked in front of the joint with a neon-blue sign that read Danny's Dive Bar. He pushed open the door with a poster plastered to it—Silicones Welcome in Our Valley—picturing a blonde with double Ds.

He pushed open the door and surveyed the dimly lit space. Over a dozen people squeezed around several wooden tables. Travis didn't appear to be one of them. Jay eyed the long wooden bar counter and the illuminated selection of alcohol. Three people sat there, gesturing as they engaged in an animated discussion. Jay hopped onto an open stool at the bar and signaled for the redheaded Irish bartender, Danny, who owned the place.

Danny grinned and slid a cocktail napkin in front of Jay. "Hey, good to see ya. What're you drinkin' tonight?"

Jay definitely didn't have money to spend, but the ten dollars in his pocket would more than cover the cost of a beer. "Guinness."

Danny poured the dark-brown liquid from the tap and topped it with the perfect amount of froth. With a smug smile, he rested it in front of Jay. "You look like crap. Can't sleep?"

Jay took a quick sip and nodded. "Something like that." He wiped the froth off his upper lip with the back of his hand. "Hey, man, one question. Have you seen that guy I usually come in here with on Tuesdays? You know, the skinny Black dude with hair sticking straight up on his head?" Unlike Tiana, who described people by their approximate height, weight, build, and hair color, Jay's descriptions were bare-bones.

"Oh yeah, Ronnie. He forgot his credit card after you two were here a couple days ago. Came back yesterday to get it." Danny scratched his goatee. "Haven't seen him since."

Jay shook his head. "No, I'm talking about Travis. The guy I'm usually here with."

Danny put his hand a few inches above his red hair. "Tall dude about this height? Skinny, Black, and comes in here with you, right?"

"Yeah." They had to have been talking about the same guy.

"Fella's name is Ronnie, not Travis. When he picked up his credit card, I checked his license. Protocol to match the names. Address on it said Stockton. I said, 'You live all the way out in Stockton?' He said, 'Yeah, he just works 'round here.'"

A chill ran down Jay's spine. "That's right. Ronnie. Ronnie... Parks, right?"

"Ronnie Coleman, if my memory isn't failin' me." Danny tapped the bar. "Let me know when you're ready for another beer." He headed down the bar to one of the trio waving an empty glass with an unsteady hand.

Jay sipped his Guinness. As the liquid trickled into his system, anger boiled his blood. Travis—Ronnie—had straight-up lied to his face multiple times. His name was just the start. When they'd first met, Ronnie had specifically told Jay he lived walking distance from the park and that he had recently been laid off from his job. Jay'd had no reason to doubt that story. Now, he couldn't for the life of him figure out why Ronnie had befriended him under false pretenses.

As Jay's gaze darted around the bar, each unfamiliar face posed a threat. They all seemed suspect. He gulped the last of his beer, slammed the ten-dollar bill on the bar, then stomped back to his car, mulling over the situation. The large knot in his belly grew, twisting with dread.

In prison, he couldn't let his guard down for a second. Danger could have pounced at any moment. He'd built a fortified wall around himself. *Damn idiot!* He shouldn't have let his wall down and allowed Ronnie into his life. The man obviously had some type of scheme going on. Jay had no idea of his endgame.

After slamming his car door shut, Jay sped home. He entered his apartment, relieved the temperature had cooled a bit. But questions surrounding Ronnie would keep him up, so instead of heading for bed, he stretched out on the couch. Maybe his parents' fighting always got worse in the summer because the damn heat kept his father awake and irritable. His father's deep, guttural voice seemed ingrained in Jay's head, and tonight, it was no different. As soon as he closed his eyes, his father hurled profanity-laced insults toward him.

You should have known goddam well nobody would want to be friends with someone who just got outta prison unless they wanted something. That brotha was up to no good. Just like you. You got played, plain and simple. Ever since you were born, you've been stupid. Got it from your dumbass mother. Watch—it'll be just your luck you get locked up again. And this time, that wife of yours sure as hell ain't waiting around. She'll leave so fast and take your son with her. Stupid ass.

He pounded his forehead with his fists, trying to force his dad's voice to flee. His phone rang, and Jay jumped. It had to be Ronnie with an explanation for everything. No one else would call at almost midnight. But his father-in-law's number showed up instead. "Martin? What's up?"

"Cut the bullshit, Jaylen," Martin said in his DA tone. "I know you were questioned at the police station tonight concerning Zoe's disappearance. What do you know?"

The edge in Martin's voice made Jay sit up straight and focus. "I already told Wanda everything that happened."

"I don't give a damn what you told Wanda! What do you know about Zoe?" Though Martin had made clear that he didn't like Jay, he'd never yelled at him like that before.

"I happened to be at the same Walmart at the same time as the girl. Look, just like I told the detective, I've never seen her before in my life. I didn't see her at Walmart. I don't have nothing to do with her disappearance. It's all just a bad coincidence." Jay purposefully let out the part about how he'd planned to meet Ronnie there. With a huge question mark surrounding the dude, he wouldn't bring Ronnie up again. "Martin, I'm one hundred percent committed to doing everything by the book. I'm getting my life back on—"

"Save it. I'm just going to say this once. I pulled every string I had so you only did eighteen months instead of thirty years to life. But if I find out you had anything at all to do with Zoe's disappearance, I'll make sure your ass is locked up for good this time." Martin ended the call.

Jay tossed his phone onto the coffee table. He had no idea why Martin was so angry or what stake he had in the whole missing-girl case. Sure, he got invested in all his cases. But he'd crossed the line by calling Jay and threatening him. Jay foresaw a long, sleepless night, but he needed to feel Tiana's body pressed against his. He crept down the hall and to their room.

He creaked the door open, and she stirred. "You coming back to bed?"

Jay shed his all his clothes except his boxers. He rested against his wife, who curved the backside of her body to him. He closed his eyes, inhaling the vanilla lotion she lathered on after her nightly shower. He laced his arms around her and tried to shut out the anxiety and fear threatening to swallow him whole.

She'd held it down throughout his imprisonment. Knowing he'd be released and coming home to her had helped him get through the hard times. Sometimes, he didn't think he would make it in confinement for another second. He owed Tiana his life. No one would ever come between him and his family again. He would do anything and everything in his power to ensure that.

That was why he had to figure out Ronnie's deal. Jay couldn't get entangled in whatever the guy had going on. But he feared it might be too late.

CHAPTER ELEVEN

The heat and Jay's tossing and turning had prevented Tiana from getting a restful night's sleep. In her office, she had to fight the urge to close her eyes and doze off. She checked her phone and sighed. *Still haven't heard from Dad* was the last text she'd received from her mom at eight that morning. Shaking her head and rolling her shoulders, she tried to circulate energy she didn't have. Only anxiety ran through her body.

She pulled up a local news website that featured the missing girl. The only new development came from the girl's family, who offered a reward of twenty-five thousand dollars for anyone who had information that led to her safe return. A knock on her office door snapped Tiana out of her thoughts. "Come in." She closed the news and opened the informational page she needed to work on.

Ava poked her head in, perfectly applied makeup on her peach-colored skin. She'd styled her brunette hair in beach waves. Ava could have been one of the stock-image models Tiana always sifted through instead of a coworker and her best friend after college. "Tiana, you can stop acting like you're working. It's just me."

She sometimes hated how well Ava knew her. "I'm reading about that missing girl."

Ava chuckled before her light-brown eyes grew faux serious. "Stop. Now. You know you become way too involved in things like that. Remember how much money you spent a few years ago after seeing those Facebook ads with the girls who needed money to go to school in Africa?"

Tiana raised her eyebrows. "It was Sierra Leone. I wanted to bring each of those girls to live with me like Oprah." She sighed. "Sometimes, it seems so unfair. We have so much, and so many other people barely have the basics to survive. I'm glad I could help back then... unlike now. I'm the one needing aid these days."

"It'll get better once Jay gets a job. But please, give the news coverage a rest. Someone just dropped this off at the front desk for you." She placed a manila envelope on Tiana's desk.

"For me? I never get mail." She shook the envelope. As the social media manager of the small startup, almost all correspondence addressed to her came through email or hits to their website.

Ava gestured toward the envelope. "Open it."

Tiana slid her finger through the corner and pulled out an eight-by-eleven photograph of the missing girl. What You Don't Know Can Hurt Her was written across it. She dropped the photograph as though she'd discovered a scorpion crawling on it. "What the hell?"

"What is it?" Ava leaned over and picked up the photograph. "Wait... what? That's the girl who's missing. You didn't mention you know her."

Palms raised, Tiana shook her head. "That's because I don't. Absolutely not. I'd never seen her before the Amber Alert on the news last night."

Ava placed the photograph on Tiana's desk. "That's freakin' creepy."

Tiana sank back into her chair. "Something weird is going on. First they questioned Jay about her. Then I saw my dad at the police station. Now this photograph."

Ava's eyes grew wide, and she picked up the manila envelope. "I'm going to ask Sheila who exactly dropped this off. Maybe she knows something that will help us figure this out." Ava left the office, a woman on a mission.

Tiana needed some of that energy to put the pieces of the puzzle together.

She snapped a picture of the photo and sent it to Jay in a text along with *WTF*. Tapping her pen on her desk, she waited for a response.

Two minutes later, Jay called her. "Tiana, where'd that picture come from?"

"Someone dropped it off at my office. I have no idea who or why. Do you? Did the police mention they think someone you or I know might be involved?"

"No, not at all. But I do have something I need to tell you."

Tiana sucked in a breath. "What is it?"

"I think it's better to talk in person."

She hung up the phone and grabbed her purse. Her phone rang with another call from Jay, but she rejected it. If he had somehow involved himself with the missing girl, she needed to know immediately.

After rushing out of the office building, she hopped in her car and dialed her dad again as she started the ignition. *Please answer.*

"Hello, Tiana," he said.

Her jaw dropped, and she turned off the car. "Dad, where've you been? Mom and I have been worried sick."

Her dad sighed into the phone. "Look, Tiana, I have something I need to tell you. Please just keep this between you and me until I have the time to speak with Mom in person. Promise me that."

With her heart pounding in her ears, she sucked in a breath. "I promise."

Silence filled the line before her dad finally spoke. "Zoe Williams, the girl who's been kidnapped... she's my daughter. As soon as I found out, I started working with the police to do everything—"

Tiana gasped for air. "Your daughter? You cheated on Mom?"

"I'm sorry you had to find out like this. I can't talk right now, but please, don't mention it to Mom. I owe it to her to tell her face-to-face. I have to go." He hung up.

Her head spun as she clutched the steering wheel. *Breathe.* Her chest heaved up and down, but she got a grip, started the car, and pulled out of the parking lot. She hadn't even thought to tell her dad about the picture. She sped home. *I gotta talk to Jay.*

CHAPTER TWELVE

Jay jumped up from the park bench and shoved his phone into his basketball shorts' pocket. He couldn't get home quickly enough. "Marcus, time to head back, buddy." He could have sworn people were staring, but when his gaze darted around the park, he didn't spot anyone watching him. The usuals were there: a handful of kids played on the jungle gym, toddlers shoveled sand into buckets in the sandpit, and the group of fitness moms did their squats next to their strollers.

"No, Dada." Marcus ran in the opposite direction and toward the seesaw. "More play."

Who the hell sent that picture to Tiana? Does someone have it out for us? After chasing Marcus down, Jay swooped him up in his arms. "Buddy, let's go."

The little boy writhed, trying to break free. "More play."

"No. We can come back later. Let's go home and find something fun to watch on TV." Jay hoped bribery would work to avoid a tantrum.

"Mickey?" His eyes lit up.

"Sure." Jay would have said yes to just about anything for Marcus to climb into the jogger stroller without a fight. He buckled him in, scanned the park again, then raced to the house in record time. Overhead, a thin gray layer of smoke lined the sky. Wildfires had become a common summer occurrence in California, and he hoped firefighters could contain this one before it became a monster like the Tubbs Fire or Camp Fire.

When Jay opened the door to his apartment, his jaw dropped. Tiana sat on the couch, her arms folded across her chest. All the color had drained from her face, and her eyes were wide and worried.

He cleared his throat. "Oh, hey, Ti. You didn't tell me you were coming home now. Are you okay?"

"Mama!" Marcus shrieked and kicked his feet to get out of the stroller. A smile spread across his chubby face.

She picked him up and kissed his cheek. "Hey, Marky. How's your morning?"

"Good." He nuzzled his forehead against her face.

Jay grabbed the remote and turned on *Mickey Mouse Clubhouse* to keep his promise. "Buddy, I'm going to put Mickey on now then talk with Mama in the kitchen."

Tiana propped Marcus on his alphabet rug next to the Legos. She placed a toy fire engine and stuffed teddy bear next to him. "Stay here, 'kay?"

Jay followed his wife the twenty feet to their kitchen and sat at the table. Gulping down a few deep breaths, he tried to overcome the fear welling up inside. Tiana and her opinion of him meant more than anyone else.

She sat across from him. "I talked to my dad. But what do you have to tell me? You go first."

"Last night after the police questioned me about Travis, I got curious about him, so I stopped by the bar we hung out at a few times. Long story short, Travis's name is actually Ronnie. Everything he told me about himself was a lie. He must have a reason for doing all that."

Tiana's forehead wrinkled. "But why? Did Ronnie know where I work? Had you mentioned it to him?"

"I might have in passing." Jay wished he'd never met the dude or told him anything about their lives. "But it seems very far-fetched that he would send you that photo. I don't think he's involved in any way with that missing girl. I just had to be completely honest with you."

"Thank you for that." Tiana placed her hand on the back of her neck.

"That's not all I wanted to tell you." Jay rubbed his chin and filled her in on what her father had said last night. "The way he spoke, it seemed like he had some type of connection to the missing girl. Something beyond work. What did he say when you talked to him?" Jay hadn't meant to throw Martin under the bus. But the more he thought about it, the more he grew convinced the missing girl had a link to his father-in-law.

"Zoe Miller is his daughter," Tiana whispered. "She's my half sister." She squeezed her eyes closed, and tears slipped out. "Had no idea he'd drop a bomb like that."

Jay rose and reached for her. "Come here."

She stood and allowed him to hug her. "I just can't believe it. I can't believe him. How could he do that to my mom?"

Jay rubbed her back. "I don't know. And we don't know why someone kidnapped her either."

Tiana broke the hug and stepped away from him. "Please don't tell anyone right now. I need to get back to work."

The whole interaction encapsulated their relationship since he'd come home from prison. Whenever he thought he'd bridged the distance between them, she put a wall back up. He lingered in the kitchen while Tiana returned to the living room. She sat on the carpet next to Marcus and massaged his thick, curly hair. Marcus giggled. Jay's heart swelled at the sight and sound of his son's glee.

Tiana stretched an arm toward their son. "Give Mama a hug. I'm leaving."

Marcus lunged into her arms. "Bye-bye."

Jay met her at the door. "You got a lot of stress and drama. How 'bout taking the rest of the day off? Hang with me and Marcus."

"I wish." Her shoulders sagged. "You know I need to get my hours."

"Right... hurry home?" He wanted her close.

"Yeah. I'll try." Her words lacked conviction.

Jay shut the door behind her. He'd never known unwavering, dedicated love like he had for Tiana and Marcus. His love had no limits, and he would do everything in his power to protect them both.

CHAPTER THIRTEEN

A crowd of professionals getting after-hour drinks competed with too-loud techno background music in an upscale downtown Palo Alto restaurant. Tiana's phone vibrated on the marble bar top, and Jay's number flashed on the screen. She picked it up and shouted into the phone, "Hey, Jay."

"Where you at, babe?"

"I stopped for happy hour with Ava. I'll be home soon. Everything okay?"

"Yeah, just thought you'd come straight home after work." He sounded more annoyed than worried.

She hadn't exactly forgotten to call her husband, but she'd had one hell of a day after her dad's confession. She and Ava had spent the afternoon trying to trace down who sent the photograph to no avail, and she needed a drink, not Jay's opposition. Ava had even offered to treat, and the air-conditioning was on full blast, so she had no desire to race home to stew in a sweltering apartment. "Sorry. It was just a crazy day."

"Well... Marcus should go to bed in thirty minutes. I know you like your bedtime routine with him."

"I'm sorry I'll miss it tonight, but just tell him that silly story about Kenny. Give him extra kisses for me. I can barely hear in here. See you soon. Bye." She ended the call, picked up her cosmo, and took a long chug. The cranberry and slight hint of lime awoke her taste buds. She regretted not being home to say good night to Marcus, but at least she'd seen him that afternoon.

Ava tilted her head to the side. "Everything okay?"

Tiana peered at her friend over the cocktail. "Other than my life imploding? Yep."

Ava let out a sigh. "Good. We need a couple drinks after everything. I'm so mad we couldn't track down whoever sent you that picture. When the courier service told me the sender's name was John Doe and couldn't give me the address, I was like, 'You're kidding, right?' I almost cussed them out for their stupidity. I mean, shouldn't they get the freakin' real name of someone using their service? The name John Doe should've raised serious stalker red flags."

Tiana raised a palm. "It's completely frustrating. But my dad's confession pretty much tops everything wrong with today."

Ava shrugged. "It makes sense, though. I could see it being some ex-con jerk who has an axe to grind with your dad."

The words felt like a punch to the gut. "Yeah."

Ava covered her mouth. "I'm sorry, Tiana. I didn't mean to say 'ex-con' like that."

Tiana waved her hand. "I hate words like that now. I know you didn't mean to offend me. I'm trying not to let anger get the best of me. But the missing girl—my dad's daughter—she's the same age as..." She choked back tears.

Ava patted her hand. "I can totally understand why you're feeling sensitive, given the similarities."

Tiana shivered. "You have no idea how my parents treated me when I got pregnant. Come to find out my dad was cheating on my mom the whole time."

The bartender tapped the surface in front of Tiana and Ava. "Check this out, ladies." He picked up three bottles in each hand, flexed his biceps, and poured the alcohol into a shaker. After adding a dash of blue curacao, he tossed the mixing glass into the air. He skillfully caught it then poured the concoction over ice into oversized glasses that he handed to the couple next to the women.

Ava clapped. "Impressive." She squeezed Tiana's arm. "We have to try whatever he just made, and the food smells delicious."

Tiana couldn't have loved her friend more. "Thank you so much. I really need this right now." She finished the rest of the cocktail then gestured to the bartender. "We'll both have whatever you made them."

"And an appetizer platter." Ava rubbed her hands together. "Can't wait."

The bartender plugged their order into the computer then put on another show as he made their drinks. He placed cocktails the color of a tropical ocean in front of them. "Enjoy."

Tiana took a sip. She winced as the alcohol burned down her throat then immediately took another one. "Nice and strong. Just what the doctor ordered." She wouldn't be able to afford a vacation anytime soon, so she would enjoy every second of that drink.

Ava had a drink and let out a whoop. "Now this is good and Instagram pretty." She took out her phone and shot a photo. "No ring, no white dress, and no cute baby, so this will have to do."

"Marriage isn't all it's cracked up to be. If I were you, I wouldn't be in a rush." Tiana drank more of the alcoholic goodness.

"Can a girl dream?" Ava frowned.

"I'm sorry." Tiana laughed a little too loudly. "You deserve happiness. I want you to have all you want and more. Hand me your phone. I'll call Brad and tell his butt to propose ASAP." She extended her arm toward Ava but almost knocked over their glasses in the process.

Ava swatted Tiana's hand away. "You can't drive yourself home after these drinks."

Tiana laughed. "I don't want to go home." She gasped then covered her mouth with both hands before bursting into tears.

"Oh no." Ava handed her a cocktail napkin. "Are you okay?"

"It's just so... hard." She hated how she sounded like a blubbering fool when she cried, but she couldn't help it. "I thought I had the dream, but it's turned into a nightmare. I'm drowning trying to keep us afloat. Every single day, I think about the baby I gave up. Every single day. Now knowing my dad got some side chick pregnant... it's just too much."

Ava blotted her friend's wet face with a cocktail napkin. "I know the adoption was closed. But is there any way you can reach out to the birth parents and ask how your child is doing?"

She shook her head. "Honestly, I left it all up to my parents. I mean, they practically gave me no choice. They convinced me when I signed the paperwork that pictures and updates would only hurt more. To just move on with my life. But I can't. I never will. And to now have a half sister who's kidnapped. It's going to devastate my mom."

Ava held up her drink. "I'm here for you, and I'm not going anywhere. Let's chill and make the most of our time. We'll eat some food and just relax."

"Thank you, Ava." Sniffling, she wiped mascara from under her eyes and tried to pull herself together. She closed her eyes, letting the air-conditioning cool her emotions and resolving to make it through the rest of the night. For the time being, with her blue drink, she was on vacation. She could figure everything else out later.

CHAPTER FOURTEEN

Jay lounged on the couch, scrolling through Twitter. The fan blasted hot air directly on his face. Someone knocked on his front door, and every muscle in his body froze. Tiana would use her key, and no one else had business at his front door at nine thirty at night. The person knocked again. If the police wanted to arrest him, they would bust his door down. *Could it be Ronnie?* No point in feigning absence. He grabbed the baseball bat from the corner. "Who is it?"

"Your favorite little brother, man. Open up," Xavier said.

Jay dropped his shoulders and opened the door. "Boy, am I happy to see your ugly face."

"Chicks would definitely disagree with your description." Xavier flashed a smile, revealing his slightly crooked teeth. Their parents hadn't been able to afford braces when he needed them in middle school, which had led to relentless teasing. But as a handsome twenty-seven-year-old making two hundred thousand dollars a year, Xavier topped the list of eligible bachelors in Silicon Valley, crooked teeth and all. He eyed the bat in Jay's hand. "Everything a'ight?"

Jay shoved the bat back in the corner and chuckled. "You wouldn't believe what's gone down. Come in."

"I'm all ears. Sorry to stop by so late without a text. Got off later than planned. I wanted to drop some cash off. Damn, it's hot in here. I forgot you don't have AC." Xavier's eyes searched the small space. "Is Tiana still up?" He sat on the couch and took out a wad of hundred-dollar bills. He counted five then handed the money to Jay.

"Thanks, X. I appreciate it." Jay tucked the money into his pocket and swallowed his rising guilt. He needed the extra cash more than he needed to placate his ego. "Tiana's out with her friend. Should be home soon."

Xavier checked his phone. "What's been going on?"

Jay propped his feet on the coffee table. "Have you seen the news coverage of the missing Black girl?"

Xavier scratched his head. "Nah, I've been too busy at work. What's that got to do with you?"

"Oh, right. Google be working the hell out of your Black ass. That's why they have all those perks, you know. To keep you there all times of the day and night." Jay laughed. "Free food, on-site gym, massages. You never need to leave."

Xavier nodded. "Yeah, all that is nice. As long as they keep giving me a paycheck, I'm happy. Shoot, I'll live there for all I care. You know Google has less than three percent Black people working there? I keep my head down, afraid they might realize I don't really belong and fire me one day."

"Come on, man." Jay lightly tapped the back of Xavier's head. "You graduated top of your class at Berkeley. You belong, and you're killin' it. Don't talk like that."

"Enough about me. What's up with this missing girl? You got me curious."

"I think Travis from the park set me up. His real name's Ronnie. He made sure I was at the same Walmart that the girl disappeared from. Now he's nowhere to be found."

Xavier's eye got wide. "For real? That skinny dude we've played with at the park? All you do is play ball together. That don't make sense."

"No, it don't make sense at all. To top it all off..." Jay pulled up the picture Tiana had sent him and showed Xavier. The knot tightened in his stomach.

"Damn! Someone's messing with y'all. You need to be real careful. We both know the last thing you need is more legal trouble." Xavier yawned.

"Yeah, I think you're right. Why don't you head home and get some sleep?" Jay could use some alone time to think about Ronnie and why the man would want to set Jay up.

"You're right. It's been real." Xavier stood and smiled.

Jay gave his brother dap. "Thanks for the cash."

"Don't keep thanking me. I wouldn't have made it through high school, let alone get a full ride to Berkeley without you taking me in. If you ever need anything, I got you. But you know who's been asking about you?"

"Yep. Janet continues to call me and leave messages." Jay rolled his eyes. "My lack of response has spoken loud and clear. My family is my everything. My relationship with her is dead and buried. Have a good night."

"Got it." Xavier left the apartment, shutting the door behind him.

Jay turned the lock and checked his phone. No notifications from Tiana. *Damn. I hope she's a'ight. She could at least call and give an ETA.* Jay couldn't help but worry the longer she stayed out. They knew the girl was Henry's daughter, and it made sense that someone had dragged Tiana into the mess. But Jay couldn't figure how Ronnie was involved. If Ronnie had planned to set Jay up, at best, he wanted to sow discord in Jay and Tiana's marriage. At worst, he wanted Jay behind bars. *But why?*

For most of his life, and especially in prison, Jay'd kept to himself and avoided making enemies. Though he'd scuffled with a couple people when they'd tried to test him, nothing had escalated to anything that would have followed him out of prison.

Needing a distraction, Jay switched on the television. The ten-o'clock news led with the expanding fire in Yountville. "Firefighters in Yountville, which in the past decade was acclaimed for having the highest concentration of Michelin-starred restaurants in the world, are working overtime to put out the blaze. Currently, less than two percent is contained."

The screen cut to a Latina newscaster with a picture of Zoe pinned in the corner. "Twenty-four hours have passed, and there has been an update in Zoe Miller's case. Police have confirmed that they suspect foul play in the ten-year-old girl's disappearance. They are now treating it as a kidnapping. There are no credible leads at this time. If you have any information at all, the police are urging you to call the number they have set up for this case." A phone number flashed on the screen. "Let's go live to the command center that's been set up in Oakland."

A reporter stood in the middle of a crowded hall, which had posters of Zoe Miller's face plastered around it. As he interviewed a police officer, a man in the back caught Jay's attention. Jay stood right in front of the TV for a closer look. Sure enough, Martin sat in the back of the room, speaking to someone. *I'll be damned.*

Once the story ended, Jay sat back down, more worried than ever. If someone had kidnapped Martin's daughter, what would they try to do to Tiana? The more he thought about it, the more concerned he grew that she was out so late. Someone could have been watching her or worse.

He called her, and it rang several times before going to her voicemail. He sent a quick text asking when she planned to be home. The knot grew even larger in his stomach. He needed her to make it home safely.

CHAPTER FIFTEEN

A midnight breeze swept through the apartment complex as Tiana struggled to jam the key into the lock. When she finally got it open, she stumbled into the dark, muggy apartment. She'd lost track of the number of blue drinks she'd had—enough to make her call an Uber for a ride. Though she'd seen a missed call and a text from Jay, she'd ignored both. Her uncharacteristic behavior would surely not sit well with him. But after all the drinks, she didn't have the mental capacity for an excuse. *Please let him be sleeping.*

When she opened the door to their room, the lamp next to Jay's side of the bed switched on and shone in her face like a cop's flashlight. *Great, he's up.*

He glared at her and made a show of checking the time on his phone. "Twelve thirty, and I couldn't even get a call from you?"

"I ended up staying out with Ava longer than expected. Sorry." She'd deserved a night to herself. Her life had been completely turned upside down in twenty-four hours.

Jay raised his voice. "You couldn't just text me to let me know? I couldn't sleep, worrying something had happened to you."

Tiana removed her clothes and left them in a pile on the floor. "I said sorry. Please lower your voice. You'll wake Marcus." She struggled with the straps on her heels then hopped up and down, attempting to pull off each shoe. If it had been a field sobriety test, she would have failed.

"I don't want to wake Marcus, but I'm not going to act like it's okay for you to stay out this late without a call or text, especially with some creep targeting you. Someone kidnapped Martin's daughter. Who knows what else they're capable of." He'd lowered his voice, but the bitterness remained.

"I had my phone in my purse. Like I said, I'm sorry. I'm an adult and can take care of myself. But in case you forgot, I waited eighteen months for you while birthing then taking care of a baby alone. So you know what? Shit happens." She stared him down, her anger surprising her.

Jay shut his eyes and kept them closed for a few seconds. "You won't ever get over it, will you?"

She attempted to lose the resentment in her voice. "I'm trying."

He reached for her. "I know. Look, we're both tired. Let's get some sleep and forget about this."

"Sure." She pulled on a tank top, placed her phone next to Jay's on the end table, then slipped into bed. Her head pounded, and her stomach felt queasy. She would certainly regret all those drinks in the morning.

A CRY RANG OUT. A DOCTOR in blue scrubs walked in with a haze surrounding him. He removed his surgical mask and focused on Tiana. "She's gone."

"No, she's not." Tiana reached her arm toward the door. "I heard her crying in the next room."

"The last time she was seen was at Walmart. No one's seen her since. She's gone." The doctor turned his back and walked away before disappearing.

Marcus's cry turned to a wail. Tiana shot out of her dreamworld and straight up in bed. The sudden movement caused her head to pound as if someone had hit her with a hammer. Nothing but sheets occupied Jay's side of the bed. She waited for Marcus to cry again. They'd been sleep training him for the past month and trying to let him fall back to sleep on his own when he woke in the middle of the night. She tiptoed to the living room. After switching on the hall light, her gaze traveled to her husband hunched over on the couch. "Jay?"

He turned to her, his eyes red and moist.

"What's wrong?" Tiana's heart raced. *Is guilt engulfing him? Did he do something to Zoe?* She stood over him, crossing her arms rather than offering comfort. "Is something going on?"

"No." He covered his head with both hands. "It's just obvious you'd rather be anywhere besides here with me." He drew a deep breath. "I can't give you the life you want."

All of her suspicion and anger evaporated, and she engulfed him in an embrace. "That's not true. I really am sorry about worrying you and staying out so late. I love you."

He pulled away. "Why, though? After what happened, the way we're struggling... how can you still love me?"

She squeezed his hand. "When we started getting serious, I told you about my past. You didn't judge me. I won't judge you, either, for what you've gone through. It's not your fault. You're still the man I fell in love with. When I said, 'For better or worse, until death do us part,' I meant every word. I still do. I always will."

Jay wiped his eyes. "I don't know what I'd do without you. When I was locked up, the only physical contact I had was when you'd come and visit me on the weekends. Holding you in my arms brought me back to life. You and Marcus mean everything to me. That's why I got so worried tonight. Someone sent you that picture, and until I find out who, I can't relax. I don't want nothing to ever happen to you."

She kicked herself for being so selfish earlier and not considering his feelings. She focused so much on how her life had changed that she neglected to understand how drastically his had too. "I'm going to talk to my dad about the photograph tomorrow. He needs to know someone's targeting me too."

"I saw him tonight on television. He was at the command center they set up to find Zoe." Marcus let out another cry. Jay stood. "I'll get him. Go back to bed." He strode down the hallway, wiping his face.

Tiana wanted to go back to bed, to lie her head on her soft pillow and wrap her body in her blanket. But her eyes hung heavy and low. She couldn't think clearly or muster the energy to walk back to her room. She stretched out on the couch and closed her eyes, wishing she would wake up to find that everything had been a bad dream. But her life never worked like that.

CHAPTER SIXTEEN

A phone buzzing on the dresser woke Jay from sleep. He removed Marcus's arm from his chest and leaned over to grab it. Tiana's phone flashed with *No Caller ID*. The fact that Tiana hadn't returned to their bed caused his heart to pound. He grabbed her phone, hopped out of bed, and rushed to the living room to check on her. Tiana slept soundly on the couch. The phone stopped vibrating, and he checked the time. *Only eight thirty?* Ridiculously early for someone to call, but they'd learned the hard way that bill collectors were relentless.

The phone buzzed again in his hand with another call from the blocked number. *What if it's Martin?* He shook Tiana gently. "Ti. Ti. Wake up. Someone's calling you. It might be your dad."

Tiana rubbed her eyes and murmured through a haze of sleep, "Answer it."

Jay tapped the green circle to answer the call and put it on speakerphone.

Tiana barely lifted her head. "Hello?"

"What you don't know will hurt her," a deep, ominous male voice said. "Tick tock."

"Who the hell is this?" Jay yelled.

The caller hung up without a response.

Tiana shot up, her bloodshot eyes wide and pure terror skewing her face. "That's what the picture said. That must have been the person who sent me the letter."

Jay's heart thudded in his chest. Whoever had called had Tiana's cell number and some damn nerve.

He ran to the door, flung it open, and quickly searched the surrounding area, but nothing seemed out of place—all of the other doors were closed, and no one was lurking outside. He shut the door, and his gaze darted around the living room to the flat-screen television on the stand, Marcus's toy bin to the right, his alphabet rug in the middle of the floor, and the coffee table in front of the couch. Everything appeared normal. Still, he couldn't shake the feeling that something was very wrong.

"Dada!"

Jay and Tiana jumped in unison at Marcus's voice. Jay held his arms out. "Buddy, come here. How'd you climb out of your crib?"

Marcus ran to the couch and into his embrace then kissed Jay's cheek. "Big Bird?" He pointed to the television.

Jay waited for Tiana's lead. Usually, she didn't want the TV on first thing in the morning, but the call had disrupted any normalcy. She switched on the television and streamed a *Sesame Street* episode. "Jay, let's talk in the kitchen."

"Good idea." He helped Tiana to her feet. Her hand trembled in his. "You good?"

"I'm scared, Jay." Her voice quivered.

He enveloped his wife in his arms, holding her close. "I'll protect you. I promise." Since bulking up in prison and keeping fit by lifting weights and playing basketball since returning home, he dared any man to try to harm his family.

Tiana sat at the kitchen table with her ear to the phone. "I'm going to call my dad."

"Good idea. I'll make coffee. I have a feeling it's going to be a long day."

Tiana huffed. "Voicemail. Again. I'll call their home number. He said he was going to tell my mom about Zoe, so he might have gone home by now." She called them on speakerphone, but after three rings, her parents' answering-machine greeting came on. "Mom. Dad. Call me as soon as you hear this."

Jay cleared his throat. "Try your mom's cell."

Her mom answered after a few rings. "Mom, I'm sorry to call you so early. Is Dad there? I really need to talk to him."

"No, Dad hasn't come home. I haven't seen him since the morning of when the girl disappeared. You actually saw him last at the police station."

Jay and Tiana exchanged glances, and Tiana shifted in her chair. "Do you know where he's been staying?"

"It sounds like you're on speakerphone. Is Jay there with you?"

Tiana bit her lip and glanced at her husband. "Yes, he is. We're trying to figure out what all this has to do with me."

"I'd feel more comfortable talking with you one-on-one, Tiana. Your call woke me up. I'll be in a much better mood if I can get a couple more hours of sleep and have some coffee. Why don't you swing by the house for lunch? Alone. I'll tell you what I know then. Bye"

Jay carried a glass of water and an aspirin bottle to Tiana. "Do you think your dad told her Zoe's his daughter? She might want to break the news to you alone."

"I hope so, or I don't know how I can stay silent." Tiana swallowed the pill then shook the bottle. "I just took the last two, and my head is pounding."

"I'll go to the store and buy more. I'll take Marcus with me so you can get some rest." He began to call Marcus to dress, but she interrupted.

"Weekends are my time with Marcus. Leave him and get some air. Take your time out."

Jay pecked Tiana on the lips then grabbed his keys. Though trying to play it cool, he'd wanted to explode with anger after the man had called and scared Tiana. He needed to calm down and think rationally in order to try to get to the bottom of things. Anger and frustration had gotten him locked up. He couldn't risk going back.

CHAPTER SEVENTEEN

Tiana's heart was still beating too quickly after the ominous call. She needed to talk to her best friend. She sighed in relief when Ava answered her phone. "Sorry to call so early, Ava. That person who sent that weird picture just called me."

"They called you this morning?" Ava asked. "What time is it?"

"It's almost nine now. He repeated the writing on the picture, something about what I don't know will hurt her." His deep, hushed voice still rang in Tiana's ears. She walked over to Marcus and ruffled his curls. Focused on Big Bird, Marcus swatted Tiana's hand. She went back to the kitchen and sat at the table. Tiana lowered her voice. "How does he have my cell number?"

Ava exhaled into the phone. "I have no idea. Who is this creep? This is getting out of hand."

"I know." Tiana told Ava about her brief call with her mom. "I just hope I can talk to my dad about the call and the photograph soon. They must be directly linked to whoever took Zoe."

"If you need anything, I'll be home, nursing a hangover. They say Bloody Marys work, right?" She chuckled.

Tiana rested her forehead in her palm. More alcohol was the last thing she wanted to think about. "I'm staying far away from Bloody Marys. Jay ran to the store to buy me some more aspirin. I might need the whole bottle."

Marcus ran to Tiana and patted her leg. "Show over, Mama. Park?"

Tiana focused on her son, who expected his usual Saturday-morning park visit. "Okay, Marky, give me one second. Ava, I'm going to walk Marcus over to the park. I'll call you later."

"I don't think that's a good idea," Ava said. "After the call you just got, I'm not sure it's safe. The person knows where you work and your cell number. What if he's watching you or something? Maybe you should wait for Jay to get back, and the three of you can go together."

"I can't let some jerk scare me. Saturday mornings are my and Marcus's time, since he's home with Jay all week." She wouldn't let anybody ruin that.

"Make sure you have your phone on you. If anything seems suspect, call the police."

"Thank you, Ava." She softened her voice. "I will."

Tiana hefted Marcus onto her hip. He'd weighed nine pounds at birth and still ranked in the ninetieth weight percentile for his age. "Let's put some clothes on you." She carried him to his room, which needed a good Saturday cleaning. Her idea of tidy didn't quite match up with Jay's. During the week, work had her too fatigued to clean, so she did it on the weekends. She dressed her toddler quickly in a pair of shorts, tank top, and hat. They would have to get in and out of the park before it got too hot. "Mama's going to put some clothes on. Play in here, and I'll be right back."

Marcus pulled the hat off. "'Kay. Park?"

"Yes, we'll go." Tiana crossed the hall to her room. She pulled on a pair of jean shorts and a white tank top, glancing at her reflection in the mirror. After having Marcus and with Jay in prison, Tiana had been unbelievably stressed. She'd had to consciously force herself to eat when pregnant, but after she had given birth to Marcus, she just accepted that anxiety filled her belly instead of food.

In the bathroom, after washing up, she ran a wide-tooth comb through her short curly hair. After Jay'd gone to prison, she could no longer afford to pay to get a weave at the salon. Not wanting chemicals in her hair, she'd cut it into a short bob. After staring at her reflection in the mirror for the first time after the big chop, she'd cried hysterically. Everything had been stripped from her, down to the hair on her head.

Tiana lined her large brown eyes with black eyeliner, applied mascara, then swiped lipstick on her full lips, a coral color that complemented her skin. Satisfied with her appearance, she left the bathroom and stopped back in Marcus's room.

"Park now?" Marcus asked.

"Yes, Marky. Let's go." She followed her son down the hallway toward the front door. He turned the doorknob to the hall closet, and Tiana retrieved the stroller and strapped him in.

AFTER A TEN-MINUTE walk to the park under the increasingly hot sun, Tiana sought refuge in the shade under a large tree over the playground. The smell of freshly cut grass and wildfire smoke clung in the air. A thick layer of haze from the fire in Yountville lined the sky like a virus infecting more and more of the horizon.

The mysterious call and Ava's warning had her on alert. She considered the park one of the only perks of their new neighborhood. She glanced at the empty basketball court, which lacked the usual crowd. She had no plan for what to do if she ran into Ronnie and hoped she wouldn't. Her mind spun as she tried to make sense of the events of the last twenty-four hours.

Marcus played on the toddler structure with a half dozen other kids around his age, squealing in delight. She watched him climb to the top of the slide. "Mama!"

She hurried over to him and stood at the slide's base. She beckoned him with outstretched arms. "Come down. I'll catch you."

He slid toward her, giggling the whole way.

She caught him and kissed his sweat-lined forehead.

"Again, Mama. Again!"

Tiana tried to enjoy the time with her son. Still, she couldn't escape her anxiety. She needed to speak with her mom.

"Morning, Teeni," someone said behind her.

Tiana froze, her pulse racing. She turned toward the voice. Devon, her ex-fiancé, stood there in a pair of black Nike running shorts. He wiped perspiration off his bald brown head with his shirt. His bare muscular chest heaved up and down. Sweat slid down his neck to his six-pack abs.

"Devon." She rolled her eyes. "You again?" Though their breakup had happened a decade before, she would never forgive him for it. Running into him far too often at the park didn't change anything.

"Out for my run." He panted dramatically. "We have to stop bumping into each other like this on Saturday mornings. This must be the fourth time in a row." His broad smile gave away that he didn't mean a word of it.

"You told me you bought a fancy new condo near Santana Row. How exactly is this park part of your run?" Tiana raised her eyebrows.

He pointed in the direction of a dirt path. "There's a trail." He focused his dark-brown eyes on her. "Plus, this park has the best view in Silicon Valley. You look more beautiful every time I see you."

She felt her cheeks grow warm. "Well, you're blocking my view of the son I made with my husband."

Devon nodded toward the play structure. "He's a good-looking boy. Everything okay with his pops? Is he working yet?"

"Cut the bullshit." She rolled her eyes again, something she did often when she spoke to him. "I denied your friend request on Facebook. I'm not giving you some type of update on my life."

"Last I checked, we still have mutual friends. We can always change our status to 'friends.' How about it, Teeni?" His voice softened.

She shielded the sun from her eyes with her hand. "You blew that. Call me Tiana."

"One, I can't get used to calling you Tiana. It's too formal. And two, give me a break." He tilted his head and smiled as the heat tanned his light-brown skin. "I'll send you another friend request. Accept it this time."

"Definitely not." She scoffed, but something occurred to her. "Hey, do you come to this park a lot other than your runs? I'm trying to find out about someone who plays basketball here."

Devon perched his hands on his slender waist. "I know a lot of people. What's his name?"

"Ronnie... but he also goes by Travis." She glanced around the park, somehow worried saying his name would cause him to appear like Candyman.

Devon shook his head. "Nope, don't know him. But I would definitely be wary of anyone who goes by two different names." Devon smirked. "What's going on with him?"

"Nothing."

"Okay, you don't have to tell me. But let's just sit for a minute. I need to stretch." Devon strolled to the bench and sat. Against her better judgment, she followed him.

CHAPTER EIGHTEEN

Jay focused on the thirty-two-foot-tall stainless-steel statue of the Virgin Mary outside the Catholic church in Santa Clara. After buying the aspirin for Tiana, he made a quick detour to collect himself and make a phone call. His heart had continued to pound in his chest all morning, ever since that phone call. The man's voice rang in Jay's ears. He wanted to scream or punch someone, but he couldn't lose his cool.

Though blocks away from Levi's Stadium, which was home to the San Francisco 49ers football team, the church was an oasis in the tech world. He'd stumbled upon it shortly after his arrest and while out on bail three years earlier. Though he wasn't Catholic, something about the enormous statue and large grassy pavilion around it soothed his spirit. But with the sky filled as if Mother Nature had taken up smoking, even the church couldn't help Jay shake the ominous feeling in his gut.

He hated helplessly standing by while someone targeted Tiana. The fact that Ronnie could have set him up—for some reason he couldn't understand—made it even worse. *What could Ronnie possibly have to do with Henry's daughter?* On top of it all, he'd lost all respect for his father-in-law. If he'd been able to hide a child from Tiana and Wanda for a decade, he could be concealing even more.

Since Jay'd been home, Martin had been on his case nonstop, harping about Jay needing to step up and put his life back together, as if he hadn't spent the last six months sending out hundreds of job applications.

A new law had passed the year before in California, making it so employers couldn't ask about criminal convictions on an initial application, but they could after deciding to hire someone. Jay'd already had four job offers rescinded after the employers checked his record. He didn't even get his hopes up anymore. For every stride he took forward, society fought against him, knocking him to his knees. On some level, he didn't understand why they'd even let him out of prison if he wouldn't have a chance to make a life for himself afterward. He'd thought long and hard about going back to school for a trade, but it would still be hard to find a job even after that. Most jobs, regardless of what type, discriminated against the formerly incarcerated, plain and simple.

He checked the time—nine thirty, late enough to make the call. He hated asking people for favors, but he had no other option. The phone rang, and after a familiar gruff voice answered, he spoke into the phone. "Harker, my man. It's Jay. How are you?"

"Jay Williams, good to hear from you. How've you been? I've been meaning to call you and take you out for a beer."

Jay hated small talk. He didn't have anything interesting to say anymore. But he didn't want to seem rude. "I'm... good. How you been?"

"You know, it's a grind. Staying out of trouble." Harker chuckled. "Or trying to, at least."

"I've never known you to stay out of trouble." He laughed. "I got a question. Is there a way to trace a blocked call on an iPhone?"

"There's a company that has an app claiming to trace blocked callers. I've heard mixed reviews of it because it can't trace all phones. What's up?"

The possibility of it working made it worth a try. "It's a long story that I don't want to bore you with. Text me the name of the app, though. And one more thing... can you run a name for me? I need any info you can find."

"Yeah, of course. What's the name and most recent place of residence?"

"The name's Ronnie Coleman. Lives in Stockton." Jay kicked himself. He should've tipped Danny better at the bar the other night.

"Will do, brother. I got a few jobs to do this morning, but I'll let you know what I find out."

"Thanks, Harker." He'd never imagined the only person he would keep in contact with after his prison stint would be a white dude. In San Quentin, very strict color rules applied, and people were segregated: whites, Blacks, Latinos, and Asians. People didn't socialize with anyone from a different ethnic background. He'd worked with Harker in the kitchen, though, and somehow, they'd formed an unlikely friendship.

Jay put the phone into his pocket, nodded toward the statue like the other people there did, then strolled back to his car. As he drove home, he doubled down on his resolve to find out who had called Tiana and sent her that photo.

He arrived to complete silence in the apartment. "Tiana?" He raced through the small space and to both bedrooms, but the place was empty.

Heart pounding, Jay ran back to his car and dialed Tiana.

She answered nonchalantly. "Hey."

"Tiana, where are you and Marcus?" He forced himself to breathe. *She's all right.*

"We're at the park like usual on Saturday mornings. Where else would we be?"

Jay slammed on the gas and navigated out of their apartment complex. "You could've let me know. I came home and freaked out not finding y'all here. That guy called this morning, remember? He's out there."

"We're fine, Jay. It's getting hot, so we're heading back pretty soon."

"I'm not taking any chances. Just sit tight. I'll come pick y'all up."
He wouldn't dare leave them at the park, where they could run into
Ronnie.

AT THE PARK, JAY SCANNED the basketball courts. A couple
teens shot around, but no sign of Ronnie. *Damn.* He almost wished
he could confront the dude and get answers. But it'd be better to do
that without Tiana and Marcus there. Jay joined Tiana at the playground. "Everything good? Anyone try to talk to you?"

Tiana crossed her arms. "Everything's fine. Nothing out of the
ordinary."

Jay sensed Tiana holding something back and squeezed her
hand. "I'm sorry I had you answer that call. I should have protected
you from him."

She looked into his eyes. "It isn't your fault."

Marcus squealed. "Dada!" He ran to Jay, sweat trickling down his
face.

"Hey, buddy. Looks like you had fun. You ready to go home?"
He picked up his son and held him toward the smoky sky.

Marcus pointed down the park. "Mommy friend?"

Jay looked at Tiana.

Tiana ran her fingers through her hair. "You're right. We should
get out of here. It's getting hot. Let's get Marky home."

Marcus shook his head and writhed out of Jay's arms. "No, no,
no." He ran back to the slide as fast as his tiny body would take him.

Jay chuckled. "Marky's got this 'no' phase down. By the way, I
called a guy, Harker, I did time with. He's a private investigator and a
hacker." Jay relayed the call to Tiana and didn't want to leave a single
detail out.

She pursed her lips. "Do you think that's a good idea? Involving
someone who was in prison? I mean, can you trust him?"

"He was in there for felony tax evasion. Yes, I do trust him. Not all people who did time are liars and untrustworthy. We're human." His heart hurt. If his own wife had such a bad perception of people because they had spent time behind bars, it seemed impossible to convince the rest of the world he wasn't a bad guy.

"Jay, you're not like them." She placed her hand on his cheek. "We've talked about this."

He took a step back. "Yes, I am. I'm like everybody who found themselves in a dark place for whatever reason, back against a wall, and did something they had to pay for. Most folks there struggled just to survive in their communities. Not everybody's born into privilege. Rich parents, private schools, college funds. The streets ain't no joke. People got a lot to worry about." He nodded.

"I have a lot of worries now." She arched an eyebrow in response.

Jay needed a reprieve from the sun beating down on him and the conversation. "Let's stop at the restaurant to get your car then go home."

"Sure. Thanks for coming to the park. I do feel better with you around." Tiana leaned in and planted a kiss on Jay's lips. "We're in this together. I'll go get Marcus."

Jay appreciated his wife's words. He had to figure out who was targeting his family and put an end to it.

CHAPTER NINETEEN

As Tiana exited the 101 freeway, she dialed Jay, who answered immediately. "I'm almost at my parents' house, and I'm fine. Please, don't worry about me."

"I'll stay on the phone till you get there. I still don't like the idea of you making a forty-minute drive out there by yourself."

"I know, but Mom made it clear she wants us to meet alone." She turned the corner and parked at her parents' expansive home in Morgan Hill. "I'm here. I'll call you when I leave. Bye."

She couldn't wait a second longer to talk to her mom. Her parents had built their million-dollar house from the ground up ten years before, right after Tiana graduated from high school and her dad had secured a position at the Alameda County District Attorney's office after working at the Solano County office for five years.

She couldn't have disagreed with Jay at the park earlier. Though she'd taken it for granted for the majority of her life, she had enjoyed privileges that many people, and especially African-Americans, did not. Married parents, plenty of income, the best schools. *I can't believe Dad ruined it all.* She jammed her key into the doorknob, swung the door open, then barged through the house. "Mom?"

"In the kitchen," her mom called.

Tiana rushed down the eerily quiet hall. Light shining through the windows illuminated the large kitchen, where her mom sat at the oak table. "Dad's still not back yet?"

Her mom sat hunched over a glass, cupping it in her hands. She hadn't styled her honey- blond hair like usual, so it lay past her shoulders, flat and lifeless. Her eyes seemed sad or tired or both. "No. Want me to pour you some sweet tea?" She gestured toward the refrigerator.

"I'll get some. Don't get up." Tiana opened the refrigerator, whose shelves brimmed with all kinds of healthy-looking food. Various items were tucked into every drawer and filled the door. She poured a large glass, joined her mom at the table, removed the picture of Zoe Miller from her purse, and laid it on the table.

Her mom's jaw dropped. "Where'd you get this?"

"Someone had it delivered to my work yesterday. This morning, the same person called me. He repeated what's written then hung up. Dad—" She caught herself. She needed to find out if her dad had come clean yet. "Has Dad mentioned any of this to you?"

A tear slipped down her mom's cheek. She brushed it away slowly. "Dad called just before midnight the day of his press conference. He said he's not coming home anytime soon. I didn't tell you yesterday because I thought he would surely come to his senses. It's not the first time he's said something like that. But we talked a little longer this morning. He said he's leaving me." Her mom exhaled a long, sad sigh.

Tiana's heart ached as if torn in two. "Did he say why?"

Her mom cradled her forehead with her hand. "No. I can't figure it out. His behavior is beyond bizarre. It makes no sense. Can he really walk away from a twenty-seven-year-long marriage this easily?" Tears rolled down her cheeks. She covered her face with her hands. "I'm sorry. You know Dad's my first and only love. I really can't imagine life without him."

Tiana stood and leaned down, wrapping her arms around her mom's shoulders. *He hasn't told her the truth about Zoe.* "It's gonna be okay, Mom. I ran into Devon at the park today, and it doesn't even hurt anymore. You'll get through this."

Her mom wiped her face and focused on Tiana. "Sit down and tell me about this run-in."

Tiana sat and eyed her hands instead of her mom. She'd purposefully avoided mentioning her encounters with Devon to anyone. A little guilt had lingered after she left it out of her conversation with Jay earlier, but she hadn't wanted him to get worked up about it. "He runs on the trail nearby. Until recently, I hadn't seen him, since... well... you know."

Her mom's voice dropped an octave, and she titled her head to the side. "Oh, I know all right. It'd be best if you found you and Marcus a new park."

"I thought I'd dodged a bullet by Devon breaking up with me. But now, it's hard not to wonder 'what if' sometimes." Tiana wanted to retract the words as soon as she'd said them. But she was relieved to finally voice what had been on her mind lately.

Her mom sipped her iced tea. "I know you've gone through a really difficult experience with Jay's conviction and fallout. You and Marcus have an open-ended offer to come stay with me here if you need some space to stretch out or cool off. But don't get the two issues confused. Never for a second forget what Devon did to you."

Tiana gave a small nod. "You're right."

The landline rang, and Tiana jumped.

Her mom rose from the table. "Let's check the caller ID." They hurried to the ringing phone in the living room, which displayed a blocked number. "Let the answering machine pick up." The recorded greeting played, followed by a beep.

"What you don't know will hurt her. But you're getting warm," the same voice that had called before said.

A lightning rod of terror shot through Tiana. *How could this man know my parents' home phone number?* Her trembling finger pointed at the machine. "That's him!"

"Whoever that is followed you here. I'm calling the police."

Tiana's phone rang next. She let out a scream. Her Dad's number popped up. "Dad? Where are you?"

"Tiana, I know you've been trying to reach me. Are you all right? You sound startled."

"No, I'm not. I'm at your house with Mom." She explained everything that had happened with the picture and two phone calls. "What's going on, Dad? Do you know who it might be?" He had to know something that would make it all make sense.

"You and Mom should go back home to Jay and sit tight. Our house is way out in the hills. He's dangerous if he kidnapped Zoe. I can't talk right now. I'll call you back when I can. Please don't tell Mom about Zoe just yet."

"Dad, wait. What about—"

The line went dead.

She couldn't move, paralyzed by fear. "That was Dad. He thinks the caller might be dangerous."

Her mom sucked in a breath. "Why would he call you seconds after that man? What if Dad's the one trying to scare me out of the house?"

"Dad wouldn't do that." Then his deception and infidelity came to mind. "But anything's possible."

"I'm calling the police." Her mom picked up her landline phone.

"Whoever Dad's worried about could be outside. Pack a bag. We should go straight to my place. We'll call the police from there."

They trudged down the hall of the six-bedroom home and into her mom's room. She'd never fully understood why her parents each had their own bedroom, but it suddenly made more sense. Her dad clearly wanted space to carry out a decade-long affair.

Her mom pulled out a few bits of clothing and rustled through the closet. "I left my carry bag in Dad's closet months ago. We'd come back from New York, and I planned to unpack his souvenirs, but I completely forgot. Would you grab it for me?"

Tiana walked next door and slid the mirrored closet door open. Inside, a perfectly organized space revealed her dad's belongings neatly tucked, hung, and stacked. The only out-of-place item appeared to be her mom's carry bag jammed in the corner. When she pulled it out, a plastic bag fell out from behind it, revealing that it contained red fabric.

Tiana grabbed the plastic bag and pulled out beautiful red velvet cloth. Her cheeks flushed—*Lingerie?* Ignoring her first instinct to shove it back in the closet, she held it up. It was a small child's dress with a huge white bow. She checked the tag, which had the number ten on it. *Must be for Zoe.*

Her mom walked into the room. "Did you find my bag?"

Tiana shoved the dress back in the bag, stuffed the bag back in the closet, then shut the door. Her throat tightened. "Yes." She tried to steady her trembling hands and gave her mom the suitcase. "Are you ready to go?"

"Yes, but how are you? You're shaking." Her mom opened her arms. She must have sprayed a few puffs of perfume in her bathroom because a lovely floral scent clung to her.

Tiana welcomed her mom's hug. In the embrace, she flashed back to her years as a youngster, when a kiss on a scraped knee made it all better and a nice long talk helped a teenage broken heart not feel quite as shattered. "I'll feel better when we're at my place with Jay."

After her mom finished packing her things, they left the house and walked to Tiana's car. Her mom slid into the passenger side. As Tiana lowered herself into the driver's seat, her gaze fell upon a folded piece of white paper stuck under her windshield wiper.

She retrieved the paper and opened it. Someone had scribbled an address with the name of an inn in Oakland on the paper. Though she didn't recognize the name or the address, the note had to be related to Zoe. Something told her there would be answers at the inn.

"What's that?" her mom asked when Tiana entered the car.

"Flyer from the supermarket that I forgot to remove earlier." She didn't mean to lie, but the desire to protect her mother had taken over. She needed to find a way to drop her mom off with Jay and head to Oakland without anyone stopping her. And quickly.

CHAPTER TWENTY

J ay stood when his mother-in-law walked through their front door with Tiana. A large pair of Gucci sunglasses shielded her eyes. A larger frown covered her face. "Hello, Wanda."

"Gamma!" Marcus clapped his hands and giggled.

"Hi there, Jay." Wanda immediately perked up and smiled as she picked up Marcus. She removed her glasses to reveal swollen red eyes. "Gamma missed you." She smothered Marcus with kisses.

Jay loved Wanda's relationship with Marcus. His mother had never even seen his son, and he had no intention of changing that. He hugged Tiana and whispered in her ear, "Is she okay?"

Tiana's gaze darted to Marcus then Jay. "Let's talk in our room."

Jay squeezed Wanda's shoulder. "We'll be right back. Make yourself comfortable."

Wanda sat on the couch with Marcus. "We'll be right here. Tiana, let's call the police after."

He paused. "Police?"

Tiana gestured toward their room. "That's what I want to talk to you about. Not in front of Marcus."

Once in their room, he shut the door. "So?"

She sat on the edge of the bed and breathlessly conveyed everything that had happened. "We have to involve the police. This whole situation's gone far enough."

"That's a lot to take in." He didn't want the police in his business ever again, but he couldn't say that. Tiana and Wanda would think he was hiding something. He needed to lie low.

"In my dad's closet, I found"—Tiana looked at her hands—"a dress for Zoe. It just hit home that the girl whose face is plastered all over the news is his daughter... my sister. The fact that he hid it from my mom and me for ten years just..." A sob stole her words.

Jay held her close while she cried. He couldn't imagine her pain. "I'm sorry, Ti."

She brushed the tears away with both hands. "The sooner we call the police, the better."

"Why don't you call in the kitchen with your mom? I'll be right out." He mulled over the new information after she left the room, kicking himself for not insisting he go with her to her parents' place. The creep calling her on their landline proved he'd followed her. Jay would never forgive himself if anything ever happened to Tiana. He had to protect her and Marcus. He pulled out his phone and dialed Harker again.

"Hello, Jay."

"I'm not calling to pressure you. I need you to check out another name while you're at it. Look, I know I'm asking a lot, so I can put some money toward it." It might mean Jay skipping a couple of meals, but he needed the information. It might prove invaluable.

Harker chuckled. "Calm down, now. I'll check out the names. No problem. No cost. What's the second name and city of residence?"

Jay lowered his voice. "Martin Moore. He's the district attorney in Alameda County and lives in Morgan Hill now."

"Whoa, a district attorney?"

"Yup, and my father-in-law. I need to know anything that stands out as unusual. But keep this between us." Tiana wouldn't want him investigating her dad. But if Martin did have his hand in something shady, Jay needed to know about it.

"Got it. I'll get back to you later today."

Jay appreciated Harker's willingness to help him out. He needed more than two hands to count the number of times he'd saved Harker's butt. Harker was always rubbing someone the wrong way in the prison's kitchen.

When Jay was young, his dad worked for fifteen years at the NUMMI auto body plant in Fremont. His dad's coworkers didn't seem to have a clue about his abusive behavior as a husband and father. The times Jay'd stopped by his dad's work, they always seemed to genuinely like him and hold him in high esteem. The nicest his father ever acted toward Jay occurred at the job. Jay's father had mastered the art of duplicity. So had Martin, apparently.

He joined Tiana in the kitchen, where she pounded her laptop keys at the kitchen table. "What happened to calling the police?"

She blew out air. "They told me to file an online police report."

Wanda fanned herself with an envelope, pacing the small space in the kitchen. "They obviously lost their damn minds."

Tiana wiped sweat from her forehead. "Budget cuts, they said."

Her mom stopped behind Tiana and peered at the computer screen. "This is serious. Why don't we go down there and demand to speak to someone?"

Jay definitely wouldn't willingly go to the police station. "I don't think that'd help. I don't see them taking it seriously. I bet they'll process the report once they get it."

Tiana grabbed her mom's hand. "Try to relax, Mom."

Marcus ran to the kitchen and tugged on Wanda's blouse. "Hungy, Gamma."

Wanda hoisted Marcus onto her hip. "What does my baby want to eat?" She carried him to the kitchen and opened a cabinet. She shut it then opened the fridge. After closing it, she looked at Tiana. "Where's the food?"

Jay's cheeks grew flaming hot. "I haven't exactly gotten around to grocery shopping yet. It's on my to-do list today."

"How about we pick up a few groceries then make lunch?" her mom suggested. "Tiana, why don't we all go?"

"Can you go with Jay and Marcus? I need to finish this police report. I also have a pile of dirty clothes for the laundry." Tiana folded her hands and smiled at Jay.

He hesitated. "We can wait for you, Ti."

Marcus whined, "Hungy, Gamma."

Wanda sighed. "Why don't we go, Jaylen? The poor boy wants some food."

Jay fought the urge to give Marcus his first spanking ever. *Is this boy really playing the starving-child role?* "He just ate breakfast not too long ago, Wanda. Tiana and I can go together later. It's a team effort, shopping with Marcus."

Arching his back, Marcus whined again. "Hungy!"

"Come on, Jay. Please take him and go to the grocery store with my mom. I need some time alone to finish this. Please." She narrowed her eyes at him.

"Ti, some stalker's on the loose. I don't feel right leaving you. Who knows what he'll do next."

"I don't think anyone would have the nerve to try anything in a packed apartment complex. I promise I won't open the door if anyone knocks. Please. Marcus is hungry." She clicked her fingernails against the kitchen table.

Jay pressed his fist to his mouth. Tiana really didn't have to rub that in with her mom there. "Fine. Call me right away if anything else happens."

Tiana returned her focus to the laptop. "Will do."

CHAPTER TWENTY-ONE

Tiana submitted the police report then jotted a quick note to say she ran to the corner store to get laundry detergent. She stuck it to the fridge with one of the magnetic alphabet letters. With luck, she would be back before Jay and her mom returned. Shopping with Marcus usually took forever because he wanted to stop and point at everything. If he did that today, it would buy Tiana plenty of time.

She grabbed her purse, left the apartment, and ran to her car. Once inside, she reread the note that had been left on her windshield then typed the address into her phone's map. Jay and her mom would be furious with her for going there, but she didn't have a choice. If anything seemed shady, she would head straight home. A gut feeling told her whoever had left her the note wanted to give her information, not harm her. With her dad staying somewhere other than at his house with her mom, Tiana had a hunch it had to do with him.

It took her fifty minutes, but Tiana finally got to the Oakland Hills location just over an hour's drive from the Yountville fire. Heavy black smoke clogged the reddish-orange sky. She could have mistaken it for a completely different planet. She slowed and surveyed the scene at the ritzy inn and a huge fountain in the middle of the roundabout. A valet worker approached her vehicle. "Would you like us to park your car?"

"No, I can park it." She needed a quick getaway if anything happened. Valets meant witnesses. She doubted anyone would try anything in front of an audience.

The valet worker pointed toward the back. "Feel free to self-park in that lot."

She continued past the valet and the tall, perfectly manicured shrubbery that lined the property, hiding the occupants' secrets from outsiders. In the parking lot, she spotted her dad's black Jaguar. She grabbed the note again, noting that it said room eight. And lo and behold, her dad had parked his car right outside the door with a number eight on it. She dug through her purse for her mace. Gripping it in her palm, she marched to the room, where she pounded on the door. She stepped aside so as not to be viewed through the peephole. The door crept open.

Her dad stepped one foot outside. "Tiana? How'd you...? What the...?"

Tiana shoved the note into his hand. "I have as many questions as you have. First one: What the hell are you doing here?"

Her dad read the note a furrowed brow. "Where'd you get this?"

"Someone put it on my car at your house. Whoever it is led me here to you. Let me in so we can talk."

Her dad didn't budge.

Tiana's stomach sank. *Someone else must be here with him. Someone he doesn't want me to know about.* "Who's here with you?" Her voice shook.

Her dad's face fell. "I don't want to do this right now."

She took a step back. He didn't want her there, and she didn't want to stay. But then again, he didn't deserve to get away with this crap. Her life had been turned upside down: Jay dragged in for police questioning, fear and anxiety caused by the photograph and calls. She lunged forward and pushed the door open.

A woman sat on the edge of the bed in the middle of the room. The straight dark-brown hair atop her head looked like a wig. Though wearing a full face of makeup, she looked worn out, her brown skin pale. The woman cast her eyes down as if ashamed to be there. Tiana didn't know the woman, but she had definitely seen her before. Then Tiana gasped. The woman had been on the news—the kidnapped girl's mother.

Tiana turned to her dad. "Is she Zoe's mother? The woman you're having an affair with?"

Her dad's mouth moved before finally settling on a response. "Yes."

Her pulse spiked. "How could you? After everything's Mom's done for you. After almost three decades of marriage. How could you betray her like this?"

"It's too complicated to explain right now. Josie—I mean Josephine—and I, we're just focused on finding Zoe."

"I'm sorry we had to meet like this." Josephine rose from the bed, seeming frail.

Tiana glared at the woman but turned her wrath on her dad. "What the hell have you done? Why did someone kidnap your daughter? Why is he targeting me? Who is it?"

"Tiana, we don't know. But Jay's name has come up at the police station multiple times. You need to keep your eyes open. With his history, you don't know what he's capable of."

"How dare you speak about Jay like that. You're a hypocrite." Her gaze darted between her dad and Josephine. She couldn't breathe. Her body refused to take in the information or oxygen she needed. She ran out of the room and to her car as fast as her legs could take her. After throwing open the door, she collapsed into her seat then fumbled with her keys until she got the right one into the ignition and started it. She sped out of the parking lot, gulping air that didn't seem to make it to her lungs.

Tears blurred her vision. She veered off the road and parked in the dirt. She wouldn't make the drive home in her emotional state. She dialed her husband. "Jay, I need you now. Please. Come. I'm in the Oakland Hills."

"Are you okay? What happened? How'd you get to the Oakland Hills?" Jay breathlessly fired off questions, his voice in a panic.

"Please, just come. I'm safe. I just need you."

"We're leaving the grocery store now. We'll head straight to you," he said.

"No, just you. Leave Marcus with my mom at our place. I'll send you my location." Tears streamed down her cheeks.

"I'm on my way."

Tiana stumbled out of her car. The midday summer heat overwhelmed her and burned her skin. The smoke mixed with car exhaust from vehicles speeding by filled her nostrils. Hands to her knees, she retched onto the gravel road. She couldn't wait for her dad to do the right thing. *I have to tell Mom.* It would crush her. Tiana had to figure out who had led her to discover her dad's affair and why. Finding the identity of the person might just lead the police to finding her half sister.

CHAPTER TWENTY-TWO

Jay checked the location Tiana had shared with him. *Why the hell is she in the Oakland Hills?* "Wanda, we need to leave now. Please strap Marcus into his car seat." He abandoned the grocery cart and returned to the car with his mother-in-law and son in tow.

He hurried to start the car, not even waiting until Wanda had fastened her seat belt to pull out of the parking spot.

She stared at him while he sped out of the parking lot. "What's happened, Jay?"

"I'm not exactly sure." He filled her in on what little Tiana had told him. "I hope she's okay." He had no idea how or why Tiana had gone to the East Bay. *Did somebody force her there?* A helpless feeling engulfed him, making him shift uncomfortably in his seat.

"That missing girl is from Oakland. I'm sure it has something to do with her." Wanda huffed. "Tiana can be so stubborn. I'm sure she sent us to the store to sneak up there."

That hadn't even crossed Jay's mind, but it almost made sense. Tiana did have a secretive side. Apparently, she'd inherited it from Henry. But Jay couldn't judge either of them. He kept plenty of secrets too.

JAY PARKED ON THE SIDE of the road behind Tiana's car then jumped out to meet her.

She ran to him, almost collapsing in his arms.

Jay held her at arm's length to inspect her. Her black eye makeup had smeared. Sweat coated her face. She was clearly rattled but seemed okay. "What's wrong, Ti? What you doing out here?"

She tried to speak, but a sob stole her words. She fell into Jay's embrace again.

Her held her close as she trembled, smoothing her windblown hair. "It's okay. I'm here now."

She wiped her tears away. "I found my dad at an inn with the other woman. It's the woman who we've seen on the news. The reality of his affair—what he's done to my mom—it hit me hard, seeing them together."

He let his mouth fall open. "Oh, Ti, I am so sorry. Does he know who kidnapped Zoe? Or who's been stalking you?"

Tiana bit her bottom lip. "No. Please, take me home. I can't drive like this. I need to tell my mom everything." She walked to Jay's car and slumped into the passenger's seat.

He joined her in the car and started the ignition. "I'm so sorry. We still gotta figure out who's been following you." He pulled out onto the road. "I'm thinking somebody who got a grudge against your dad. I mean, he's a prosecutor. He's spent decades locking people up. I'm sure there's hella people who want revenge." He didn't mention it but wondered whether Martin had prosecuted Ronnie at some point.

Tiana nodded. "That would make sense. But my half sister's in serious danger. Even though I'm furious with my dad, I still want his daughter found safe. Who knows what her kidnapper has done to her."

Jay squeezed her knee. "We gotta stay positive. Let's not talk 'bout worst-case scenarios."

He couldn't believe what Martin had done, but he hated the man following Tiana even more. He'd purposefully led her to discover her dad's affair. If that had been his plan all along, he should have been satisfied... but Jay worried it was just the beginning. Martin's daughter had been kidnapped. Jay feared what else the person was capable of and how far he planned to take his dangerous game.

THEY ARRIVED HOME TO a sweltering apartment and found Wanda in the bathroom. She sat next to Marcus, who splashed in a bubble bath with a huge smile on his face. He clapped his hands, forming small bubbles. "Dada!"

"Well, there you are, Tiana. What got into you? Where have you been?" Wanda shot rapid-fire questions at Tiana. "You had Jay and me worried sick, taking off like that. Marcus was upset, too, when Jay had to leave to meet you. He cried for at least half an hour. I thought he would make himself pass out, so I ran him a cool bath."

"It's a long story. We need to talk." Tiana's eyes brimmed with tears, and her voice quivered. "You're not going to like what I have to tell you."

Wanda stood and wiped her hands with a towel. "All right, but I'm starting to think coming to your place wasn't the best idea. My house has AC. Maybe all of us should head back over there."

Marcus splashed his hands in the water. "Bubbles, Dada."

Jay cleared his throat. "You two should talk. I'll let Marcus soak a little longer. We can talk about the AC after."

Jay wouldn't go back to Martin's house, even if it did have air-conditioning. Staying in the middle of nowhere in Morgan Hill did not sound smart. He would prefer to sweat it out in the safety of his own spot. With a kidnapper and stalker targeting his family, he didn't want to take any unnecessary risks.

CHAPTER TWENTY-THREE

Tiana marched down the hall, her belly filled with dread. Her tank top stuck to her with sweat. She carried the burden of her dad's affair like a loaded gun she would have to aim at her mom.

At the kitchen table, her mom fanned her reddened face with Tiana's electricity bill, which she'd picked up from the counter. "Sit and tell me what happened."

Tiana sucked in a breath, trying to draw from a well of courage that had run dry. "I found Dad at an inn in the Oakland Hills. He was with another woman there. His mistress. She's not just any woman. She's the kidnapped girl's mom."

Wanda gasped then covered her mouth with both hands.

Tiana held back tears. "I'm so sorry. I thought you should know. I feel horrible."

Her mom tilted her chin up, gazing at the ceiling. "Tiana, I already knew about Dad's affair. But I never for the life of me would have thought her child was the kidnapped girl on TV."

"Wait, you knew Dad was cheating on you?" She searched her mom's face for answers. There was no way Wanda could have accepted her dad's infidelity.

The older woman closed her eyes. "I found out about it around the time that you and Devon started dating the end of your junior year, and—"

"Over a decade ago?" Tiana couldn't fathom her parents hiding a secret like that for so long.

"I have threatened to leave so many times." She shook her head. "Every time, Dad promised me he would end it. Wash, rinse, repeat. We've gone through the cycle so much that I've lost count. It killed me to pretend we had a happy marriage all these years. Ever since you left for college, he spends at least half the weekends out of a month away. Maybe more. But like I said, I never knew she had a child." Her mom's eyes looked like the affair had broken her.

Tiana's stomach turned. She couldn't believe her parents could have hidden something like a decade-long affair from her. "It's not just her child. Dad said the kidnapped girl is his daughter."

"Excuse me?" She pursed her lips and narrowed her eyes.

"Zoe Miller is Dad and that woman's daughter. Whoever kidnapped that girl knows intimate details of his life. He wanted me to find out about the affair and my half sister." Tiana couldn't fathom having a sister, let alone one who'd been kidnapped.

"Dad lied to you." Her mom cursed under her breath. "Your father had a vasectomy after your birth. That girl is not his child."

A chill ran down Tiana's spine. "That's what Dad said. That's why he was at the police station. People get vasectomies reversed, or they fail. That's what must have happened with Dad. They both said the girl is theirs."

"Absolutely not." The color drained from her mom's face. "That bastard! Take me to him, Tiana. We need to confront him."

Tiana's pulse spiked. The possibility of what her dad might have done rendered her almost mute. "Let's go," she whispered. As she headed toward the door, a silent panic overwhelmed her. Part of her didn't want to return to the inn. Something told her she would never be the same if she did.

TIANA AND HER MOM TOOK Jay's car. When they arrived at the inn, her dad's Jaguar still occupied the same parking space. Neither woman had spoken since they left. Tiana broke the silence. "He's in room eight."

Her mom hopped out quickly. They hadn't even discussed a plan of action. Tiana stood a couple steps back from the door as Wanda pounded on it. The door cracked open. Her mom barged into the room.

"Wanda, come on." Her dad's face contorted in a grimace. "What do you think you're doing here?"

Her mom pointed her index finger right at her dad. "Don't you dare get that tone with me. You're my husband. You have the nerve to ask me what I'm doing here? You owe me answers." She pointed at Tiana. "You owe us both answers."

Her dad stood in front of the door. "After Tiana stopped by, I arranged for private security at our house and Tiana's apartment. They should be there by now. You both can go back either to our place or Tiana's place and be safe. I took care of it. Please. Leave."

Tiana stepped forward, backing her mom up. Her dad had some nerve acting like throwing money at the situation would solve everything. They deserved answers, not just rent-a-cops. "That's the last thing on our minds right now. We need to talk. It's up to you whether you want to make a scene or not."

He rolled his eyes then waved them both into his room. "Come in. Let's get this over with."

Once inside the room, Wanda scowled at Josephine. She then directed her full rage at her husband. "I only came here for one thing. Whose child is Zoe Miller?"

"She's Josephine's and my daughter," he whispered without making eye contact.

"Tell the damn truth, Martin!" her mom yelled.

Sweat beaded her dad's forehead. He mumbled incoherent words.

"Don't tell me you could possibly have done what I think you did, Martin."

He focused on Tiana. "I did what was best for everyone."

A thick cloud of horror descended on Tiana. It rested on her shoulders, rendering her immobile. Every muscle in her body itched to activate, to take her as far away as possible. But she couldn't move. She had to hear the truth.

"Admit what you did!" The neighboring occupants had to have heard her mom's pleas.

"Tiana, you had your whole life in front of you." Her dad stepped toward her, raising his palms. "The best solution to the predicament you'd gotten yourself in was to take her away."

The word "her" stabbed Tiana in the chest. "What are you saying?"

"Zoe—the missing g-girl"—her dad stammered—"is..."

"No," Tiana said.

"Zoe is your daughter." He released a loud sigh as if unlocking a vault he'd kept from her.

She can't be. She stumbled backward, the whole room spinning under her feet. "You forced me to give her up for adoption. You wouldn't even let me hold her. And you've had her this whole time?"

"Josephine and I... we've loved Zoe like she was our own." He backpedaled toward the other woman.

Josephine reached toward Tiana. "We've done nothing but love Zoe."

"Don't you dare talk to my daughter!" her mom yelled at Josephine. "Love has nothing to do with stealing someone's baby and claiming her as your own. Nothing! It's twisted!"

A scream escaped from the deepest depths of Tiana. She fell to her knees.

Her dad hurried toward her, but Wanda shoved him backward. "Don't touch her. You're a monster, Martin! An absolute monster! Both of you." She pulled Tiana to her feet.

Sobs racked Tiana's body, and she choked on her tears. The full weight of the trauma she'd experienced ten years before threatened to swallow her whole. "I gotta... get out... of here." She clawed at the door then tumbled outside, her head throbbing. Her phone rang—a blocked number. "What do you want from me?" she screamed into the phone.

"Tick tock. There's even more to know," the same ominous male voice said.

She scanned the parking lot. The scenery blurred through her tears. "Leave me alone!"

Her mom grabbed the phone. "Look here, you son of a—" She eyed the screen. "Coward. He hung up. We need to get out of here. I'll drive."

Tiana climbed into the passenger seat and closed her eyes. Her heart pounded so hard she feared it would explode. "I have to find her, Mom. I have to find my daughter." She had no idea where to start, but she would do everything in her power to bring her daughter, Zoe, home.

CHAPTER TWENTY-FOUR

Jay's stomach bottomed out the second Tiana walked through the door. Bloodshot and swollen eyes gave away that she had been crying for a while. "Ti?"

She fell into his arms, her whole body trembling.

"Mama?" Marcus said.

Wanda came in after Tiana, her face pale and sullen, but she put on a smile as she scooped up her grandson. "There's my big guy." She patted Tiana's back. "I'm going to take Marcus to his room so you can talk to Jay." She turned to him. "Whoever's been watching Tiana called her when we were at the inn. He's obsessed with her and our family. I don't know what he's capable of. We need to put our heads together and come up with a way to make the police take this situation seriously."

"Ti's safe here." Jay led Tiana to the couch while Wanda carried the toddler down the hall. "What happened?"

Tiana took a deep breath. "Zoe Miller's not my half sister." Her voice came out so weak that Jay had to strain to listen. "She's my daughter, the one my dad forced me to give up for adoption my senior year of high school."

He pulled her close. "Ti, that's horrible. This is beyond effed up. You and Zoe don't deserve this. The dude called you when you were there?"

Tiana sobbed. "Yes. He said there's more to know. I need to find my daughter, Jay! I want to meet her. Hold her. Love her."

"We'll find her. I promise." He would have moved mountains to help his wife reunite with her daughter.

"We need to go straight to the police station. If they won't take me seriously over the phone, I'll make them in person." Tiana braced herself to stand.

He recoiled at the suggestion. "And say what? You'll sound like a crazy person claiming out of left field that you're Zoe Miller's mom. Do you have any paperwork? Like a birth certificate? I don't want you humiliated by the police. They're real good at doing that."

"No, I don't have anything. They didn't even let me name her. They just took her away. I can't sit around, doing nothing. What can I do if I don't go to the police?" She stared at him, pleading for answers with her eyes.

"We need to put the app Harker told me about on your phone. We can trace any calls that come in. We'll at least have something to give to the police." Jay took out his phone, looked for Harker's text, then showed it to Tiana. "Sign up for this app. I'm going to make a call."

"Call?" Tiana furrowed her brows. "What kind of call?"

"I'll call my PI friend again. He told me about all kinds of crazy jobs he worked. He's real good at what he does. I'll ask what he thinks about Zoe's kidnapping. I bet he can help us." Harker had to have worked on missing person cases before. Calling him would definitely be better than doing nothing.

Tiana grabbed her phone out of her purse. "Okay, I'll download the app. Go ahead and contact him."

Jay called Harker then cursed when voicemail picked up. He sent a text. "He'll get back to me." He rested his arm around her shoulder. "Remember when I said there was something weird after the police questioned me and kept showing me all those pictures of Zoe?"

Tiana nodded. "Yeah."

"What I didn't say is that"—Jay peered into his wife's eyes—"she looks just like you."

Tiana burst into tears.

A loud banging on the door startled Jay. He got up, grabbed the bat, then peered through the peephole. "A dude wearing all black and an earpiece is outside our door."

Tiana hurried to his side. "Do you think that's the person who's been following me?"

Jay shrugged. "Who is it?" he called.

"Adan Alvarez," the man replied. "I'm paid security for Tiana Williams and her family."

Tiana patted Jay's shoulder. "My dad did mention he had hired security."

Jay relaxed his shoulders a bit. "Hold your security badge up to the door."

Adan did as instructed.

Jay placed the bat down and opened the door. "I'm Jay Williams, Tiana's husband. You need something from us?"

Adan shook Jay's hand. "Not right now. Let me know if you need anything from me. I'll be stationed right outside the door."

Marcus ran toward Jay, his hands balled into fists and tears lining his red cheeks. "Dada." He raised his arms. Jay picked him up.

Wanda came up behind the boy. "He's been rubbing his eyes. Someone needs a nap. The novelty of having Grandma over has worn off."

"I'll put Marcus down and be right back." Jay carried Marcus down the hall, contemplating the agony he suffered after Tiana gave birth to their son. Jay hadn't been able to be there or visit with either of them for over a month, so he thought he understood Tiana's pain. Her parents had forced her to give up her baby, which he'd known, but never in his wildest dreams had he imagined Martin could be so cavalier to raise the girl as his own. How heartless to deprive Tiana of a relationship with her own daughter.

When Jay placed Marcus in his crib, the boy kicked his feet. "Not tire, Dada."

"You need a nap, buddy. Just close your eyes and sleep." Jay closed the blinds to darken the room then stepped out while his son screamed in protest.

Jay walked back toward the living room and could hear Tiana ask tersely, "Did you know Dad took my baby?"

He reached the two women and stood silently.

Wanda cringed as if the thought pained her. "No, honey. I had told Dad we could help you raise the baby. But he was adamant you put her up for adoption. He insisted he'd handle everything. I never imagined he would give her to that woman. It's disgusting. I was so naïve. I'm sorry."

Tiana's shoulders slumped. "Ten years. For ten years, Dad has raised my daughter as his own. Now she's gone. I might never get the chance—"

"Don't talk like that." Jay spoke up. "We're going to find Zoe."

"Yes, Tiana. After the shock has worn off, we'll talk to Dad and figure out what to do next. We'll find her and bring her home." The worry lines in her forehead belied her confident voice.

"I'll never speak to that man again or forgive him. He's ruined my life. He robbed me of a relationship with Zoe. Now she's gone."

Tiana spoke with such conviction that Jay believed every word. He'd never seen his wife so upset. That meant a lot, considering the hell they'd endured for three years.

"I know you're hurt. I'm hurt too." Wanda reached out to Tiana. "But we have to do what's best for Zoe. That means working with Dad to bring her home. I know your father. He didn't want to see your future ruined because of an unplanned pregnancy. He did the wrong thing, but I know he did it out of love."

Tiana shot to her feet. "How can you possibly defend him? There's absolutely nothing you can say that justifies him stealing my daughter. He's been raising her with his mistress. Lying to my face for ten years. You might be able to make excuses and somehow come to terms with him cheating on you for a decade, but I can't. I won't. Never!"

"Ti." Jay raised his palm toward her. "We understand how you feel. You have every right in the world to be upset. But what your mom is saying is—"

"My daughter's face is plastered all over the news because of him." She waved to the television. "Someone's kidnapped her. I may never have the chance to ever hold her. After I gave birth, my dad's doctor friend wouldn't even place her in my arms. You have no idea how that's torn my heart apart. Every day, I've regretted giving her up. The only thing that consoled me was imagining one day being reconciled with her. I imagined her turning eighteen and me finding her. But now this!" Her face reddened, and she pointed a trembling finger at Jay then Wanda. "Don't either of you stand here and say you understand how I feel. You have no right to tell me what I should do."

Jay's loyalty lay with his wife. He wouldn't try to keep the peace between Tiana and her parents. "You're right. I'm sorry. I'm behind whatever you wanna do."

Wanda reached out to Tiana. "Tiana, all I'm saying is that sitting around and pointing fingers at people won't bring Zoe home. We need to—"

"No, *we* don't need to do anything." Tiana's nostrils flared. "I'm an adult. I don't have to take your or Dad's bullshit anymore. You two tried to control my every move and plan my life when I was young. Those days are over. Just go home. Dad said there's security at your place. Besides, whoever's been following me wants *me* for some reason, not you." Tiana turned to Jay. "I'll stay here with Marcus. Please drive her home."

"I don't want to leave you so upset." Wanda softened her voice. "I'm sorry about all this."

Tiana stormed past her mom and down the hall. Their bedroom door slammed closed.

Jay headed after Tiana. Marcus still screamed, protesting his nap. Jay opened the door to their room first. After surveying her, he stepped forward and caressed her face. "I'll take Marcus with me to drop off your mom and head straight back. He'll fall asleep in the car. But Ti, promise me you won't take off again. Stay safe here with Adan watching our place."

"I promise." Tiana flounced across their bed and rested her head on her folded arms.

Jay crossed the hall to Marcus, who stood in his crib, his face beet red from crying in the heat. He stretched toward Jay. "No nap, Da-da."

Jay picked him up. "You're in luck today, buddy. Let's go for a ride."

Marcus grinned broadly in Jay's arms. He hiccupped as his rapid breathing slowed.

Wanda waited by the front door. "I feel horrible."

Jay patted her shoulder. "We both do." They stepped outside, and Jay mumbled a hello to Adan. "Can you make sure no one gets in the apartment? We're not expecting nobody."

Adan gave a quick nod. "Absolutely."

Jay planned to drop Wanda off as quickly as possible. He refused to leave Tiana alone for a second longer than needed. The mystery of Tiana's connection to Zoe Miller had been solved. Now Jay had to figure out who had known about it.

THOUGH JAY'D TRIED to make small talk on the drive to Wanda's house, neither of them could muster it. Too much had happened. He silently grappled with everything and assumed she was doing the same. The temperature on his dash read 101 degrees, and he was grateful for the car's AC.

He pulled into the roundabout at Wanda's perfectly manicured house. A dark SUV with tinted windows had parked in the driveway. Jay stopped behind it. A man wearing a suit and wired earpiece stepped out of the SUV and approached his window. Wanda leaned over. "I'm Wanda Moore. I live here."

The man walked around the car and opened Wanda's door. "Nice to meet you, Mrs. Moore. I'm Sergio Jimenez. Your husband hired me to surveil the property. Let me know if you need anything."

Jay checked behind him, where Marcus slept soundly in his car seat. Jay wouldn't dare leave Marcus in the car alone. He stood outside the door. The oppressive heat from the merciless sun surrounded him. "Wanda, be safe. I'm a call away if you need anything."

"Thanks for the ride, Jaylen." Wanda opened her front door and disappeared into the expansive house.

Jay gave Sergio a salute then escaped the sweltering heat, climbing back into the car and cranking the AC. He backed out of the driveway then slammed on the gas, intent to return home quickly. They had to come up with a plan to figure out the identity of the mysterious caller. He hoped that finding that person would lead to Zoe.

CHAPTER TWENTY-FIVE

Tiana lay on her bed in a tank top, tears streaming down her cheeks. Grief, fear, and rage mixed inside of her like a Molotov cocktail. The fan in her room provided no relief, and she swore the heat was making everything worse.

But the heat paled in comparison to the agony and heartbreak caused by Zoe's kidnapping. Since she'd downloaded the tracing app and paid for a subscription, she both wanted the stalker to call again yet feared it. The instructions told her to decline the blocked call, which would automatically forward it to the tracing company. They would use their software to unmask the caller then send a report to Tiana. She just hoped it would work.

The traumatic turn of events and the recent run-ins at the park transported her back to high school and her relationship with Devon. She weighed whether she should involve him. He'd broken her heart their senior year in high school by calling off their engagement and disappearing a month before Zoe's birth. She'd vowed never to forgive him or forget what he'd done to her, but she would be a complete hypocrite to keep the knowledge of Zoe's relationship to him a secret, given what her own father had hidden from her.

She grabbed her phone and searched the internet. Devon Price, South Bay Venture Capitalist populated immediately. She called his listed number but got voicemail. *Damn, voicemail. Does anyone pick up the phone anymore?* "Devon, it's Tiana. Look, I have something very important to talk to you about. Please call me back." She left her phone number then hung up.

The phone rang minutes later with Devon's number flashing on the screen, and she answered on the third ring.

"Tiana, I got your message. I'm surprised to hear from you. Pleasantly."

She hadn't expected such a quick response but welcomed it nonetheless. "Brace yourself." Tiana took a breath. "What I'm about to say is going to be one hell of a shock."

"Tell me," he replied without hesitation.

She mulled over the best way to drop the bomb. "Have you seen the coverage of that little girl from Oakland who's been kidnapped?"

"Yeah, of course. It's all over the news." Devon huffed. "What's that have to do with me?"

Tiana bit her bottom lip. "That little girl is our daughter." Tears slid down her cheeks as the reality sank in all over again.

"Not funny, Tiana. Not funny at all." Devon's voice had turned cold as ice.

Tiana choked back tears. If only the whole situation had been a sick joke. "I'm serious. She's the daughter I gave up for adoption."

Devon broke a brief silence. "Where are you? I need to come over. I need to see you face-to-face, so I know you're not trying to get me back after all these years."

"I would never do that." Tiana gave Devon her address then hung up.

Everything she'd known for the past decade had been a lie. Though she didn't know exactly how, she hoped Devon having a stake in the search for Zoe would help bring her home.

TIANA WAS APPLYING makeup in her sweltering bathroom when her phone rang again. She froze, paralyzed by fear. Glancing at the phone, she felt a rush of relief at Devon's number appearing. It'd been twenty-five minutes, and she didn't know when to expect him or if he would actually show up. "Hey. Are you still coming?"

"I'm at your place. The security guard outside won't even let me knock on your door. Since when do you have security guarding your apartment, by the way?"

She'd completely forgotten about Adan with everything else going on. "I'll be right there." She double-checked her appearance, blotted the sweat beading on her forehead with a cold face towel, then hurried through the house to the front door. "Hey, Adan, Devon's fine to let in. He's a... friend I invited over."

Adan looked Devon up and down. "Are you sure? Your husband made it clear not to let anyone in the apartment when he left earlier."

"Yes. My dad's the one who paid for the security for me and my family, not Jay. Don't worry." She gestured for Devon to come inside.

Devon glared at Adan before following behind Tiana. "Why did your dad hire security? What's going on?"

Tiana closed the door. They stood in her living room. When her mom had left, Tiana had closed the blinds and turned off all the lights to keep the apartment as cool as possible, but it still hovered close to a hundred degrees inside. Conscious of her tiny hotbox of an apartment, Tiana regretted inviting Devon over. But she'd promised Jay she wouldn't go anywhere. She needed to push aside her embarrassment and let go of her pride. Her daughter's life was at stake. "Let's sit at the kitchen table." She switched on the ceiling fan and took a seat.

"Teeni, you look terrible." He looked around the apartment. "Where is everyone?"

"My husband and son should be back any minute. He drove my mom home. She and my dad bought a house in Morgan Hill after our breakup. They thought new scenery would help me after everything that happened between us." Tiana glanced at the refrigerator and contemplated offering Devon something to drink but decided against it. She didn't want to appear overly friendly.

"This place is... hot. Definitely smaller than your folks' old place." He took the seat across from her.

She rolled her eyes at his unnecessary, obvious statement. "I didn't ask you over to criticize my home or make small talk."

"I'm sorry. That didn't come out right." He knocked on the table. "Let's get straight to the point. Tell me everything."

Tiana recounted the sequence of events, beginning the morning she received the photograph at her office. She purposefully left out the police questioning Jay the night before. By the time she recalled her dad admitting he'd been raising Zoe with Josephine for ten years, she could barely see—tears and sweat covered her face.

Devon rose and put his arms around her. "I can't believe it. We'll find our daughter. I promise you. We'll find Zoe."

She pushed him away. "This is your fault."

He sat back down. "What?"

"How could you have left me like that?" The question had burned in Tiana's mind for a decade. "Of course the pregnancy was unexpected, but you were the one who reassured me throughout that we could do it. But then you just left us. Disappeared. I would never have let my parents pressure me into giving her up if you had stayed. You completely and utterly broke my heart. I didn't have the emotional or mental energy to keep our daughter. I just gave up. Someone wouldn't have kidnapped Zoe if you didn't abandon us."

"Teeni—"

Tiana slammed her hand on the table. "Don't call me that, dammit! You were the first love of my life. I gave you everything, including my virginity, and what did you do? You got me pregnant then left me high and dry." Tiana shoved her chair away from the table and stood. "I shouldn't have asked you to come over."

"Please, sit down. I'm so sorry. Every time we've run into each other at the park, I've told you how sorry I am. There's a lot more to the story than me just breaking up with you. I've tried to come up with a way to tell you what really happened whenever I've seen you. You've never given me a chance. If you let me, I'll explain everything." Devon's soft brown eyes pleaded with her.

Tiana wanted to kick Devon out and never see him again. But if he had another version of the story to tell, she owed it to Zoe to listen. She sat. "Tell me."

CHAPTER TWENTY-SIX

Jay's phone rang as he sped down the highway. He hit Answer on the steering wheel. "Hey, Harker. I've been waiting to hear from you."

Harker laughed. "That's definitely a change from my ex-wife's attitude whenever I have to pick up my kids." All humor left his voice. "I'll warn you upfront. I know you've had a lot going on, and the information I'm about to tell you has the potential to make things substantially worse. Are you ready?"

Jay took a deep breath. "Ready or not, right?"

"That Ronnie fellow popped up immediately when I searched his name. Guess where?"

"Where?" Jay tightened his grip around the steering wheel.

"Megan's List. You know, the database for convicted sex offenders. Apparently, he was charged and did time for sexually abusing a young girl about fifteen years ago."

Nausea overwhelmed Jay. He had no idea Ronnie was capable of that. "That's so messed up. I can't even..."

"That's also not all. I did more research on this Ronnie guy, and I've matched him to a profile that's all over the dark web and various black-market sites. If it's the same person, Ronnie is quite the salesman in all kinds of goods. Drugs. Guns. Organs. Jay, do me a favor?"

Stunned into silence, Jay could barely get his words out. "What's that?"

"Stay the hell away from this dude."

The hairs on Jay's arms stood on end. "You're right, Harker. Things just got much worse."

"As for your father-in-law, the only thing that stands out is he filed for bankruptcy about six months ago. Considering he has multiple properties, one in Morgan Hill and the other in the Oakland Hills, I'm surprised."

"What? Martin Moore? Are you sure?" That made absolutely no sense.

"Yep, I'm sure. I have a couple other jobs to do today, so I can't really dig into it. If you want, I'll share my Pacer information. That's the online system for federal court that includes bankruptcy. You can do some research into the exact debt that's caused him to file. It's a bit tricky to navigate, so I'll give you instructions when we have time."

"I definitely want to check it out." Harker had turned out to be even more useful than Jay had imagined. "Harker, have you ever worked on a kidnapping case? I'm wondering if you can help us find my wife's daughter. Martin Moore's been raising her. The whole situation is a mess, but I could explain it when you got time."

"Definitely sounds interesting. Absolutely. I've worked my fair share of kidnapping cases. With new technology, kidnapping and human trafficking has exploded. I hate to say it, but if Ronnie has something to do with your stepdaughter's kidnapping, he might have intentions of trafficking her."

Jay's heart sank. "God, that's awful."

"Jay, it's a crazy world. We served time with a lot of guys in there for drugs, theft, fighting, parole violations. But you have no idea how many corporate bigwigs and their cronies get away with abusing kids and desperate women. It absolutely disgusts me. Some people guess about fifty thousand people are trafficked every year in our country. About half of them are children. I'll definitely help you and your wife. I'll check my schedule and get back to you about a time I can stop by."

"I appreciate it, man." Jay let out a sigh of relief.

"Talk to you soon," Harker said before hanging up.

Jay looked in the rearview mirror at Marcus, who still slept hard as ever. Jay could never in his life imagine Marcus or any child being passed around for the sick pleasure of deranged adults. He needed to find Zoe faster than ever. *Should I tell Tiana that Ronnie might be involved with Zoe's kidnapping?* He had to be very careful because the information he had about Ronnie was more than enough to get him dragged back down to the police station. Jay didn't want to hide anything. But he decided not to tell Tiana what Harker had said about Ronnie yet.

Jay pulled into the carport at his apartment and carefully removed Marcus from his car seat. Jay rested his son on his shoulder and carried him through the complex. When Jay approached Adan at his front door, he put his finger to his lips then pointed at Marcus. Adan gave him a thumbs-up in reply.

Jay opened the front door but stopped in his tracks at the sight of Tiana and a man he'd never seen before sitting at the kitchen table. Dressed in a light-blue polo shirt and khaki shorts, the man belonged on the golf course, not in his home. "Tiana?" Jay whispered.

Tiana rose. "Jay, this is... Devon. I invited him over to tell him in person what's going on with Zoe."

Blood rushed to Jay's face. "Oh. Devon." Jay had no idea Tiana had planned to involve her ex-fiancé, let alone invite him over. "I'll put Marcus in his crib and be right back." Jay stomped down the hallway, his mind racing. *Why the hell would Tiana invite her ex-fiancé over? Where'd the dude come from all of a sudden?* After he gently put Marcus in his crib, Jay sped back to the kitchen for answers.

Devon stuck his hand out when Jay approached the table. "Sorry we have to meet under these circumstances."

Jay hesitated then shook Devon's hand. "Yup."

"Look, I should go. I have calls to make to get the ball rolling." Devon turned back to Tiana. "We're going to find Zoe. We'll find our daughter. I promise."

Jay cringed at "our daughter."

"Keep me updated." Tiana walked Devon to the door then closed it behind him.

Jay marched to the living room. "What was that all about?"

Tiana raised her eyebrows. "Excuse me?"

Jay gestured toward the table where Tiana had sat with Devon. "Explain to me why I just came home and found you with your ex."

Tiana's jaw dropped. "I just learned that the daughter I gave up for adoption was kidnapped. Do you really have the nerve to be mad because Devon came over? Get over yourself."

Jay started to talk but then shook his head, clearing his initial response. "Get over myself?"

"Yes. It's not about you." She glared at him.

He couldn't believe her. "Don't for a second forget how he dogged you. He ain't allowed here again."

"You have no right to tell me what I can do or who I can invite over. I pay the rent, remember?" Tiana grabbed her purse and rushed out the door. "I need some air."

"Where are you going?" he called after her.

But she ignored him and left the apartment.

Jay seethed with anger. He started to follow her then stopped when he heard a brief exchange between Tiana and Adan. She told him she was fine and would be right back. Jay pulled out his phone and called Xavier. He needed a voice of reason to stop him from running through the complex to find Devon and having a full-blown confrontation. When his brother answered, Jay let out a frustrated yell. "I need you talk me off a ledge right now."

CHAPTER TWENTY-SEVEN

Heading through the apartment grounds, Tiana huffed hot air mixed with wildfire smoke. Another hundred-degree day, and the exchange with Jay had her heated as if the flames surrounded her. She dialed Devon. "Did you take off already?"

"I'm pulling away now. You need something?"

"I hate to ask, but I left my car in Oakland earlier today." She took a couple breaths, weighing whether to proceed. Jay had interrupted Devon's explanation of why he'd broken off their engagement. She wanted to continue that conversation, so she pushed aside her doubt. "I kinda need a ride."

"Meet me at the stop sign on the corner. I'll take you straight there." His serious-but-generous tone put her at ease.

The oppressive heat slowed her. The blazing sun radiated off the concrete, and sweat dotted her forehead before quickly turning into drops running down her face. She wiped the sweat away and tried to keep her face expressionless when Devon rounded the corner in a red Mercedes coupe. He parked, exited the car, and jogged around to open the door for her. "Hurry in. I have the AC on."

Tiana eased herself into the car. The cold air instantly refreshed her. "Thanks."

Back in the driver's seat, Devon buckled his seat belt. "Where in Oakland is your car?"

Tiana reached into her purse and pulled out the paper that had the address to the inn. She handed it to Devon. "This is the note that person stuck on my windshield earlier. My car is about a block away."

Devon typed the address into the fancy console dashboard that also displayed icons for his text messages, his home security system, the weather forecast, and a newsfeed. After he set the navigation, he faced Tiana. "I hope your husband isn't too mad about me coming over."

Tiana sighed. "Mad" didn't even scratch the surface. "He'll get over it."

Devon blew out a long breath. "I'm glad you called me today to tell me about Zoe. We're in this together now." His vehicle sped down the street and toward the highway.

"So what were you going to tell me?" Tiana asked.

Devon cleared his throat. "It might change the way you look at me."

Fear rose in Tiana's throat. She swallowed hard and sank back into the seat. She couldn't handle a final, lethal blow from Devon. "Go ahead."

Devon glanced at Tiana before fixing his eyes on the road. "When I broke up with you like that..." He took a couple breaths.

The same spot ached in Tiana's heart at the memory—it felt like poking a bruise. She assumed he would proceed to tell her about another woman he'd fallen for at the time, someone he loved more than her. Maybe they were still together. "Go on."

"You were seventeen. I had turned eighteen the beginning of senior year. Toward the end of the pregnancy, your dad gave me an ultimatum. He said either I break up with you and let you move on with your life, or he would report me for statutory rape. That he'd make sure I did jail time. That I would have to register as a sex offender the rest of my life. I was too young to know the intricacies of the law or if he could even legally do any of it. All I knew was that a district attorney was threatening to lock me up. I didn't want to go to jail or ruin my reputation and record like that." Devon's voice grew tender. "I loved you with everything I had. But I was too scared to stick up to your dad and face the consequences. I'm so sorry that I left you. I didn't know you were going to give up Zoe. I thought I'd wait until you turned eighteen, come back, and we'd be a family. When I found out you'd given up Zoe, I knew you'd never forgive me. I've never forgiven myself either."

Tiana stared straight ahead but snuck a glance at him. "I don't believe you. Why wouldn't you have just told me?"

His chin quivered. "I was a coward. I should have stayed with you. I'm sorry I left. I moved out of the state, and my parents relocated to Japan in the fall. It's haunted me to think about the pain you must have been in. I suffered too." Devon clenched the steering wheel until his knuckles turned white.

Tiana glanced out the window. Her surroundings suddenly seemed foreign. Her whole life had turned upside down in less than twenty-four hours. She'd hated Devon with such a passion since he abandoned her. If she dared to lift even a fraction of that hate from her heart, she feared what else she would find. Too stunned to reply, she sat in silence.

"I promise you that I'll find the asshole that's been stalking you. I won't rest until I find our daughter." Devon glanced at Tiana. "Do you think your husband will accept us working together? That's the only way we'll find Zoe."

Putting herself in Jay's shoes, Tiana admitted it must have been a hell of a shock to come home and see Devon in their home. "Yes, I hope he'll come around to the idea. One minute, it's just our family, and the next, I suddenly have a daughter and her father in the picture. It'll be an adjustment. But so have the past three years." Truth be told, she still hadn't adjusted either.

"That must have been terrifying when you found out that he was going to prison, huh?" Devon whispered the word "prison" as if he didn't want to say a bad word aloud.

Tiana tried to focus on the scenery zooming by, but the smoke lining the atmosphere hampered her view. She would rather not remember Jay's plea bargain. She worked hard every day to try to move beyond his situation and not dwell in the past. It exhausted her.

Devon tapped Tiana's leg, drawing her out of her thoughts. An electric bolt coursed through her body at his touch. "I'm sorry. I shouldn't have brought that up. Look, I read online that there's a makeshift command center set up to find Zoe. It's not too far from the inn. Do you want to head over there after I take you to your car? We won't say anything about our connection to Zoe. But it would make me feel like I'm doing something useful."

Tiana wanted to be of use, but Jay had said he'd spotted her dad there on the news the night before. She couldn't stomach another run-in with him. "I'm not sure that's a good idea. My dad might be there."

"Don't let him stop you from helping find Zoe. He's already kept her away from us for ten years. I don't want to add another second."

"I guess you're right." When they neared the inn, Tiana directed Devon to her car. Her Honda looked unimpressive compared to his Mercedes. He navigated to the side of the road. Outside, the sun shone bloodred.

They exited the car, and Devon engulfed her in a tight hug.

She wanted to pull away but couldn't. His arms brought warmth and familiarity. It'd been a decade, but she couldn't help but remember that at one point, she desired nothing more than to spend the rest of her life with him. She broke the hug, not wanting to dwell in that memory. "We should get going."

He took a step back. "You're right."

Tiana's heart pounded in her chest. Once inside her car, she put both hands on the steering wheel and tried to focus. She longed to feel Devon's arms around her again, knowing full well how wrong that was. *That cannot happen.* She needed to get it together.

Devon knocked on her window. She rolled it down, embarrassed she hadn't noticed him standing there. "You good?"

"Yeah, of course." Her face burned. "I'm just trying to prepare myself for the command center. Go first. I'll be right behind you."

He smiled, revealing a set of perfectly straight white teeth. He'd had his braces taken off the year before he'd met Tiana. "See you there." He took off slowly.

Tiana dreaded seeing her dad or Josephine, but no one would stop her from searching for her daughter.

CHAPTER TWENTY-EIGHT

Jay paced the twenty feet between the back of the couch and kitchen table while Marcus watched cartoons. As if worrying about Ronnie possibly being involved in kidnapping and trafficking Zoe didn't occupy enough mental space, he now had the additional burden of Devon being back in Tiana's life. He didn't know anything about the dude other than that he'd gotten Tiana pregnant. He'd ended their engagement, disappeared, and broke her heart. Based on the way Devon had looked at her in the apartment, he clearly still loved her, but pacing wouldn't get Jay any answers. He grabbed his laptop off the shelf in the living room and sat on the couch next to Marcus.

After bringing up a web browser, he typed, *Devon Price San Jose*. Jay hadn't even known Devon lived locally, but considering how the man had appeared at the apartment in no time, he must have. *Devon Price, South Bay Venture Capitalist* showed up with various social media and industry-related profiles. As Jay scanned the various websites, one thing came across: the dude had serious money. Jay didn't see any mention of a wife or kids, like a lot of men in Silicon Valley. The thought of Devon being a rich, eligible bachelor in the same city as Tiana made the knot in Jay's stomach tighten.

After a few minutes, he'd seen enough. He shut the computer and sank into the couch. He'd fought the urge for over an hour, but he finally gave in and called Tiana. It rang before voicemail picked up. Instead of leaving a voice message, he sent her a quick text. *Just checking in. Sorry bout earlier. R u ok.* Though not completely apologetic, he wanted to make amends as soon as possible. If Jay's hunch proved correct and Devon hadn't completely gotten over Tiana, he would have to get ready for a fight.

Jay had casually dated before he'd met Tiana, but he had never truly been in love until her. After witnessing the mess of the marriage between his parents, he never had a desire to settle down with anyone.

When he met Tiana, he knew she was way out of his league. He never thought they would become anything serious. But within a short period of time, he had fallen for her. She encapsulated everything about a perfect woman: beautiful, smart, accomplished, loving. When she'd returned his affection and they married, life became perfect in a way he hadn't imagined possible. Especially after his legal troubles, she'd supported him in a way nobody ever had. The thought of losing her sent Jay into a panic. That caller could want to cause her physical harm, and now he worried about Devon.

The man surely lived in some huge, million-dollar home that definitely had air-conditioning. The list of things Devon could probably offer Tiana that Jay couldn't made his blood boil. He rose from the couch then picked up all of Marcus's toys and stored them in the play bin. He moved to the kitchen, where he retrieved the Pine-Sol and rags from under the sink. He scrubbed the countertops and sink, washed the remaining dishes, then dried them. Sweat dripped down his face. He had a lot more to do.

Jay scooped Marcus from the couch and shut off the TV. "Let's clean your room, buddy."

Marcus pouted. "Watch Mickey."

Jay carried Marcus through the house then perched him on the soft, child-sized roll-out sofa in the room and handed him a Mickey Mouse book. "Try this instead."

As Marcus flipped through the book, Jay tidied the room. It amazed him how much clutter the toddler could generate each day.

Jay couldn't help but blame himself for the mess his life had become. Even if he didn't have a job, he had an opportunity to prove himself. *He* would somehow have to be the one to find Zoe and bring her back home.

With his tank top completely drenched in sweat, Jay surveyed the newly tidied room. He'd done well. Marcus needed to be removed to prevent him from overturning it again. Making their way back through the house, Jay summoned the courage he needed to confront his father-in-law.

He plopped Marcus into his high chair in the kitchen and handed him a short plastic spoon and some fruit. "Here's some peaches, buddy." Picking up his phone, he dialed Martin. He anticipated the call would go to voicemail—Martin usually avoided him. But the man answered abruptly. Jay fumbled for words. "Martin... hey, it's Jay. I'm racking my brain, trying to figure out this whole situation going on. Tiana told me everything. That Zoe's her daughter and—"

"If you're calling to lecture me, save your righteous indignation," Martin said. "You of all—"

"No, I'm not. I wanna help. Somebody's after your reputation and my wife and her daughter. I have a hunch money's got something to do with it. So, I'm gonna just ask. Are you in some type of financial trouble? I know you filed for bankruptcy. Is someone trying to blackmail you or something?" Jay wiped the sweat dripping down his face.

"How do you know that?" Martin hissed.

Jay couldn't show his hand just yet. "Bankruptcy is public record. I love Tiana more than anything. I wanna find her daughter. Just be straight up. Is something going on with you?"

"Absolutely nothing is going on. How dare you call me and act like I would have anything to do with Zoe's kidnapping. I would ask you the same thing, but I already know you're in financial trouble.

Not to mention the police took you in for questioning. So what are *you* hiding?"

"Nothing. I ain't got nothing to hide." Martin had flipped the tables on Jay like the expert district attorney he was. And Jay had Ronnie's past to contend with—it would not look good if the two of them were found to have been connected. "I'm gonna let you go. Hit me up if there's anything I can do to help."

"Jaylen, don't call me again." Martin hung up.

Frazzled by the call, Jay sent Harker a quick text asking what time Harker could swing by. If Martin wouldn't help Jay figure anything out, maybe Harker could. They would have to search deeper into Martin's bankruptcy and figure exactly who his debtors were. Jay called Tiana again. Still no answer. He slammed the phone down. Anxiety raced through his body. He followed the call with a short text. *I'm sorry, Ti. Come back home.*

CHAPTER TWENTY-NINE

Devon turned the Mercedes into a church parking lot, and Tiana followed. She parked next to Devon, her heart pounding in her chest. She'd ignored Jay's calls out of spite. After the hell she'd been through with her dad, she would not tolerate Jay's insecurity. Still, she checked the text he'd sent, making sure nothing crazy had happened. Her heart softened a bit at seeing the word *sorry*. She began to respond to the text and let Jay know she'd be home in about an hour. Devon tapped on her window. She tucked her phone into her purse and left her car. "So, this is it?"

"Yeah. Let's check it out." Devon led the way toward the gray-walled church. It had a steeple topped by a spire pointed toward the ashen sky. A silent church bell rested at the side of the building.

Tiana and Devon climbed up stairs to the structure, which appeared centuries old. They headed in the direction of the chatter of voices, which led them to a large hall. Tiana's head spun with all the commotion. People packed every inch of the space, shouting at each other to be heard over the noise. Several long tables were cluttered with papers and people answering ringing phones and typing on their electronic devices. "Devon, it's an absolute madhouse."

He scanned the room. "Yeah, there's a lot going on. I'm sure we can figure out a way to help with something."

At the nearest table, Tiana picked up a flyer with Zoe's picture, the same photo as the one on the news. Up close, she could see Zoe's resemblance to her own elementary school pictures. With her hair in two braids and wearing a pink shirt with a gold star in the middle, Zoe looked innocent, precious.

Tears came to Tiana's eyes. She blinked them away and wiped the ones that had escaped with the back of her hand. She didn't know who had kidnapped Zoe, but she prayed with all her might that he hadn't done anything to her. Aside from stalking Tiana and leaving her clues, he obviously had a motive and wanted to expose her dad and his lies. *But he must want more.* Tiana had to figure out what he wanted so she could give it to him and get her daughter back.

Devon also picked up a flyer. "She looks just like you."

"That's what Jay said." The mention of her husband reminded Tiana that she still needed to respond to him. She pulled out her phone. Before she could send him a text, a heavyset elderly woman approached her and Devon.

"Take as many flyers as you'd like. We're trying to post them everywhere and could use all the help we can get. What's your relationship to Zoe?" The woman had deep wrinkles in her full, mahogany-colored face.

Tiana moved her lips to respond but couldn't find the right words.

"We're concerned like everyone else." Devon scooped up a stack of flyers. "We can definitely help post these. With all the people here, I'm sure every corner is already covered."

"Around here, yes. But as I'm sure you know, the Bay Area is expansive. We want these posters plastered far and wide. We need word about Zoe's disappearance to spread like wildfire." The older woman paused. "I guess we shouldn't use that phrase around here anymore, huh?"

Tiana cringed. The world seemed broken, with one disaster following the last. Her personal tsunami threated to drown her. "So Zoe went to church here?"

"Oh, yes. I've attended this church for over five decades. For the past ten years, Zoe, Josephine, and Josephine's brother, Kirk, would be seated in the second row every Sunday. Since she turned three, Zoe sang her heart out in the children's choir just like an angel. I know her beautiful singing touched God's heart in a special way. She touched all of ours." The woman's voice broke. "We just want her found safe and sound."

Tiana hated the fact that a stranger knew her daughter better than she did. "Is Josephine's brother the man at the press conferences with her?"

"Yes, he sure is." The woman had a wide smile. "They're very tight. He's like a dad to Zoe."

Devon looked over his shoulder. "Are they here?" He glanced around the room.

Tiana looked, too, not sure what she would do if she had to face Josephine again.

"No. After the press conference, the media set up camp at Josephine's house. Word is that she's staying somewhere nearby. Her phone is glued to her hand because she's hoping she gets a call from Zoe. She still believes that it's all a big misunderstanding, that somehow, Zoe got lost. She wouldn't want to be here with all the noise and commotion and miss a communication from someone who found her. Kirk was here earlier, but he left about an hour ago."

Devon huffed. "What fantasy world is she living in?" His words came out bitter.

The woman nodded. "It's denial, for sure. Thinking that it's all a big misunderstanding is easier than imagining the worst. While I certainly wish for the best, I'm not going to just sit around when I can be here, trying to find her. Faith and deeds, right?"

"Yes. Absolutely." Tiana nodded. Once the woman had left and disappeared into the crowd, Tiana turned to Devon. "Josephine really was up here living a lie. Worshipping every Sunday while having an affair with my father and raising the daughter that they stole from me. Unbelievable." Tiana would have never allowed someone to kidnap Zoe right from under her nose. She didn't trust Josephine for one second.

"I couldn't agree more." Devon held up the posters in his hand. "But posting flyers will be helpful. Let's walk through this place to see if there's anything else we can do then get out of here."

A few tables down appeared to be a social media hub with several laptops and tablets. "We're using this hashtag." A young man who appeared to be in his twenties handed Tiana and Devon postcards with a picture of Zoe and a hashtag of FindZoeNow. "The news coverage is cool, but we want this to go viral. Twitter, Facebook, Instagram, TikTok. Use whatever you got. We want every corner of the US to know about Zoe's kidnapping."

Tiana took out her phone. As a social media manager, she could definitely do a lot in that department to increase visibility. "That's a brilliant idea. Thank you. I'll post now." She and Devon stepped away from the table to post messages to their social media accounts.

Tiana appreciated having tangible actions to take. But deep in her gut, she couldn't help feeling like all the busywork happening in the command center could be for naught. She'd seen her dad prosecute multiple repeat offenders who'd committed heinous crimes. He would talk about his cases with her mom and her, always using them as lessons for Tiana to learn. *What if someone like that kidnapped Zoe?* Posters and tweets would do nothing to loosen her daughter from the grip of someone like that.

A large circle of people holding hands and praying occupied the space between the next two tables. A stocky, gray-haired man wearing all black and a reverend's white collar led the prayer. Many of the women cried, anguish on their face like fresh makeup. Tiana believed in God, as did her parents and Jay. They'd always been Christmas-and-Easter Christians. Now, though, listening in on the prayer, the reverend's pleas to heaven soothed a part of Tiana that ached. *Please, God. Bring my baby girl back.*

With a tug on Tiana's elbow, Devon urged her to move forward. He seemed more perturbed than moved by the prayer. They made it through the crowd and headed for an exit on the far end of the hall. A lady at the door handed them another flyer. "If Zoe's not located by tomorrow, there will be a search for her. We'll meet at nine in the morning at Walmart in San Jose where she was last seen. We'll scour the location until dusk."

Tiana took the flyer. "Thanks. Hopefully, she'll show up before then. But if not, I'll be there."

"Same here," Devon said. They walked toward the door to the parking lot.

"Excuse me?" A woman with olive skin and long black hair hurried behind them and gestured for the pair to wait for her.

Tiana and Devon paused. "Yes?" Devon asked.

"I have information that will help you find your daughter," the woman said. "I'm a psychic."

A chill coursed down Tiana's spine. *How could this woman know we're Zoe's parents?* "Excuse me?"

The woman ran her fingers through her hair. "Zoe's your daughter, right?"

"Leave us alone! You won't get a penny from us." Devon pressed his hand against Tiana's back. "Let's get out of here."

The woman shoved a card into Tiana's hand. "He's dangerous."

Does she mean the guy who has Zoe or Devon?

Before Tiana could ask anything else, Devon pushed her through the back door and shut it behind them. He shook his fist toward the door. "That woman should be ashamed of herself. Vulture."

Tiana's hand trembled as she shoved the card into her purse. "How could she have known we're Zoe's parents, though?"

"I'd say lucky guess. Anyone with eyes can see the resemblance between you and Zoe. I'm sure she tried to pull that crap on other people there too." Devon led Tiana around the back of the church to where they'd parked. When they reached her car, he checked his phone. "It's still early. Do you want to grab dinner?"

Tiana pulled out her phone. She had another missed call from Jay. "I should head home. I hadn't planned on staying so long. My husband's worried."

"Yeah... sure. I'm glad we came." Devon held out his hand. "Why don't you give me your flyers? I'll drive around and put them up."

Tiana handed him half her stack. "I'll put up a few in my neighborhood too. Like they said, the more people who know, the better."

"Take care, Teeni. Hopefully, Zoe will be found before the search. If not, I'll see you there."

"Yeah, hopefully we won't have to go." Before Tiana knew it, Devon had embraced her.

Tiana's phone rang, and she backed away from him. "I have to take this." She hopped into her car and picked up. "Jay, I'm on the way home."

"Where you been? Where you at now?" He didn't yell, but anger seeped out of his voice.

"Devon took me to pick up my car. After, we stopped by the command center set up to find Zoe and helped out a bit. I'll be home in less than an hour." She sped out of the parking lot. The sooner she returned home, the less mad Jay would be.

"Did you see my calls and texts? I mean, you could have... never mind. I'll see you when you get here. Drive safe. Bye."

Tiana zoomed down the freeway. A thousand conflicting emotions collided inside her. Complete strangers at the command center had shared in her daughter's life for the past ten years, while Tiana had been deprived. Still, she had nothing but gratitude for all their effort to help find the girl.

Even if they did find Zoe, everything wouldn't magically fall into place. Zoe knew only Josephine as her mother. Tiana had signed Zoe's birth certificate, but she'd also signed various other documents her dad had presented her with. If Josephine had legally adopted Zoe, Tiana had no rights to her. Tiana had carried Zoe for nine months and brought her into the world, but that meant nothing to a ten-year-old. Zoe had never even met Tiana or Devon. Having two strange adults impose themselves wouldn't be easy for anyone.

Why hadn't Devon told the truth about Dad threatening him and forcing him to break up with me at the time? It only added to her disdain toward her father, but that anger wouldn't bring Zoe home. The guilt over giving Zoe up suffocated Tiana. If she never found her daughter, Tiana could never forgive herself. She would do everything possible to make sure she had an opportunity to share in her daughter's life.

CHAPTER THIRTY

After Tiana disappeared with her ex, Jay spent hours imagining all the worst-case scenarios that could unfold in their lives. Though thankful she'd called him and was on her way home, the tightness in his chest wouldn't lift until she safely walked through the door.

He got a text from Harker, who had said he'd stop by at nine that night.

Drenched in sweat, Jay sniffed under his arm and cringed. He definitely had to hop in the shower before Tiana returned. He placed Marcus in his crib with a few toys then jogged across the hall to his room. After undressing, Jay hit the bathroom and turned on the shower. He stepped into the cool stream, which soothed his tight muscles. He'd been wound too tightly ever since the police interrogation.

Decades earlier, his dad would punish him by forcing him into a scalding hot shower. His screams of agony would infuriate his dad, who would yell, "Stop screaming like a little girl!" When the torture ceased, Jay would leave the bathroom, his skin bright red from the burns. Towel around his waist, he would walk right past his mother, Janice, who always seemed to have tears in her eyes but never once stepped in to make the abuse stop.

He cupped his hands over his face. His hot breath in his palms reminded him that he'd survived. *You're okay, Jay.* He finished scrubbing his body then got out and toweled off.

"Dada!" Marcus screamed. "Out, Dada."

Jay climbed into a pair of shorts. "Coming, buddy!" He hurried to Marcus's room then stopped and couldn't help but smile as Tiana lifted their son from his crib.

"Mama's here now," she said softly.

Marcus nuzzled his curly head against Tiana's neck. "Hi, Mama."

Jay tried to welcome her. "Oh, hey. It's... you're... back. I just took a three-minute shower."

Tiana's face was painted with fresh grief. She attempted to smile at him, but her mind seemed to be miles away, and her puffy red eyes and downcast expression spoke louder than words. "The apartment looks amazing. Thanks for cleaning."

Jay wrapped his arms around her and Marcus. He kissed Marcus on the cheek then gave Tiana a quick peck on the lips. At least for the time being, he had his family. "Now that we have a full fridge, I can start dinner. What do you feel like?"

"I have no appetite. Just make something for you and Marky."

"Buddy, what do you want to eat?" Jay patted his son's round belly.

"Apple-saw!" Marcus's eyes lit up.

Tiana yawned. "I'll give you some applesauce to hold you over until dinner."

"Ti, you look real tired. Why don't you go lay down while I cook?" Jay reached toward Marcus, who lunged into his arms. It'd taken a good two months for Marcus to get used to Jay after he'd come home from prison, but they'd become inseparable.

"I've barely seen Marcus all day. I'm fine." Tiana yawned again, quickly covering her mouth.

He fought the urge to argue with her and spoke in his least confrontational tone. "What if you rest in bed, and I'll put on a show for Marcus in there?"

They crossed the hall to their bedroom. Tiana kicked off her shoes then sat on the bed. Jay fluffed her pillow. "Come lie down."

She rolled her eyes but did it anyway. "You're being dramatic, Jay."

"Did you get another call from the blocked number when you were out?" Jay wanted to put the app to the test.

"No, he hasn't called. But when I declined your call..." Tiana paused. "Sorry about that, by the way. But after I declined your call, I got a notification in the app that led me to a caller report. It gave your name, phone number, and address. So it definitely works."

Jay perched Marcus next to his wife, trying to mask his irritation that she'd ignored him on purpose earlier. "That's great news. Let that jerk call you again, and we're nailing him." He put on the Disney Channel then rested on the edge of the bed next to Tiana. Though tinged pink with heat, her skin looked paler than usual. "You look sick. Can I get you something? I could go to the store and get ginger ale and crackers."

She huffed. "I'm not sick."

Jay squeezed her hand. "All this is a hell of a shock. You're in shock." He held the back of his hand against her forehead.

She swatted his hand. "I definitely don't have a fever. I'm fine."

He kissed her lips. "I got you, okay? I love you."

"I know." She pressed her hand against his face. "I love you too."

"Kiss, Mama." Marcus pointed to his cheek.

She did as requested. "We love you too, Marky."

"Ti, I'll go cook. My friend Harker is coming at nine. So let's put you-know-who to bed after dinner so we can talk with him. I'll let you know when dinner's ready." Jay stood to leave.

"Are you sure it's a good idea, having him come over?" Tiana arched an eyebrow.

He nodded. "He's cool. I think he can help. I'll be in the kitchen if you need me."

In the kitchen, he gathered the ground beef and dried spaghetti. Tiana definitely possessed the culinary skills in their family. Still, Jay could hold his own. He'd had to step up his cooking skills when his brother had moved in with him during Xavier's freshman year of high school. Eating fast food every night had quickly run its course.

"Dada." Marcus ran into the kitchen, pointing toward the bedroom. "Mama sleeping."

"Good. Mama's tired." Jay picked him up. "Do you want to help me cook?"

Marcus clapped his hands. "Cook, Dada."

Jay plopped the boy down on the counter and took out a few sticks of spaghetti. He held both ends and broke the noodles in two. "Now you try." He gave a few more sticks to Marcus, who followed his example and broke the noodles. "Good, buddy!"

As Jay and Marcus worked through the box of spaghetti, he remembered the men serving life sentences at San Quentin. They would never have the opportunity to enjoy quiet moments with their children in the comfort of their own homes, though a select few lifers were granted overnight visits through the family visiting program. Jay'd never seen it, but he'd heard the prison had a cottage where the men stayed with their families for the weekend. He almost had survivor's guilt that he'd made it out. So many men like him never did.

Tiana's phone rang in their bedroom. Jay placed Marcus in his high chair and raced through the apartment. He couldn't wait to decline the call if the blocked number showed up. He didn't want the call waking Tiana. When he got there, Devon's name flashed on the screen. He quickly declined the call.

He waited a couple minutes then checked the tracing app. The app had sent Devon's name, phone number, and address to Tiana. Jay snapped a screenshot, texted it to his phone, deleted the outgoing text, then gently placed her phone back on the nightstand. If push came to shove, Jay knew exactly where to find Devon.

CHAPTER THIRTY-ONE

The ringing phone woke Tiana from sleep. The illuminated screen pierced the empty, dark room. Her shaking hand reached for the nightstand, anticipating that a blocked number would show up again. Every time she'd gotten a call from the unknown man, something bad had happened. When she picked up the phone, relief washed over her. "Devon? What's up?"

"Are you okay? You didn't answer earlier. Since you didn't call me back, I got worried."

"I'm just waking up from a nap. I must have slept through your other call. Do you have news?" Her heart sped. Maybe they'd found Zoe.

"No, nothing new. I wanted to say..." Devon exhaled into the phone. "I'm really sorry about everything. If I could go back in time, I would never have left. Please, believe me."

Jay opened the door and poked his head in the room. "I thought I heard your voice. Are you on the phone?"

"I gotta go." Tiana hung up and placed the phone back onto the nightstand. "No, I'm not anymore. I just woke up."

Jay walked to her and kissed her forehead. "I'm glad you're up. I didn't want to wake you, but my friend Harker got here about ten minutes ago."

She sat up. "Where's Marcus? What time is it?"

Jay patted her hand. "Marcus is in bed for the night. It's a little after nine. You slept through dinner. There's plenty of spaghetti left if you're hungry."

Tiana climbed out of bed, trying to shake off the sleep. The recent traumatic days had apparently affected her a lot more than she'd realized. "Why'd you let me sleep so long? I should have put Marcus to bed. That's the second night in a row I've missed."

"You were up late last night, and it's been a hell of a day." Jay shrugged. "I wanted to let you sleep if you needed it. I'm sorry."

She dismissed the comment with a wave. "I shouldn't have snapped at you. I feel guilty. I'm not doing anything to find Zoe, so the least I could do is my job for Marcus." She huffed. "I'll be right out to talk with you and your friend. Give me a minute."

"Take your time." He left the room.

Tiana started to send a quick text to Devon, apologizing for ending the call so abruptly, but she stopped herself. She didn't owe him an apology. Instead, she checked her texts. Her mom had sent several. Tiana briefly skimmed them with no plans to respond. Ava had also sent a couple, so Tiana sent her a message about the search for Zoe tomorrow in case her friend had time to attend.

Tiana stepped into the bathroom. In the mirror, puffy, red eyes stared back at her. No wonder Jay had thought she'd fallen ill. She had morphed into a hot mess. After washing her face, she reapplied her makeup and combed her short hair into place. Once satisfied with her appearance, she left the bathroom.

In the living room, Tiana examined Jay's friend, an older white man probably in his early fifties, sitting on their couch. He had a blond crew cut, strong dark features, and a muscular build. He didn't look like the type who had done time in prison, but she had to check her own implicit bias.

The man stood when she approached, extending his hand. "Harker."

"Hi, Harker. I'm Tiana." She reciprocated his firm handshake. "Thanks for coming over." She looked at Jay, who had also stood. "Please, let's sit. No need to be so formal."

Harker cleared his throat. "I'm sorry to hear about your little girl. Jay filled me in on the picture delivered to your office, the calls, and the note. I'm glad he called me. I want to help you find her."

Though Tiana appreciated the sentiment, having Harker refer to Zoe as her little girl pained her. Having a daughter she'd never had the chance to know seemed so cruel. "Thank you. Jay said you're a private investigator."

He chuckled. "Yes, among other trades. After Jay called me, I did what any private investigator would do and—" Harker paused and smiled mischievously. "Searched the web. There's a ton of press. I hate to say it, but that's unusual for a missing black girl."

"Excuse me?" Tiana pursed her lips. She immediately regretted her decision to let this guy come over. "That's my daughter you're talking about."

"I'm sorry. That came out wrong. I've been doing this a long time. There's a name for it." Harker hooked his two index fingers to make air quotes. "'Missing white woman syndrome.' Lots of people of all ages disappear every day. But usually, it's the attractive blondes that get the media coverage. White victims receive three times as much attention as minorities—I'm sorry, people of color. Anyway, if you're not a white girl or woman, the kidnapping has to be sensational or the family has to have a lot of money and importance in the community. After Jay explained your father's involvement, it makes more sense."

Tiana glared at Jay, who shrugged. "Do the police have any leads?"

Harker laughed. "Sweetheart, the police are the last people in hell that will talk about leads."

"Aren't they supposed to keep the public up-to-date on developments?" Though she didn't like Harker's demeanor, he did seem to have insider knowledge that could be valuable. She wouldn't kick him out just yet.

"Think about it." Harker tapped his temple. "If the cops released information to the media prematurely, the suspect could take off, destroy evidence, or plant ideas into supposed witnesses' heads. If the cops make private information public before the missing person is found, they might ensure they never find them."

Tiana leaned forward. "Well, what can I do?"

"Not much." Harker raised his chin.

Tiana glanced sideways at Jay. *Why did he invite this jerk over?*

Jay cleared his throat. "Harker, we were hoping that—"

"I know what you were hoping. Don't worry. Like I said, I can help." Harker had a smug look on his face.

"How? Exactly? You're talking a lot, but what can you actually do?" Tiana asked.

"There's going to be a big search tomorrow for the girl. While everyone's busy doing that, I'm going to check out the Walmart security camera footage. I'll interview some people that work there. Basically, I'll do what the police won't tell you they've already done."

Tiana eyed Jay. "How much will it cost?" They literally had no money to spare. But she would come up with the cash to help find Zoe. Maybe Devon could help.

"Jay's saved my butt a couple of times. I owe him. It's on the house." Harker tapped his chin with his index finger. "Though I do accept tips in the form of alcohol. Preferably Jack Daniel's."

Jay held up a palm. "Hold up." He disappeared into the kitchen. A minute later, he reappeared with a brown bag. He held it out to Harker. "I was hoping you'd say that. I stopped at the store earlier and picked that up for you."

Harker accepted the bag and peeked inside then twisted off the cap and took a long swig. "This will definitely do. I'll be in touch." He headed toward the door, and Jay and Tiana followed him.

Tiana stopped Harker. "I really hope you're not all talk."

"Sweetheart, I'm very good at what I do. But talk is cheap. I'll be back with the proof sooner than later. In the meantime, why don't you two come up with a list of anything that seems out of the ordinary lately. Especially you, Tiana. A woman's intuition is powerful. Write down anything you can think of. Jay, I shot you an email with information to log in to search the federal court website. Check it out when you can." Harker tipped an imaginary cap and opened the front door.

Tiana would be glad to see Harker and his know-it-all attitude go. Still, a bit of hope swelled inside of her. *Maybe he can find Zoe.* "Thanks for coming over."

"We'll find your daughter." Harker turned to Jay and shook his hand. "Good seeing you."

"Same. I'm glad you're on board. We'll find Zoe." Jay's voice held conviction.

After shutting the door, he extended his arms to Tiana. "Come here."

Tiana leaned against his chest. "I can't believe it, Jay. I just can't." Tears slid down her face.

Jay held her close. "We're going to get through this. I promise."

She couldn't imagine how. She no longer trusted anyone's word. When she'd gone into labor her senior year, she'd begged her mom to call Devon and let him witness their baby's birth. Though her mom had called, Devon hadn't answered or returned the call.

"I'm so sorry, Tiana." Jay squeezed her tightly. "We're gonna get through this."

Every fiber in her itched to scour the entire state of California to find her daughter. *I must bring her home.*

CHAPTER THIRTY-TWO

Jay wiped the tears from Tiana's eyes, wishing he could take his wife's pain away. "Harker means well. He's just a bit rough around the edges." Jay had always appreciated Harker's candor. But he'd seen firsthand how it caused problems.

"Yeah, definitely rough." Tiana winced.

"Why don't we work on the list Harker suggested?" Jay got up and fumbled around in the junk drawer for a pen and notepad. He grabbed two beers and returned to Tiana.

"Thank you, Jay. You've been so good to me." She opened her beer and sipped it.

A smile crept onto Jay's face. Regardless of the tension earlier, his wife appreciated him. Maybe he'd been overly insecure about Devon. "Has anything stood out to you? Have you felt weird or whatever?"

Tiana arched her shoulders. "I've been trying to think about the last few weeks. I realized we've been in complete survival mode with you out of work. I can barely remember what it feels like to wake up and not have anxiety. Whether it's how we'll pay the bills. How much more overtime I can get. Is there room left on my credit cards to buy groceries? Or *something*. It's like an elephant lives on my chest."

Jay's face fell. "I'm so—"

"I know you're sorry. I got it. You've said it over and over again." Tiana narrowed her eyes. "Then the police showed up at our door and took you to the station. That was definitely out of the ordinary."

His face burned with embarrassment. Everything Tiana said had truth to it. Even if he tried, any response he came up with would sound like an excuse. Not to mention, if Ronnie really had something to do with Zoe's kidnapping, the police could definitely come up with a reason to tie Jay in as an accomplice. He couldn't mention what Harker had uncovered about Ronnie. He had to redirect the focus. "Ti, I found out your dad filed for bankruptcy. We spoke earlier about it, but he won't tell me what happened to lead to that. If he's having money trouble, that's something else that could factor into Zoe's kidnapping."

Tiana rested her hand on her forehead. "That makes no sense. I've been thinking about my dad too. He prosecuted a case about a two years ago involving gang members who'd kidnapped, raped, and murdered a teen. After the jury found them guilty, another member of the gang confronted my dad outside the courthouse and told him he better watch out. That they know all about his wife and pregnant daughter and said neither of us were safe anymore." Her voice shook.

"Why didn't you tell me that, Ti? That's awful." His rage swelled. *How dare that man threaten Tiana and Marcus, then in the womb.*

"You'd just gone to prison. I had too much else on my mind. My dad ordered security for me and my mom for about two weeks. After consulting with his colleagues, they ruled out the seriousness of the threat. Now I'm wondering if this whole thing could have been planned out and orchestrated by the gang." Tiana's shoulders slumped forward, the whole ordeal physically weighing her down. "They could've dug into my dad's past and found out about all this somehow."

Jay clenched his fist. His pregnant wife's life had been threatened, and he hadn't even been able to protect her. "I'm sor—we definitely need to bring that up to your dad and—"

"Hell no. There's no way I'm speaking to that man ever again." She leaned back and swigged her beer.

He wrote down a couple sentences summarizing what Tiana had told him. "Maybe I can talk to your dad instead." He paused, weighing whether to broach the subject that had occupied his mind all afternoon. He took a deep breath and proceeded. "What kind of feeling did you get, hanging out with Devon? Anything feel off about him?" He took a long gulp of his beer.

"No, nothing weird at all." She said it so quickly that she hadn't seemed to think about the question. "He's Zoe's biological dad. No way he could be involved with her kidnapping."

"How'd he react when you told him someone had kidnapped the baby you'd given up for adoption?" He fixed his eyes on her face, observing every intimation of her feelings for Devon.

She furrowed her brows. "He was shocked and upset like me. There's no way to get back those first ten years of Zoe's life we missed out on. All we can do now is try to get her back."

Jay set the pen on the coffee table next to his beer. *We.* He took Tiana's beer and rested it next to his. He leaned over and drew her into a tight hug. "I know this is hard. I know the past three years have been hard too. With Harker working with us, we're on the right track. I'll do everything in my power to bring Zoe back."

"Thanks. I'm glad Devon's involved too. He has a lot of financial resources. With all of us and the police searching for Zoe, I feel like it's only a matter of time until we find her." She grabbed her beer, drank the remainder in one long gulp, then stood. "I'm going to give Devon a quick call."

She left the room, and the knot in Jay's stomach twisted. Her words, "our daughter," rang in his ears. If Devon succeeded in finding Zoe, the chances seemed high that he'd try to win Tiana back too. Jay had to make sure neither of those things happened.

CHAPTER THIRTY-THREE

"**D**ada!" Marcus cried. Tiana rolled over to see Jay's silhouette rising from the bed. She couldn't recall when either of them had fallen asleep. They'd gone to bed a little after midnight, and she had tossed and turned until slumber won the fight.

Moments later, Jay reemerged carrying Marcus. He planted their son in the middle of the bed and lay back down. Marcus rested his cheek on Jay's shoulder, instantly falling back to sleep. Tiana closed her eyes and tried to do the same, but Zoe's face and large, innocent brown eyes came to mind. Her gaze focused on the ceiling. She couldn't sleep with her daughter missing.

After easing herself out of bed, she slipped on her robe and tiptoed to the living room. She turned on the television and hit the power button on her laptop. Since it was almost one thirty in the morning, all local news broadcasts had ended. She flipped on the cable news. Zoe's disappearance hadn't gone national. She shut off the TV and focused on her computer.

Tiana skimmed the latest news articles about Zoe's disappearance. Plans for the massive search for Zoe dominated the stories. She'd confirmed with Devon that they would meet up and search together. Tiana navigated to Facebook and found herself poring over Devon's page. His latest post linked to an article about Zoe's disappearance. He'd captioned it with the words, "Anyone with information about this should immediately go to the police."

Scrolling through his feed, she couldn't help but be surprised by how successful he'd become. He came across as intelligent, athletic, and hardworking. Her dad's words when Devon had broken up with her rang in her mind: "He's an idiot who will never amount to anything. His best chance at making anything of himself would be to join the service like his father. But he's too cowardly to do that. Count yourself lucky. You dodged a bullet."

Tiana had found no solace there. From the moment Tiana's dad had met Devon, he'd hated him. When they'd told her parents about the pregnancy and their plans to marry her senior year, Tiana thought her dad would end up in jail for murdering Devon.

Breaking the news to Devon's parents had proved equally challenging. Having raised him in a very strict military household, his devout Christian mother couldn't understand or easily forgive the young couple's sin, and his dad couldn't believe his son's irresponsibility. As an army sergeant, his dad grew adamant that Devon should enlist in the military to provide for the family he would have.

Navigating through Devon's Facebook pictures, her breath caught in her chest. He'd posted a throwback picture of the two of them at junior prom, on their first date. She hadn't seen it since she'd torn up all their memorabilia after he dumped her. She'd regretted it immediately after doing it, but it had been an effective way to distance herself from Devon and all the memories of their relationship.

Now all the emotions returned. Peering at the photo, Tiana couldn't believe how happy they both looked. Tiana had felt so lucky that out of all the girls at their school, Devon had picked her to be his girlfriend. *How has he even kept this picture for so long?*

"Tiana?" Jay called.

Tiana slammed the laptop shut. "What are you doing up?"

Jay glanced at the computer. "Just checking on you. Everything okay?"

Tiana pressed her hands together. "Yeah. I can't sleep. Just checking if anything's changed with Zoe's case."

Jay sat next to Tiana. "I'm joining the club."

"I have to get up early to go to the search. I wish I could sleep."

Jay squeezed her shoulder. "Marcus and I can come too."

"Thanks, but I don't really want Marcus there. Some weird woman claiming to be a psychic came up to Devon and me yesterday, and she freaked me out." Tiana shivered at the memory. "I think something like this tends to bring the crazies out."

"Do you think either of your folks will be there?"

Tiana hoped not. "I don't know. My mom keeps calling me. I can't bring myself to answer. I mean, what could she possibly say?"

Jay put his hand on her knee. "Sometimes people do the wrong thing for the right reason."

She brushed his hand away. "You would say something like that."

"This ain't about me. I don't want you to lose your relationship with your mom. You two are hella tight. You need her." The sincerity in his voice almost made Tiana reconsider her position toward her mom.

"All I need is to find Zoe." Tiana stood. "Like I said, I have to be up early. I'm going back to bed."

"I'll be in a little later." Jay lay on the couch and faced the television.

In bed next to Marcus, Tiana stared into the darkness. She had so many questions for Devon. What had he been doing the last ten years? Did he end up enlisting in the military? Did he have a girlfriend? How had he become so successful? Where were his parents now? Against her better judgment, she sent him a quick text: *How are you?*

She assumed Devon must be sleeping. *Is he sleeping alone? Stop it, Tiana.* She couldn't go there. It was none of her concern at all.

Her phone vibrated with a text from Devon: *You can't sleep either?*

Tiana sighed. *Yeah.*

We have the search in the morning. We both need sleep.

I know. See you then. Tiana placed the phone under her pillow.

Her phone vibrated again. *I can't wait until then. Can I see you now?*

She sucked in a breath. She couldn't possibly explain to Jay that she wanted to leave the house at one thirty in the morning to meet her ex-fiancé.

Please, Devon texted.

Okay. Meet me at the park in 15. She slipped out of bed, dressed quickly, then went to the bathroom to apply some makeup. After she left the bedroom, she headed through the living room.

Jay paused the movie streaming on the television. "You're going out?" He stared at her, a grimace on his face.

Tiana avoided eye contact. "Yeah, to clear my head. I can't sleep."

Jay stood. "You're gonna go see him? Don't go, Tiana."

Tiana slipped out of the front door without answering. A man dressed in black, who must have switched shifts with Adan, slept in a chair next to their apartment door. Crisp summer night air nipped at her skin. She wrapped her arms around her chest and hurried to her car.

Darkness blanketed the usual scenery, turning her neighborhood foreign. *Could the caller be following me now?* She brushed aside the worry and sped to her and Devon's meeting spot. Her phone rang with Jay's number. She ignored it. When she arrived, Devon's Mercedes already occupied a parking space. He got out and opened her door. "Come in my car. There's more room."

Tiana stepped out and then slid into Devon's passenger seat. "Is this illegal?"

"Depends on what *this* is. Do you have drugs you want to do or something?" Devon smirked.

Tiana chuckled. "I meant loitering in a park."

"Loitering—maybe but probably not. What we used to do in parking lots like this one—definitely."

Tiana's face burned at the memories. "So..." She tried to think of how to change the subject. "What'd you do after the search?"

"I called everyone I know, trying to see if anybody had useful insight or information that could help to find Zoe." His face fell.

"No luck?" All the hope she'd had for Devon finding Zoe seeped out like air leaving a balloon.

"Not exactly. Several people assumed your father probably has the most power in this situation as a district attorney. You know how closely the DA's office works with the police department. I wonder if he plans to use it. And even if he does, and we find Zoe, what happens then? I mean, is he going to fight us so he and Josephine keep her?" His hands opened in a question.

"I'll fight back all the way if he tries to do something like that." Rage stoked by her father's deceit burned inside her. "I keep thinking about what hypocrites he and Josephine are."

Devon arched his eyebrows. "Elaborate."

Tiana held out up her palm. "The Ten Commandments. Thou shall not commit adultery. Thou shall not steal... someone else's baby."

"I'm not religious, but you're absolutely right."

"I'm hoping we find a clue that leads to finding Zoe alive and well tomorrow." Tiana didn't want to sound pessimistic, but she doubted it. From what she'd seen on TV and in the news, usually, if people recovered anything during a search for a missing person, it was a body, not a living being. She didn't dare speak that thought. "What if whoever has been following me has Zoe locked up somewhere? He must want something in exchange. I wish I knew what it is. I'll give him whatever he wants. Anything."

"Me too. I'd give the world to know who's been following you." Devon scratched his chin.

Tiana nodded. "Jay and I were just talking about this exact same thing and trying to come up with names of anyone who seemed suspicious. We're stumped."

Devon softened his tone. "What about Jay?"

"What do you mean?" Tiana squinted, trying to read him.

"I'm just saying, you told me Jay's been out of work since going to prison. I mean, he *was* in prison, after all. Who knows who he connected with in there or what kind of scheme he could've come up with." Devon's steady gaze and firm expression held no trace of humor.

"I know Jay well enough to know he's not involved. He's my husband, after all." She started to regret coming out to meet Devon. The fact he could even imply Jay had anything to do with Zoe's disappearance caused her body to tense.

"Did you know him well enough to think he'd go to prison for killing someone?" Devon apparently had no intention of backing down.

Tiana grabbed the door handle to leave, disgusted with Devon's heartlessness. "You have no idea what happened or what Jay's been through."

Devon reached over and grabbed her hand. "I'm sorry. Don't be mad. I just want you to keep your eyes completely open."

She shook her hand free from his grip and slammed the door behind her. Her phone vibrated, and Jay's number lit the screen.

"Tiana, when are you coming home?" His voice shook with anger.

Any man calling his wife to get her whereabouts at two in the morning would probably have sounded the same. "I'll be back soon." She got into her car and drove away without a second glance at Devon.

"Soon isn't good enough, dammit." Jay's voice lowered an octave. "Come home now. You're my wife. It's the middle of the night."

"I know. I'm on the way." She hung up. She couldn't get Devon's words out of her mind as she drove. Her heart couldn't believe Jay would ever have something to do with kidnapping anyone, but she couldn't let love blind her. He had served eighteen months in prison. He was getting desperate for money. He had been spotted at Zoe's last known location. But whoever had been following her must know all that too. They could have set Jay up. *Who can I trust?* From the recent research she'd done on missing children and her dad's previous cases, the longer Zoe remained missing, the lower the chance they would find her. The clock was ticking.

CHAPTER THIRTY-FOUR

Jay's computer screen illuminated the otherwise pitch-black living room. He'd spent the last forty minutes reading every piece of information about Devon he could find online. Among the various articles about his career and success as a venture capitalist, one thing seemed to be missing. He'd joined the field by investing a large sum of money in a startup straight out of high school, around the time he'd dumped Tiana. That startup beat all expectations and eventually became a Fortune 500, making Devon a huge amount of cash. Since then, he'd had a knack for investing in the right companies at the right time. But one question remained. *Where'd Devon get the money to invest in the first place?*

From what Jay'd read, Devon had come from a military family. They moved around a lot, and Devon had first relocated to the Bay Area his junior year. Based on a military salary, Jay doubted the money could have come from Devon's family. *But who?* Jay sent Harker a quick text: *Last name, I promise. Look up Devon Price for me. Anything and everything you can get.* The front door opened, and Jay shut his laptop.

Tiana stepped into the apartment. "You didn't have to wait up for me."

Jay stood and took a step toward her. "Let's get one thing clear. I will not tolerate you ever leaving the house in the middle of the night to see Devon or any man ever again. I'll admit times are tough, so I'll forgive you this time. Once. If there's ever a next time, don't expect me or Marcus to be waiting around for you."

"Is that a threat?" She glared at him.

"You can call it whatever you want. I'm letting you know exactly what I will and will not put up with. I made a mistake that landed me behind bars. I've told you how sorry I am because of it. You know how sorry I am. I'm not gonna apologize again or let you walk all over me because of it. You would never be okay with me leaving at this time of night to meet another woman, let alone my ex-fiancée." His chest heaved.

"It won't happen again. I'm going to bed." Tiana tried to walk past him, but he stepped in front of her.

"No man would meet another man's wife at this hour unless he wanted her back. Tell me what he said about me." Jay regretted the way he'd treated Devon when he'd found him in his apartment earlier. Apparently, Jay had come across as the type of guy Devon could walk right over, the type of guy who wouldn't fight for his wife. But that impression was incorrect. He wanted to go back in time and slug Devon in the face. A couple of times.

Tiana stared at the ground. "He didn't say—"

"Don't lie to me." Catching himself yelling, Jay lowered his voice. "Tell me what he said."

"He thinks you might have come up with a plan to kidnap Zoe while you were in prison. It's ridiculous. I told him that." Tiana grabbed Jay's hands. "I'm sorry for leaving tonight."

Jay engulfed Tiana in a hug, needing to impress on her the fact that she belonged with him and not Devon. "I could never do anything to hurt a child. Never. Let's go to bed. We have to be up early for the search tomorrow. I'll ask Xavier to watch Marcus because I'm going with you." He shot her a laser-focused gaze. "I'll meet you in bed in a few minutes."

Tiana left the room, and Jay took out his cell phone. It was two fifteen in the morning, but he still dialed his little brother. Either they'd both inherited some type of insomnia gene from their dad, or their shared childhood trauma made them light sleepers. After a couple rings, Xavier answered. "Hey, Jay. Everything okay?"

"Yeah, sorry to call you at this hour. Tiana and I are having more drama. I need to ask you a huge favor. Can you watch Marcus tomorrow?" He explained everything had just happened. "X, I really need this." Jay hated to beg, but he couldn't stand the thought of Devon poisoning Tiana's mind with more lies.

"Okay, brotha. I'll do it. What time?"

Jay cringed. "We gotta leave at eight thirty. Search starts at nine."

Xavier huffed. "I'll be at your place at seven thirty."

Before Jay could say thank you, Xavier had hung up.

Jay turned off the light in the living room and walked through the dark to their bedroom. Inside, Tiana had fallen fast asleep next to Marcus. He stood over her for a minute to see if she would stir. When she didn't, he reached toward the nightstand and grabbed her phone.

He hurried out of the bedroom, silently closing the door behind him. On the couch in the living room, he pulled up Tiana's texts with Devon. He cringed reading that they'd just met up at the park. The last one read, *Teeni, I'll see you tomorrow.*

Teeni? Jay's body smoldered with anger. *Just go to bed, Jay. Leave it alone.* Jay started to return to their bedroom and take his usual spot next to his wife. Regardless of Devon's attempt to shove a wedge between them, she would still come home to Jay, at least this time. But Jay wouldn't be able to sleep if he left Devon unchecked.

With Tiana's phone to his ear, he called Devon, who answered immediately.

"You still can't sleep, Teeni?" Devon asked.

"My wife's name is Tiana. Cut the 'Teeni' bullshit. Given the stories you're trying to tell her, you are very aware I was in prison. Don't for one second think I won't come at you if you disrespect me again. If you ever ask my wife to meet you in the middle of the night, you'll be the next one missing. Got it?" Jay kept his voice low but made sure Devon heard every single word.

"Your threats don't scare me. I'll do whatever it takes to get my daughter and Tiana back." Devon scoffed. "Hope you sleep tight."

Jay placed a pillow from the couch over his mouth to muffle his curses. He took out his phone, pulled up the text he'd sent with Devon's address, pasted the address into his map app, then grabbed his keys. Devon would pay for threatening to get Tiana back.

"Dada! Dada, come!"

Jay ignored Marcus's cries and continued toward the front door.

Marcus yelled louder. "Dada!"

Jay squeezed his eyes closed and blew out a long breath then dropped his keys and Tiana's phone on the coffee table. He forced himself to put one foot in front of the other until he made it to his room, where he paused at the sight of Tiana trying to soothe Marcus back to sleep. He pounded his forehead with his fist. *Get it together, Jay!* He wouldn't let anyone separate him from his son and wife. Not Devon. Not even himself.

CHAPTER THIRTY-FIVE

Banging on a door woke Tiana. She sat up, her heart pounding. Marcus stirred next to her and rubbed his eyes.

Jay ran out of their bedroom. "We overslept. That must be Xavier. I'll tell the security he's fine to let in."

Tiana hopped out of bed, frustrated her alarm hadn't woken her. She searched the nightstand and the floor below but couldn't find her phone. *That's strange.*

Marcus flung his legs over the bed and slid down. "Uncle!" He ran down the hall on tiny feet.

Tiana hurried to the bathroom. Though she didn't look forward to attending the search with both Jay and Devon there, she still had to arrive on time. Telling Jay what Devon had said about him surely only added to the animosity between the two men. But after leaving the house in the middle of the night, she owed it to Jay tell him the complete truth.

After washing up, Tiana took extra time with her makeup. She tried to tell herself it had nothing to do with Devon, but she couldn't help the butterflies in her stomach as she remembered their embraces the day before. She hadn't felt emotions like that in a long time. Somehow, Devon telling her the truth about why he'd left all those years ago unlocked a part of her heart, and it scared her.

But she also hated the way he'd talked about Jay. She had to rein in her emotions because she couldn't afford to make another bad decision like meeting Devon in the middle of the night. Jay had made it clear he wouldn't be so forgiving next time.

But what if I turned Jay's words around on him? I can't forgive you for what you've done to our lives anymore. I've given you enough time to get your life back on track. I've had enough.

She pushed the thoughts away. Loving someone, taking vows and having a child to raise with that person, meant it didn't work that way. That was how she differed from her dad and Devon. She could never turn her back and walk away from the people to whom she had committed, no matter how bad it got. No matter how tempting. No matter what it cost.

Dressed in a green tank top and jean shorts, she joined everyone in the living room. Xavier sat on the couch in shorts and a T-shirt, bouncing a giggling Marcus on his muscular knees. Even though he worked crazy tech hours, Xavier kept himself in great shape. His bloodshot eyes gave away that he hadn't slept much. Tiana hugged him. "Thanks for coming over. I feel bad, making you get up so early on a Saturday."

"Don't feel bad at all. I'm sorry for what you're going through. Watching Little Man is the least I can do. We'll have fun today, right, Marky?" Xavier gave Marcus's round belly a squeeze.

Marcus grinned and clapped his hands. "Yep, Uncle. Fun."

"I'll go get ready." Jay tossed Tiana her cell phone. "It was out here all night."

"Oh, thanks." Tiana headed toward the kitchen. "Xavier, do you want some coffee? I'm going to make a pot."

"Yeah. Lots." Xavier chuckled. "Marcus is like a little engine that never runs out of energy."

Tiana started the coffee then met Jay in their room. "Hey, you just about ready?"

"Yeah. I'm dressing light. It's supposed to be another hot one. I'm sure we'll be out there for a while." Already in a pair of gray shorts, Jay pulled a light-blue shirt over his head.

Tiana retrieved her sneakers from the closet. "I hope we can move past last night. There's nothing between me and Devon."

"You literally left our bed to meet him and didn't get home till after two in the morning." Jay pointed to their empty bed like evidence. "Do you think I'm an idiot?"

Tiana huffed. "Seriously, Jay, stop being like this."

"Being like what?" He raised a hand in question. His intense gaze focused on Tiana. "Do you still love him?"

Tiana hadn't expected that question. "I'm married to you."

"Answer the question," he hissed.

Tiana took a step backward. She couldn't remember Jay speaking to her with so much anger before. "I don't appreciate you talking to me like that."

"You've done a lot in the past twenty-four hours that I don't appreciate. Do you love him? Answer the question." Jay stepped toward her.

Tiana stared her husband in the eyes. "No." Her voice shook. "I don't even know him anymore. Jay, I love you."

"He wants you back, Tiana. But don't forget he dumped you and left Zoe."

Jay's comment hit Tiana like a dagger. Without thinking, Tiana blurted out, "He told me my dad forced him to break up with me. He didn't want to."

Jay scoffed. "That's a great story. I don't believe a word of it. If it's true, what does that mean to you? You're married to me. We have Marcus. Does that change anything?"

Tiana couldn't admit that it changed everything. "No, it doesn't. Look, we need to go. I don't want to be late. I'm going to grab our coffee. Meet me in the living room when you're ready."

She returned to the kitchen and poured Xavier a cup of coffee.

Marcus sat next to his uncle on the couch, clutching his favorite teddy bear. The noise of the loud TV bounced off the living room walls—Xavier had obviously tried to drown out Jay and Tiana's argument.

He turned the TV down and accepted the coffee. "Everything a'ight?"

Tiana rubbed her forehead. "I hope so. It's a bad situation. There's no script for something like this."

"I don't know when or how, but it will get better, Tiana. I'm rooting for you and your daughter. Actually, I'm rooting for your whole family, including my knucklehead brother." He squeezed Tiana's hand.

She wiped away a tear that slid down her cheek, hating how her emotions threatened to overtake her at every moment. "I'm rooting for us too."

"If you need anything, I'm here for all of you. I wouldn't be where I am now without Jay. He sacrificed a lot to take me out of our dysfunctional home and support me. I'll never be able to repay him," Xavier whispered.

"Jay doesn't mention it, but I know you help us out financially. I really appreciate it. We're hanging on by a thread right now." Tiana swallowed the tears again. "I'm hoping Jay gets a job soon. It's not easy."

Xavier shook his head. "Don't mention it. But even when he... you know... he was looking out for—"

"I'm ready, Tiana." Jay walked into the living room, a scowl plastered on his face.

Tiana's phone rang. Every cell in her body tensed. Instead of a blocked number or Devon's, her mom's number appeared on the screen. Ignoring the call, she let it go to voicemail.

Jay glared at Tiana and the phone in her hand.

Tiana held up the phone, which showed the missed call. "It was my mom. I'm not ready to talk to her."

"I know y'all are in a hurry, but Jay, can we talk for a minute?" Xavier asked. He placed Marcus on the couch and stood. "In the back."

"All right. Ti, give me a second." Jay stomped down the hall with his brother on his heels, then the men disappeared into the bedroom.

Tiana hated the tension between her and Jay. She just hoped nothing would happen between Jay and Devon at the search. She already had enough to worry about.

CHAPTER THIRTY-SIX

Jay paced the short distance between the door and the chest of drawers in his and Tiana's bedroom. "What's up, Xavier? I can't make Tiana late for the search."

Xavier placed a hand on Jay's shoulder. "Look at you. Steam is almost coming off your head. Can you promise you'll be cool at the search when you see Tiana's ex?"

"Nah, I can't promise that. If he even tries to come at me crazy, it's over." Jay's heart pounded in his ears.

"You can't go. No way. There's too much at stake. You need to sit this one out and get your emotions under control."

"I gotta go. I ain't letting nobody punk me like that." Jay walked toward the door.

Xavier stood in front of the door with his hands out. "Nope. You've come too far to get caught up again. Tiana and Marcus are worth more than your ego. Do you want to get locked up again?"

The eighteen months behind bars flashed through Jay's mind. *I can't go back.* Jay took a few steps back and sat on the edge of the bed. He cradled his head in his hands. "I can't lose her, X."

"Tiana loves you. But if you mess up in any way and violate your parole, you'll be right back in prison. I know Tiana won't be able to go through that again. You can't risk a fight with her ex right now. You have to be smart and work on finding her daughter."

Jay didn't want to leave Tiana alone with Devon for the day. He could only imagine the lies Devon would feed her. But he didn't think he could control the anger threatening to explode. "I hate to say it, but you're right. I'll tell Tiana now. Thanks for having my back." Jay mustered his self-control and walked to the living room.

Tiana stood by the door, keys in her hand. "We're gonna be late."

"I'm gonna stay here with Marcus. Go without me." It took all the restraint Jay had to plop himself on the couch next to Marcus.

Tiana eyed Xavier, who nodded. "Okay, wish me luck. I'll be back as soon as I can. Hopefully with some good news."

After Tiana left and closed the door, Xavier sat next to Jay. "You did good letting her go. She'll be back."

Jay huffed. "It's too convenient for Devon. The daughter he's never known gets kidnapped, and all of a sudden, he's back in the picture with his Benz and money, trying to get back the family he abandoned. He's never known the girl. Who does he think he is, playing concerned dad now?" Each word tasted like bitter disgust.

"Benz and money?" Xavier winced. "Stiff competition."

Jay clenched his fist. "It shouldn't be a competition. Tiana's married to me. All the dude can say is he left her when she needed him the most. And he's even trying to spin that now. He told Tiana her dad forced him to break up with her. It's a damn lie."

"You need to do your homework and learn everything you can about him. If something is off, you'll find out. Try not to worry too much." Xavier shrugged. "Tiana loves you and Marcus. I doubt she'd leave what she has for anyone."

"But what can I offer her? I got no job, no money, no prospects." Jay's reality sounded even worse aloud.

"That's all temporary. I have one hundred percent confidence that you'll be back on your feet soon." Xavier patted his brother on the shoulder. "I'll help you get there."

"Thanks for coming over, man. You're free to go. If you're not too tired, you can still make it in to work." Jay picked up Marcus's hand and waved it. "Say bye to Uncle."

Marcus curled his bottom lip. "No leave."

"Why you trying to get rid of me? I'm already here. Let's grab breakfast, on me." Xavier patted Marcus's stomach. "Want some food?"

Marcus clapped. "Food, Uncle!"

"That sounds good. Let's go." Jay needed a distraction from thinking about Tiana meeting up with Devon again. A grown woman with her own mind, Tiana had to decide who she wanted to be with. He needed her to choose him.

JAY GRINNED AT MARCUS, who had stuffed his mouth with silver-dollar pancakes. "Slow down, buddy." His phone beeped, forcing his smile to fade. Of course Janice had to call and ruin his breakfast.

"What's wrong?" Xavier gestured toward the phone.

"It's your mother. She has some type of uncanny ability to call at the worst time." Jay dropped his fork onto the plate.

"Come on." Xavier nodded to his plate. "Don't let her ruin breakfast. She means no harm. Eat."

Jay picked his fork back up. "No harm? She ruined my life. But you're right. I ain't gonna let her mess this meal up too." He forced the food down, though it had lost its taste.

"She's sorry, you know?" Xavier didn't take his eyes off his plate of eggs, sausage, and hash browns.

"Yeah, she is sorry. Always has been. But that's never helped me once in my life. It won't now either. I wish she'd just leave me the hell alone."

"Lee' me the hell a-lone!" Marcus repeated with his eyes scrunched closed and a frown on his face.

Jay and Xavier exchanged a glance before both burst into laughter. Marcus giggled too.

"You look just like Marcus when you're mad." Xavier smiled widely at Jay.

Jay couldn't stay angry for long around Marcus and Xavier. "Whose side are you on?"

"Marcus's side, obviously. Came all the way over at seven thirty just to see the little dude, remember?" Xavier reached across and squeezed Marcus's arm. "Right?"

Marcus swatted Xavier's hand away. "Where Mama?"

Guilt overwhelmed Jay. While he sat in an air-conditioned restaurant, enjoying a big breakfast, Tiana braved scorching temperatures to search for her lost daughter. He wished with all his heart that he could be with her. But Xavier had been right. *I can't be nowhere near Devon.* At some point, the men would come face-to-face, and Jay had to have the restraint not to do anything that would land him back in prison.

"Mama's out today. She'll be back home later." The words came out easily. But how easy would it be for Tiana to return home? The more Devon tried to get her back, the harder the decision might become. Jay would need to touch base with Harker and see if he'd found anything out about Devon. Devon obviously didn't mind playing dirty, so Jay wouldn't either. He would use anything he could find to bring Devon down.

CHAPTER THIRTY-SEVEN

Smoke polluted the sky above as Tiana pulled in to the Walmart parking lot. After parking, she opened the car door, and heat mixed with smoke enveloped her. Due to the forecast of temperatures in the high nineties and the worsening wildfire, public health officials had declared a Spare the Air day. But based on the number of cars, the warning to limit time outside hadn't deterred many people from the search.

She crossed the parking lot and joined the large crowd. More than half of them wore medical-grade masks to keep the smoke out of their lungs. Uniformed police officers and agents wearing FBI shirts milled about in the group.

Her heart swelled to know that so many people cared about Zoe, but she felt as insignificant as a grain of sand at the beach.

A thin woman with curly blond hair extended a flyer with Zoe's face toward Tiana and pointed to a line leading to a table manned by police officers. "If you're here for the search, please sign in and get a mask."

Tiana accepted the flyer. "Thanks. I am."

"Great. We leave in fifteen minutes." The woman moved on through the crowd.

She gazed at the flyer with Zoe's picture as she stood in line. *My beautiful daughter.* When her time came to check in, she showed her driver's license and wrote her name and phone number on a list. Knowing that the police wanted a record of everyone volunteering provided her some comfort.

A man with an unruly white beard who smoked a cigarette held his flyer up next to Tiana's face. "You two related?" Smoke escaped with each of the man's words.

Tiana winced as the stench filled her nostrils, unsure how to answer. "I'm concerned like everyone else."

He inhaled another drag. "It's a shame. Let's hope she turns up today—not just her body."

Tiana glared at the man and moved away. She jumped when someone tapped her shoulder. She turned around then screamed, "Ava! I can't believe you came." Tiana hugged her best friend tightly.

Ava wore jeans, a yellow tank top, and tennis shoes. Somehow, they'd picked out almost identical outfits, other than the color of their shirts. Ava had pulled her brunette hair into a ponytail. A mask hung around her neck. "Of course I came. I didn't expect so many people. If Zoe's anywhere nearby, I'm sure we'll find her."

Tiana squeezed Ava's hand. "You're the best. Thank you for coming." She looked past Ava, searching for Devon. Her emotions were mixed about seeing him after what'd he'd said about Jay.

Ava looked at the crowd. "Are you meeting someone here?"

"Not exactly, but Devon said he's coming." She couldn't imagine him not showing up.

Ava arched an eyebrow. "Devon, huh?"

"It's not like that. But you know..." Tiana shrugged. "He's Zoe's father."

"And your first love, who broke your heart." Ava's eyes grew stern.

Tiana wished that Ava and everyone else didn't feel the need to remind her of that. "It was high school. Literally over a decade ago. We've both grown up a lot since then. So much has changed."

"Yeah, one of those changes is your marital status." Ava elbowed Tiana in the side.

"Attention." A woman dressed in a black T-shirt and black jeans, as if to give a middle finger to the scorching heat, addressed the crowd through a bullhorn. "Thank you all for coming. Our plan to-day is to search far and wide for Zoe Miller. These first days after a child goes missing are absolutely critical. That's why we are out here. We have one goal, and that is to locate Zoe and bring her home. If you haven't done so already, please sign in at the table in the front. We appreciate each and every one of you being here today. Should you find anything that you deem important while searching, please bring it to the attention of law enforcement personnel immediately. Again, thank you. We'll form lines and slowly comb through every inch of the field. Let's get going."

A dozen FBI agents with bloodhounds led the pack. Tiana, Ava, and a couple hundred people started walking behind them. Tiana checked her phone. Devon hadn't texted her. She didn't want to pursue his whereabouts further in Ava's presence. After all, Ava was right. Tiana had married Jay, and her allegiance stood with her husband.

The blazing sun mixed with the smoke from Yountville assaulted Tiana like a gardener pointing a leaf blower in her face. The mask added more heat but did prevent her from inhaling the worst of the smoke. She wiped her sweaty forehead with the back of her hand. Leaving the confines of the parking lot, they turned onto a dirt path that opened into a huge field that ended at a reservoir. "Did Brad mind you coming? I know he works so much, and the weekends are all you really have together."

Ava rolled her eyes. "Are you kidding? He's going to have a few uninterrupted hours to play his video games without me nagging him for attention. What has Devon been up to the past ten years? I'm assuming quite a bit has happened since he broke up with you and fell off the face of the earth."

Tiana didn't need the reminder. "I think he's just been playing video games."

"Ha. You mentioned he drives a Mercedes. Apparently, he's done well for himself. Is he in a relationship now? Does he have any other kids? I mean, it's kind of weird how the man just pops back up into the picture when Zoe disappears, don't you think?"

Tiana hadn't mentioned their run-ins at the park the past month because of Ava's exact attitude toward him now. Tiana had known Devon since they were teenagers. He definitely couldn't be up to anything shady. "We've been so focused on Zoe that we haven't really had time to catch up. I'm sure I'll learn more in due time. Right now, the main goal is finding our daughter. Can we focus on that, please?"

"I'm sorry. You're absolutely right." Ava wrapped her arm around Tiana's shoulder. "You're my best friend, and I don't want Devon to hurt you again. You've already gone through so much pain because of him. Just know I got your back. I'll always be here for you."

"I appreciate that, Ava. I don't know what I'd do without you." Tiana's phone rang. Though expecting Devon, a blocked number popped up. She silenced the call, determined to send it to the tracing app. It'd take a few minutes for the app to send the caller's identification back to her.

Ava looked at the phone. "Do you think that was the guy who called earlier?"

"Yes, I think so." A voicemail notification popped up. "He left a message."

She played the voicemail on speaker. The same man's ominous voice came through the phone. "Looking in all the wrong places. But green looks good on you."

Tiana froze. Her eyes ventured to her green tank top. She scanned the crowd. People streamed by in front of her, on her side, and behind her. The man had to be there. He could have been anybody. The murmur of the people around her grew unbearably loud. She covered her ears, pushing her way out of the crowd. She stopped at a patch of brown grass away from the search. "He's here. Watching me."

Ava's gaze darted around the crowd. "This has gone too far. We're surrounded by law enforcement. You have a voicemail as proof. I know the police didn't take it seriously, but it's time you talk to someone else here."

"You're right. Let's go back to the police table. I don't want to continue the search, knowing this guy is here. He could do anything." Tiana and Ava hurried back to the search home base. She checked the tracing app. "Dammit!"

"What's wrong?" Ava glanced at Tiana's phone.

"The tracing app sent a message saying that caller can't be traced. It says some phone services can't be unmasked if they are routed through a company or don't have a number to show. Whoever is calling isn't some lone weirdo. It's an organized effort." Tiana headed straight to the table where uniformed police congregated.

"Tiana," a man yelled.

She turned. "Dad?" Her shoulders tensed further. *Dad's the last person I want to talk with.* Dark bags hung under his eyes. Tiana swore more wrinkles lined his face than when she'd confronted him yesterday.

"Tiana, I need to talk to you." He glanced at Ava. "Alone."

"What do you want?" If it were up to Tiana, her dad would be jailed for kidnapping Zoe.

"To talk. Please." Her dad gestured to an empty spot near a garbage can.

Ava glared at Tiana's dad. "I'll be right here if you need me, Tiana."

Tiana followed her dad away from the policemen. *Whatever he has to say better be good.*

When her dad stopped walking, he sighed. "Tiana..."

"What?" All she could see was a liar and cheater. "After all you've done to me, Zoe, and Mom, what can you possibly have to say?"

"I'm sorry about everything that's happened. It was wrong and selfish to keep Zoe from you all these years. That was never the plan. I wanted you to get settled into college and graduate. Then I'd reintroduce you to Zoe like a wonderful surprise. But then you met Jay, and Josephine and Zoe had such a strong bond. The time never seemed right. I regret the decisions I've made. Please know that. I want your forgiveness."

"There's no way words can heal what you've done. I will never forgive you or look at you the same. But I have more pressing issues. I need to find Zoe, and I believe the person who led me to you knows where she is. The person is here." Tiana held up her phone. "He left me a voicemail. I was on my way to talk to the police before you stopped me. I'm going to try to get them to listen to me."

Tiana's dad's face grew red. "The person's here?" He searched the crowd.

Tiana played the voicemail for her dad. "I need to do something. Why is he targeting me?"

"I don't know." Her dad ran a hand over his head. "There are a million possibilities. Money. Revenge. A personal vendetta against me. He led you to discover that Zoe was your daughter. It's someone who knows intimate facts about our lives. But the police are already involved and searching for Zoe. You going to the police now—it won't help anything. It will only complicate—"

"*Your* life, right? Forget that it might help find *my* daughter." Tears of rage shot down her face. "I can't believe you."

Her dad folded his arms over his chest. "I didn't want you to end up like your mom and me." With a heavy sigh, he seemed to unmask the façade he'd put on. "We married because she got pregnant with you. We were just kids in our last year of high school. Don't get me wrong. Having you was the best thing that ever happened to me. But once you commit to marriage and a family, so many doors close. I saw you in the exact same position your mom was in. I didn't want you to go through what we did." He reached his hand to touch Tiana's.

Tiana yanked her arm out of her dad's reach. The combination of the heat, smoke, and her dad's bullshit had her on fire and feeling dizzy. "You're a successful prosecutor. What on earth are you talking about?" He would have to come up with a better explanation for his behavior. Blaming her mom becoming pregnant with her wasn't cutting it.

"I know I am. But your mom had dreams too. She put them on hold for you and me. She became bitter and jealous of my success." He held out his palm to Tiana. "I didn't want that to happen to you. I wanted you to be free to pursue every opportunity available."

"So you're blaming Mom?" He had some nerve. "She's done nothing but love and support you. Never once has she acted jealous of your success."

His eyes pleaded with Tiana. "I wanted more for you. Can you understand that?"

Tiana shook her head. They would never see eye to eye. "No, and I never will. But right now, I need your help. Maybe if you intervene with the police, they'll take me seriously."

Tiana's dad took a step closer and lowered his voice. "Tiana, I can't do that. If this gets out—"

"What part? That your daughter got pregnant at seventeen? Or that you've been raising her daughter as your own with your mistress from a longstanding affair?" Tiana purposely yelled so anyone walking by could hear.

"All of that." Her dad shifted nervously. "I can't drag my and Josephine's names through the mud. She can't handle that right now."

"*She* can't handle that? Really? But I deserved to have you lie to me and kidnap my baby? And my daughter deserves to be held captive by a crazy person because you can't face the consequences? You're a selfish man who only cares about himself." Tiana turned her back. She would leave and permanently sever the relationship with her dad.

Her dad placed his hand on her shoulder. "Wait. What are you going to do?"

Tiana now had the proof she needed: the voicemail. "I'm going to talk to the police and help them find Zoe."

Pulling out a card, her dad handed it to Tiana. "Here's the detective who's handling the case at SJPD. Go speak to him directly. I'll put in a call now, so he'll be expecting you. Like I said, the plan was always to reunite you with Zoe. I never changed her guardianship to Josephine legally. You still have every right as Zoe's mother. So the police have to let you in on the case once I explain everything."

Tiana grabbed the card, grateful her dad had finally done something right. She walked back to Ava. "I'm going to the police station."

Ava walked with Tiana toward the parking lot. "Do you want me to come with you?"

Tiana shook her head. "I can't ask you to do that. There's going to be a lot of waiting. When I talk to the detective, they'll want me alone. But I'll call you later tonight." When they reached the parking lot, Tiana hugged Ava again. "Thank you for coming and being the best friend ever."

"Don't thank me. But please, be safe." Her worried gaze focused on Tiana. "Until we find Zoe, everyone is a possible suspect."

Tiana shivered. Ava only spoke the truth. *Who can I trust?*

CHAPTER THIRTY-EIGHT

When Jay, Xavier, and Marcus arrived back at the apartment, Harker stood outside, talking to Adan. Jay approached his friend. "Harker, what's up?"

Harker shook Jay's hand. "Jay, sorry to just show up. I have to talk to you about what I've found."

"I'm Xavier, Jay's brother." Xavier shook Harker's hand.

"Right on. Jay talked a lot about you in—" Harker looked at the security guard and abandoned the sentence. "Can we go inside?"

The knot in Jay's stomach tightened. Harker must have found something serious. "Yeah, of course." Jay opened the door and stepped into his apartment. Even though he'd set all the fans to high before leaving for breakfast, the apartment could have doubled as a broiler. He brought out Marcus's Legos. "Buddy, make me the tallest building ever. We're going to talk in the kitchen."

Marcus stacked two Legos. "'Kay."

Jay crossed the room and pulled three kitchen chairs out from the table. "Let's sit here and talk."

Harker glanced at the fridge. "Got any cold beer?"

"Yep." Jay felt grateful he actually had some beer. After retrieving three, he handed one each to Harker and Xavier. He sat and opened his. "I have a feeling I'm going to need this."

Harker cracked open his beer and took a long gulp. "Your feeling's right."

Jay's phone rang with a call from Tiana. "Hey, Tiana. What's up? How's the search?"

"I actually left twenty minutes ago." Tiana relayed what had happened at the search.

"I'm glad your dad's finally done something to help. But can you come home first? Harker's here at our place." Jay glanced at Harker, who set up his laptop on the table. "He has information that he said is real important."

"I'm focused on speaking to the police. Just tell me what he says later. I'm in no mood to see that jerk."

Jay turned down his phone's volume, hoping Harker didn't hear that. "What Harker knows might help when you go to the police. Come home first and hear what he has to tell us. The police station will still be there after."

Tiana huffed into the phone. "It better be worth it. I'll head home for a second. I have to go straight to the police station after."

Harker cleared his throat. "No offense, but Jay, do you feel comfortable discussing this with your brother here?"

Xavier furrowed his eyebrows and blew out air.

Jay needed to calm the tension suddenly in the room. "Xavier's cool. He already knows everything. Anything you say will be kept in this room."

"Can I speak freely right now?" Harker chugged his beer, his gaze focused on Jay.

Jay looked at Xavier, wondering what Harker could want to tell him. "Yeah, absolutely."

"What I found looks bad for you. I stopped at Walmart early this morning and got some more dirt on Ronnie. When your wife gets here, I'll show her what I have. But it's up to you to decide what you want to do with it." Harker held up his beer can. "You got another one?"

Jay sat motionlessly, trying to process Harker's words. He wanted to get up, but dread weighed him down.

Xavier stood and went to the fridge. "I'll get you one, man." He grabbed a beer and handed it to Harker. "What you got exactly?"

Harker snapped open the beer, chugged a few gulps, then wiped his mouth with the back of his hand. "Before we talk about that, I got your text when I woke up and looked into Devon Price. Nothing remarkable at all. No convictions. No debt problems. Nothing, really. One thing stood out to me. He invested one hundred thousand dollars in a startup at age eighteen, straight out of high school. I'm wondering, where'd he get that money? That first investment basically opened the door to his career. It took off after that startup did well. Like I said, it's not like there's a trail of dirty money. But I have a feeling there must have been more than luck for him to come up on money like that."

Jay had thought the exact same thing. But unfortunately, Harker didn't seem able to help him solve the mystery.

Keys jingled at the door, then Tiana walked through. Streaks of sweat and dirt lined her face. "I got here as fast as I could."

Marcus squealed and dropped the Legos in his hand. "Mama!"

Tiana picked him up and peppered him with kisses. "Hey, Marky. I missed you." With Marcus rested on her hip, she headed toward the kitchen table.

Harker eyed Marcus. "Is there somewhere the boy can go while we talk?"

More dread squeezed into Jay's already tense body. "Tiana, why don't you put him in his crib with some toys? Just for a few minutes."

Tiana bit her lip. "Sure. I'll be right back."

When she left the room, Jay looked at Harker. "Is it that bad?"

Harker nodded. "Yeah."

Tiana returned and sat in the empty chair at the table. "What do you have, Harker?"

Harker punched his password into his laptop and pointed at the screen. "I've viewed twenty-four hours of Walmart's surveillance footage from the day Zoe disappeared. I wanted to show you all some of it." Harker brought up a video and pressed play.

"Wait, how'd you get this?" Tiana asked.

"Let's save the questions until after I show you the video. See, this is Zoe entering with Josephine." Though hard to see Zoe's face because of the camera angle, the video showed a slender little girl with two braids entering the store, holding hands with a woman with Josephine's rail-thin frame. Harker sped up the video. "Jay, they got you and your boy. You came about twenty minutes after Josephine and Zoe. Now, this is where things get crazy because Josephine alerts the staff she can't find Zoe. The staff start searching the store."

Jay snapped his fingers. "That's why I heard them calling her name over the loudspeaker."

"This is you leaving about five minutes later." Harker sped through the video then pressed stop. "That's all twenty-four hours. Know what's missing?"

"What?" Jay and Tiana asked simultaneously.

"Zoe never leaves." Harker stared at Jay. Then Tiana. Then Xavier, for emphasis.

A chill raced through Jay. The reality of being in the same store as Zoe at the same time hit him hard. *I wish I could've helped her.*

Tiana raised her palms. "What happened to her?"

Harker rewound the video. "This is the kicker. See this man? He entered the store by himself about thirty minutes before Zoe and Josephine. He walks around without picking up a single thing. He joins Zoe in the same aisle. Then he leaves with a little boy. See, looks like that boy is sleeping on his shoulder." Harker froze the screen and zoomed in, revealing a child who looked like Zoe wearing an oversized sweatshirt. With her hair hidden by a baseball cap, she appeared asleep in the man's arms.

Goose bumps dotted Jay's arms. "That's Zoe, isn't it?"

"I'd bet money on it." Harker took another long gulp of his beer. "Josephine's story is that she and Zoe shop for their church's outreach program every Thursday down here at Walmart in San Jose after she picked up Zoe from school. A church member manages the store and gives them a huge discount. The Walmart store clerk I spoke to said that day and time is unusually quiet for the store for some reason. Anyway, Josephine says she sent Zoe to grab a few items in the row over like she usually does. Zoe never came back. Josephine frantically searched the store. When she still couldn't find her about five minutes later, she alerted the store's staff. Now, this man could have known all about their routine and somehow caught Zoe alone in the aisle. He must have somehow sedated her, maybe a quick injection in the arm. She looks to be completely knocked out when he carries her out of the store."

Tiana pointed at the screen. "Who is the man? Can we get a closer look?"

Harker glanced at Jay and raised his eyebrows.

Jay gave a slight nod. He didn't know how it could affect him. He had nothing to hide.

"I'll zoom in." He clicked the mouse several times to enlarge the man in the image.

Jay gasped. "Hell no. No way."

Xavier stared at Jay. "What's wrong?"

Jay's heart pounded in his ears. He pointed at the screen. "That's—that's Ronnie."

Tiana leaned in to get a closer look at the image. "Are you sure that's Ronnie? I mean, why would he take Zoe? How could he even know her? Jay, what the hell is going on?" Her pitch grew higher with each word.

Harker sat back in the chair without saying a word.

Jay's voice trembled. "I don't know what's going on. That's him, though."

Xavier put both his hands on his head. "And you still haven't talked to him?"

Jay balled his fists. "No. He fell off the face of the earth. He ain't called or texted me back. Nothing."

Tiana narrowed her eyes at Jay. "What do you know about this Ronnie guy?"

Jay wrung his hands, which were coated with sweat. "I don't know no more. He lied 'bout everything." That's the most truth Jay could tell at the moment. He definitely wouldn't bring up what Harker had found out about him. That could cause Tiana to panic.

Tiana rose from the table. "We need to go to the police with this information. We know who kidnapped Zoe."

Harker threw his hands up. "Whoa. Technically speaking, you don't know any of this. I obtained Walmart's surveillance footage through back channels that I promised would stay anonymous. So you can't cite this footage if you go to the police. But I'm sure the cops have reviewed this exact footage. They're on top of this already."

"There hasn't been information about any of this in the media." Jay rose from his chair.

"Like I told you, if they have a suspect, they're not going to disseminate the information all over the place." Harker gestured to the flat screen. "If Ronnie turned on the TV and saw his face plastered on the screen, he might do something drastic. That's the last thing anyone wants to happen."

"There's gotta be a good reason for all this." Jay paced the floor. "I can't see Ronnie just kidnapping a little girl, let alone Zoe."

Tiana glared at him. "Where does he live? What does he do for a living? Does he have a family?"

Jay hung his head. "I don't know. I can't believe this. He couldn't have kidnapped her. Could he?"

"We have the proof right here!" Tiana slammed her hand on the table. "Your friend kidnapped my daughter. We need to go to the police and talk to the detective my dad told me about. You have to tell them the friend you were supposed to meet there has completely disappeared, and something seems off."

Xavier joined them standing. "Wait. Jay can't just walk into a police station and act like he has information on Zoe's case. Not only does he have a history of incarceration, but he's a Black man in America. They'll find any reason to lock him up again."

Harker shut the laptop. "Xavier's got a point."

"If Jay didn't do anything wrong, they can't lock him up. My daughter's life is on the line." Tiana faced Jay. "You have to do what's right. You owe that much to me."

Jay's fists banged his forehead. The room swayed around him. *How the hell did I get caught up in this?* Everything in him wanted to run to Marcus's room, pick his son up, and get the hell out of there. The prospect of going to the police station and possibly implicating himself in a crime seemed beyond stupid. But Tiana had a point. He owed her. He would put his life and freedom on the line to prove that he loved her without a doubt. "I'll do it. But you have to do something also."

"What's that?" Tiana asked.

"Taking out what Harker's told us, you need to tell them everything 'bout your dad, Josephine, Devon, no matter how crazy it sounds." If Jay could go down, everyone else would have to fall too.

"I will," Tiana said.

Xavier shifted nervously. "You two go to the police, and I'll stay with Marcus. He's been with me all morning, so he'll be fine. Go now. It will be better if he doesn't see you leave." Once again, Xavier had Jay's back.

Jay walked to his brother and gave him a tight hug. "Thank you, X. I appreciate you." He turned to Harker, who held his laptop in its case. "You came through, man. It's not what I wanted, but it'll help."

Harker waved his hand to dismiss the gratitude. "After what you did for me, we're still not even. You got about one big favor left. But be cool at the police station. Let me know when you get back home."

Tiana grabbed Jay's hand and tugged him toward the door. He took a long look at his home. It was possibly the last time he would have the freedom to see it. Though he wanted to hug Marcus and say goodbye, he didn't want to make it worse for Xavier, so he pledged to himself he would do everything in his power to make it back home.

CHAPTER THIRTY-NINE

With Jay dragging his feet behind her, Tiana rushed into the police station and to the police attendant's window. "I have information that's related to the missing girl, Zoe Miller." She slid the policewoman the card her dad had given her under the bottom of the plastic window separating them. "I need to speak to this detective."

The policewoman nearly rolled her eyes. "We've had over five hundred people with so-called information since the reward was posted. What information do you have, exactly?"

"That I'm her birth mother. My name's Tiana Williams." Tiana slid her driver's license under the window to the policewoman.

"And I was brought in for questioning Thursday night. I have more information that the police will want," Jay added.

Tiana squeezed Jay's hand. He had a lot to lose by coming forward. She appreciated his braveness.

"Birth mother?" The woman arched an eyebrow.

"Yes." Tiana tried to sound convincing. She still had trouble believing it herself at times.

The policewoman pointed to the metal benches in the lobby before leaving the counter. "Have a seat."

TIANA AND JAY WAITED for what seemed like an eternity in the busy lobby before a man wearing plain clothes and a badge opened the door and called Tiana's name. She and Jay rose and approached him. "My name is Detective Kent McDaniel. Thank you for coming in. We'll see you two separately. Mrs. Williams first." The man gestured for Tiana to follow him. "Come with me."

Tiana followed the lanky man down a narrow hall and to a small room. A chill coursed through her body. The police had taken her into a room like that after Jay's arrest. They'd interrogated her for hours until her voice had turned hoarse.

The detective pulled out a chair then sat in another one across from her. "Please, sit."

Tiana lowered into the chair. Even though the police station held a chill from the air-conditioning, her whole body heated under the harsh fluorescent lights.

The officer leaned toward Tiana. "Tell me what information you have."

Again, and for what felt like the umpteenth time, Tiana relayed the events that had unfolded over the last few days. She showed him the photograph and notes then played the voicemail from the man on her phone. It sounded so bizarre. She would completely understand if McDaniel not-so-politely asked her to leave.

But instead, once she was done, he folded his hands on the table. "I'm so sorry for everything you've gone through, Mrs. Williams. Your father called me. After we spoke at length, he sent me a copy of Zoe's birth certificate. I will be more than happy to inform you of all the efforts undertaken to find Zoe. However, I have to speak with your husband first."

Tiana smiled, grateful the officer took her seriously. "Absolutely."

"You're very brave for coming in here like this. Feel free to wait in the lobby. We'll call you when we're ready."

Tiana followed Detective McDaniel back out. She didn't feel brave. She was desperate. Her child's life was on the line.

Though still bustling, the lobby no longer had Jay in it. She waited in line to speak with the attendant. "Hello. Is my husband, Jaylen Williams, still back there?"

The policewoman nodded. "Yes."

Tiana shifted uncomfortably. "Do you know when he'll be out?"

Without a word, the woman shook her head.

"Do you know how long they'll question him?" Tiana tried to hide the panic welling up in her.

The attendant looked past Tiana. "Next."

Tiana slid into the gray bench against the concrete wall. *Did I make a mistake in guilting Jay into speaking with the police?* It made no sense that his friend could have been the one to take her daughter. If the police took Jay into custody, it could only be if he had done something wrong. And if he had, though it would hurt, that would be the end of their marriage. There could be no other way.

Taking out her phone, Tiana noticed a missed call from Devon. She definitely couldn't tell him what Harker had told them. Still, she didn't see a reason not to call him back. "Devon, what happened to you at the search today?"

"I'm still here now. I had to handle something at work this morning. I came straight here after. Where are you?" Devon shouted over the crowd's noise in the background.

Tiana shuddered, thinking about the voicemail she'd received earlier. "Whoever's been following me was at the search. I decided to go to the police. I'm at the station now."

"What's happening? You should've told me. I would've gone with you."

"Jay's here with me." Tiana stared at the door, willing it to open and for her husband to reappear.

"I'm Tiana's dad. I should be there. I'll head there now."

"No. There's nothing you can do here. Your name isn't even on Zoe's birth certificate. You're more useful at the search."

"We've covered a lot of ground. But no one has found anything of note. I'm anxious for some kind of lead. Anything."

Tiana mulled over all the new information Harker had given them. She couldn't find a way to mention it to Devon without letting on how she found out about it. "Look, Devon, I just wanted to say, about last night... that can't happen again. I shouldn't have met you so late. It really upset Jay. He doesn't deserve that."

Devon laughed. "Did I deserve to have him call me last night and threaten my life?"

"What are you talking about?"

"Last night, he called me from your phone and threatened me. He's dangerous, Tiana. You have to be careful. You don't know who he really is at all."

The door opened, and Detective McDaniel approached her. "I have to go." Tiana hung up and tucked the phone in her purse. She now knew why her phone had spent the night on the coffee table. *Is Devon right about Jay?*

"We're going to keep your husband a bit longer. To be frank, we need to make sure he's not involved with Zoe's kidnapping before we tell you any more information about the case," McDaniel said. "You can wait for him or go home. Either way, we'll speak more with you tomorrow."

Tiana sighed. "Fine. Do what you must. I'll wait for Jay." She didn't know the truth, but the police were trained to find it. She would wait until they made a call and would accept it whether she liked it or not.

WHEN THE DOOR FINALLY opened and Jay walked out, Tiana didn't know how to feel.

He approached her. "Let's bounce before they change their minds about letting me go." He hurried to the exit and held the door open for Tiana.

Pausing, Tiana questioned where she'd be safer: at the police station or with her husband.

"Let's go, Ti." Jay nodded toward the parking lot.

Tiana reluctantly followed him outside. The early-evening sunset fought to shine through the haze of smoke, casting a burnt-orange glow on everything. Though it'd cooled down some, heat still radiated off the concrete sidewalk. They walked silently to the parking lot. Jay unlocked the car and sat inside. He turned on the ignition and blasted the air-conditioning. Putting both hands on the steering wheel, he took several deep breaths.

"How bad was it?" Tiana broke the silence.

Jay shut his eyes tight. "Bad. They grilled me for almost an hour and kept threatening to send me back to prison. I don't know nothing. At some point, I think they finally believed that. Hope so."

"What'd they say about Ronnie?" Tiana leaned forward.

"They wouldn't give anything away, but they're onto him. Even though I was scared to come here, I think it will look better in the long run. It shows I have nothing to hide." Jay slammed his hand against the steering wheel, blowing the horn. "Everything is so screwed up right now. Everything!"

Tiana started to rest her hand on Jay's shoulder but pulled it back. "I'm glad you talked to them too." If they let him go, he must not have done anything criminal. Devon didn't know Jay the way Tiana did. He didn't know Jay at all. But she couldn't shake Devon's warning. She brushed aside the thought to bring up the conversation between the two men. Jay'd already gone through enough. Tiana couldn't blame Jay for his reaction to Devon.

Neither of them spoke on the drive home. When they parked at their apartment, Tiana noticed a piece of paper taped to the back window of the car. She opened it then showed it to Jay. Someone had written *Lights, Camera, Action* on a blank piece of paper.

Tiana inspected the paper. "What the hell could this mean?"

Jay grabbed the paper. "This dude has some nerve following us to the police station. Once I find out who it is, it's over!"

Tiana took note of Jay's more frequent outbursts. "He does have a lot of nerve. That's what scares me. I don't know what this note means, and I'm afraid to find out."

CHAPTER FORTY

When they arrived at their apartment, the night security guard stood watch. Jay gave him a nod and opened the door. Xavier and Marcus both sat on the floor, surrounded by what appeared to be the entire contents of Marcus's toy bin. "Hey, X. Looks like y'all been busy."

Xavier rose. "Boy, am I happy to see your face back here. We had a good time kicking it, but I'm one tired uncle. I'm 'bout to take off. Everything a'ight?"

"Yeah. I'm home. That's all that matters. I hope we're closer to finding Zoe." Jay turned to Tiana. "I'm going to walk Xavier out and go for a drive. I need to unwind a bit."

Tiana shoveled the toys back into the play bin. "Take your time. And thanks again, Xavier. I had no idea we'd stay out so long."

Following the concrete path toward his parked car, Xavier patted Jay on the back. "You sure you okay?"

"Man, you have no idea. It's incredible how my already-effed-up life seems to get worse and worse." Jay usually didn't like to dwell in negativity, but it seemed like nothing but bad shit kept happening to him. He needed a reprieve. "I can't believe Ronnie kidnapped Zoe. But we literally saw the proof of it."

Xavier stopped walking and focused on Jay. "Like I said before, it looks like someone set you up. I no longer think it was a coincidence that you two met at the park. Ronnie had his eyes set on you and your family. Now the question is, what could he or whoever orchestrated this kidnapping want from you?"

Jay pulled his pockets out of his shorts. "I literally don't have a dime."

Xavier pointed back toward the apartment. "You have a beautiful wife and little boy. Someone's trying to take them away from you. Whoever it is wants to ruin your life and see you back behind bars."

"The only person who had the nerve to say exactly that to me is Devon." Rage coursed through Jay's veins. He balled his fists. "I bet he's somehow behind all of this. I'm gonna figure out how."

Xavier continued walking to his car. "I don't particularly like Harker, but he knows what he's doing. It would be good if you two can get more information on where that money Devon invested came from."

"You're right." They stopped at the car. Jay gave his brother a quick hug. "I owe you for today."

"Don't ever say that again." Xavier chuckled then shut the door to his black Mustang and drove off.

Jay hopped into his car and drove fifteen minutes to the church. He got out and walked up the stairs and to a bench facing the large steel statute of the Virgin Mary. He leaned down, elbows to knees, and folded his hands. He wouldn't have called himself the praying type, but he needed some divine intervention.

As a young boy, his mother would always tell him to say his prayers before bed. But praying never stopped the yelling between his parents or his mom's crying. Praying never made his dad become a better person. Jay figured his prayers didn't deserve to be answered. Like his dad, God must have thought Jay would never be anything but a failure. If Jay's own dad didn't love him, surely God wouldn't think Jay worthy of love either.

While Jay had given up on formal prayer early in life, he sometimes found himself talking to God since his arrest three years before. Now he just asked for clarity. Looking up at the illuminated statue of Jesus's mother, he asked her for help to find Zoe. Even if Jay didn't deserve it, certainly poor Zoe and Tiana did.

Jay removed his laptop from his backpack and connected to the church's Wi-Fi. He hadn't wanted to search the federal court's website at home with Tiana there. He typed in the information Harker had emailed him the day before then searched through the court documents for Martin's bankruptcy case. The major debts he owed included Stanford Hospital, $100,000, Natural Solution to Cancer Oakland, $75,000, and St. Michael's Catholic School, $25,000. *Martin has cancer!*

Without mulling the situation over, Jay called his father-in-law.

"What, Jaylen?" Martin already sounded annoyed by Jay.

"Martin, I'm sorry for what you're going through. Why didn't you just tell us you have cancer?" Surely, Tiana would soften toward her dad once she learned about his diagnosis.

"I don't have cancer, you idiot."

"You don't have to lie to me." Martin's pride always got in the way of a relationship between the two of them. "I know you've gone bankrupt paying for medical bills."

Martin sighed into the phone. "I don't know how you found out about that. It's not me. It's Josephine. She's dying. After everything she's gone through the past year, she might die without ever seeing Zoe again."

Jay's jaw dropped. "Oh, man. That's all bad. Tiana and I talked with the detectives at SJPD today. I think they're close to finding Zoe."

"Those idiots don't have a damn clue what they're doing. We're running out of time. I don't even know where to look."

Jay had to tread carefully. "What about Devon? It seems like Zoe's disappearance is way too convenient for him. When he was eighteen, he invested one hundred thousand dollars in a startup. Do you have any idea where he got that money?"

"Jaylen, if I were you, I'd stop sticking your nose where it doesn't belong. Devon is Zoe's biological dad. He doesn't have anything to do with her kidnapping. If you spent this much time trying to find a job instead of snooping in other people's business, you might have one by now." Martin hung up abruptly.

Jay had certainly hit a nerve when he'd asked about the money. Though Martin clearly didn't want to talk about it, he also didn't seem surprised about it either. *Could Martin have something to do with the money?* If so, he clearly had something to hide. Jay stared at the statue of Mary. *Please, make it make sense.* He stuffed his laptop back into his backpack. Needing to have a long talk with Tiana, he raced back to his car.

WHEN JAY WALKED INTO his apartment, everything had been returned to its normal place. He found Tiana and Marcus fast asleep in his and Tiana's bed. Though Jay had so much he wanted to tell Tiana and talk to her about, she looked too peaceful to wake. Plus, she needed the sleep. He, on the other hand, needed to find out who set him up, because that person most certainly would lead to Tiana's daughter.

CHAPTER FORTY-ONE

Tiana's alarm chimed, alerting her to wake up and get to work. She hated going in on Sundays, but she needed to put in at least half a day to make overtime. Plus, she had a backlog to catch up on, since she hadn't finished anything on Friday. Receiving the photograph had completely ruined her productivity.

Jay stirred. "Do you have to go in? I was planning on taking Marcus to toddler arts and crafts at the community center this morning. Why don't you come with us?"

"I don't have a choice if we want to pay rent this month." Tiana rose and headed toward the bathroom.

Jay stretched, and Marcus stirred with a yawn. "Right. I'll put on the coffee." He left the room, carrying Marcus on his hip.

Tiana checked her cell phone. She had a few texts from Devon. *Did Jay read them last night?* She sent a quick text saying she'd just woken up. On autopilot, she got ready in the bathroom, her mind in a million different places.

Once in the kitchen, the aroma of coffee clung to the air. She sat at the table, where Jay had set out coffee and a toasted raisin bagel.

Jay pecked Tiana's lips. "Just the way you like it."

Tiana took a bite of the bagel, the sweet raisin juxtaposing perfectly with the cream cheese. "Yep."

"Not everything's changed, right?" Jay focused on her, pleading with her.

The life they had before Zoe's kidnapping seemed like a lifetime ago. Tiana forced the thought away. "No, not everything." She sipped the coffee and munched on the bagel while Marcus ate Cheerios and sliced bananas. Thoughts of Zoe and Devon swirled in her mind. *What would my life be like with them both in it?*

"What you thinkin' 'bout?" Jay sat next to Tiana with a bowl of instant oatmeal.

Tiana focused on her bagel. She couldn't admit the truth. "Everything that has changed."

Jay squeezed her shoulder. "I talked to your dad yesterday. There's something I need to tell you."

She rose and quickly washed her dish. She still missed having a dishwasher. "Does it directly lead to finding Zoe?"

"No, it's 'bout—"

"Then I don't want to talk about it right now. Let me make it through work. I should be in a better space when I get back home. You can tell me then."

Jay hugged Tiana. "I love you. Have a good day."

"Love you too." She hoped returning to work would provide some much-needed normalcy to her life. Everything had become so chaotic and uncertain. She craved routine.

She plodded to her car, the blazing-hot sun already shining in the hazy, soot-filled sky. Last she'd heard, the wildfire in Yountville was continuing to expand. She doubted firefighters would contain it anytime soon. The devastation caused by the increasingly common and deadly wildfires wreaked havoc on the lives of everyone in the affected areas, and the smoke and anxiety spread to more people miles away. She paused in the parking lot, weighing whether she should go back to the apartment to grab the mask she'd gotten at the search, then noticed at least five news vans had parked in the carport. *What the...?*

Reporters surrounded her. "Ms. Williams, is it true that the missing girl, Zoe Miller, is your biological daughter?" A woman shoved a microphone in her face while a man recorded them.

"Is District Attorney Martin Moore responsible for Zoe Miller's disappearance?" another reporter asked.

"How does it feel to find out the daughter you gave up for adoption was kidnapped?" another person shouted.

Tiana's stomach somersaulted with panic. She had seen scenes like this too often on the news. "No comment." She hurried past the crowd of reporters to her car. She backed out of the parking space slowly to avoid hitting any of the newspeople swarming it. The reporters darted her windshield with their business cards. The note came to mind: *Lights, Camera, Action.* That punk had gone to the press.

She took out her phone and dialed Devon. "I just walked outside to drive to work. The media is camped at my apartment building. Whoever's been following me leaked the story to the press."

Devon cursed under his breath. "Unbelievable. What's most important is your safety. Why are you going to work on a Sunday? Will other people be there in case something happens?"

"I need the overtime. I'm probably going to be the only one in the office. Now I don't think that's the best idea."

"No, not at all. Why don't you come to my place? My community has a gate and a security guard. No one can trail you in."

Tiana hesitated for a moment. Jay certainly wouldn't want her at Devon's. But she liked the idea of leaving her complex so the media would disperse. She wouldn't stay long at all.

"Strictly platonic. I promise," Devon added.

Tiana felt like a child. "You didn't have to add that. I know." Her phone beeped with a text.

"I just sent you my address. I'll see you soon."

Tiana stepped on the gas, navigating out of the apartment complex without a second thought.

WHEN TIANA ARRIVED at Devon's townhome community on Santana Row, a valet attendant greeted her and promptly took her car before escorting her through the building.

Devon waited for her, dressed casually in a pair of jean shorts and a polo shirt. "Did anyone follow you?"

Tiana shook her head. "I don't think so."

"I turned on the news after we spoke." He let out a loud breath. "It's the lead story right now."

Tiana bit her lip, willing herself not to cry. She wished she had a cave she could hide in.

Devon must have sensed her feelings, because he wrapped her in a tight embrace. "We're going to get through this. I promise."

Tears sprinkled Tiana's face. "Why me? What did I do to deserve all this?"

"It's your dad's fault. He never should have forced me to leave. Not to mention he could have been straight up from the beginning about his intentions to raise Zoe. None of this would have happened." Devon pulled back and wiped Tiana's tears with his fingers. "Come inside. Want something to drink?"

Going into Devon's place would cross an invisible line. Jay would not be happy. But she'd already come so far. "Okay."

Devon led Tiana through the perfectly manicured gardens before stopping in front of a townhome. They all looked identical, except for their color—his was a soft blue with white trim.

Though in her mind, she imagined Devon living in a bachelor pad, the reality inside proved to be quite different. Modern and tidy, his place could have been featured on an HGTV show. Elegant ivory leather furniture adorned the living room. She could picture Marcus taking a marker and scribbling all over it. No way she could get away with that color furniture. She ventured to a kitchen that had brand-new stainless-steel appliances and granite countertops. Fresh fruit filled the bowl next to a juicer that contained green residue.

With a diet like that and his exercise regime, it made sense Devon stayed in such great shape.

Tiana couldn't hide her envy. "Your place is awesome."

Devon shrugged. "I can't complain. I feel lucky to have nabbed it when I moved back to San Jose six months ago."

Tiana didn't even know where Devon had lived the past ten years. "Where'd you move from? Why'd you come back?"

"I worked for a VC firm in New York the past seven years. I'd been wanting to branch out on my own for a while. I decided to move back to the Valley, where a lot of funders are located." Devon opened a cabinet and displayed an assortment of Keurig pods.

"Water is fine." Tiana sat on a stool at the island in the middle of the kitchen. She placed her hands on her cheeks. "I'm so embarrassed."

Devon poured her a glass of water and placed it in front of her. "Don't be." He stood behind Tiana and massaged her shoulders. "You aren't to blame for any of this."

She took a couple of deep breaths, trying to calm down. "It's like all my skeletons are out of the closet and literally being featured on cable news." She moved away from his impromptu massage and rose from the stool. "Let's see how bad it is. Can you turn on the TV?"

"Sure. Let's go to the living room."

Tiana followed him and sat on the white sofa.

Devon pointed the remote at the huge, curved flat-screen TV mounted on the beige wall. "Are you sure you want me to?"

"Yeah. I need to see this." Tiana prepared for the worst.

Devon clicked on the TV and navigated to CNN. "Oh shit!" Devon said.

The screen showed Tiana's dad swarmed by news cameras outside the Oakland Hills inn. "In what is a bizarre twist in the case of the kidnapped ten-year-old Oakland girl, it is now reported that District Attorney Martin Moore is Zoe Miller's biological grandfather.

After an intensive search yesterday, the police still do not have a suspect."

Tiana gasped. "This could ruin his career."

Devon muted the TV. "That's the least of what he deserves."

Tiana's phone rang. She answered it. "Jay... hi." She had no idea how she would explain stopping by Devon's place.

"Where are you?" he yelled.

Tiana's heart pounded. "What's wrong?"

"I turned on the TV and saw you on the news surrounded by reporters at our place. Then when I called your office, you didn't answer. Are you okay?"

"Yes, I'm fine. I'm actually on my way back home now. I wanted the media to leave our complex. I'll see you soon. Sorry for the worry." Tiana hung up and rose from the couch, placing her purse strap on her shoulder.

"What happened?" Devon asked.

"That was Jay." She walked toward the front door. "I need to head home."

"Are you sure? You just got here." Devon followed her.

Tiana faced him. "This was a mistake. I shouldn't have come."

He reached for her hand. "Don't say that. You're free to do what you want."

She yanked her hand away. "I'm not free, Devon. I'm married. What I do affects him and our family."

Devon grimaced. "What about what he's done to you? Committing a crime. Getting locked up for a year and a half. Making you work overtime on a Sunday because he doesn't have a job. Possibly kidnapping our daughter. Come on, Teeni. You're being naïve."

She didn't have a response. All of Devon's points seemed valid. She opened the front door and headed toward the valet.

"I'm going to follow you home. I want to make sure you make it safely." Devon sped past her, headed to the parking garage.

"No, Devon. You'll only make things worse." Tiana hurried away, preparing for Jay's wrath, which she deserved.

CHAPTER FORTY-TWO

Jay paced the small living room, waiting for Tiana for what seemed like an eternity. She sounded fine, so she hadn't crashed her car escaping the news vans or anything like that. *But where'd she go?* One person came to mind.

"I'm fine. You can go," Tiana said outside.

Jay opened the front door to find Devon with her. Blood rushed to his face. He walked past Adan, who stood at attention next to the door. "What the hell are you doing here?" He stepped toward Devon.

His wife blocked him. "He just wanted to make sure I got home safe." She faced Devon. "You can go," she repeated.

Devon avoided Jay's gaze and stared directly at Tiana. "If you ever want to stop by again, you now know where I live." He turned his back to leave.

Jay couldn't contain the lava-hot anger bubbling up in him. He charged at Devon and shoved him to the ground. "Don't you ever talk to my wife again."

Adan rushed in between the two men. "Hey. Break it up."

"Just leave, Devon." Tiana turned to her husband. "Jay, it's not worth it. Calm down. Go inside."

Jay pointed at Devon. "Don't you ever step foot on my property again. Stay the hell away from Tiana."

"Your property? Your broke ass doesn't own anything." Devon smirked.

Jay lunged at Devon again. He would smack that smug look off Devon's face.

Adan held Jay back and addressed Devon. "Mrs. Williams already asked you to leave. Either you go now, or I'll call the police."

Jay stared Devon down until he turned and walked away.

"Dada?" Marcus stood at the entrance to their apartment, his tiny face scrunched up and on the verge of tears.

Jay glared at Tiana. "I can't believe I was worried about you."

Marcus reached his arms up. Not wanting his anger to infect his son, Jay stormed past him.

Tiana picked up the boy and carried him into the apartment after Jay. "I'm sorry. I stopped to talk to Devon for a few minutes about what's going on. That's all. I didn't think you'd get so upset."

Jay took shallow breaths and tried to calm the rage welling inside. He needed to get some distance from Tiana. "Don't turn this around on me and make this about my anger. We already talked 'bout this. Why go to his place?"

"I didn't know what to do." Tiana placed Marcus on the couch. "I freaked out when the reporters approached me."

"And your first thought to was run to Devon?"

"No, it just happened."

He ignored her, skulked into the kitchen, flung the cabinet door open, and grabbed a glass. He splashed orange juice into it, thinking that drinking something might help him gather his composure. "You promised me you wouldn't run off to see him. You don't need him. He dumped you when you were at your lowest. Remember? Now he wants to help you? Hell no. I don't want you nowhere near that bastard!"

"Jay, you're making it sound like Devon's some type of monster. I know this is a lot, but he didn't kidnap Zoe. Whoever did is the person we need to find and blame. Right now"—she pointed at him—"*your* friend is the only person on video, kidnapping my daughter."

Jay slammed the glass on the counter so hard it shattered. Broken glass pierced his hand, and orange juice sprayed all over the counter and floor. "I'm being set up!"

"How am I supposed to believe that?" Tiana threw her hands up.

Marcus ran into the kitchen. "Uh-oh." He covered his mouth and stared at the mess.

"It's okay, Marcus." Tiana shooed him toward the living room. "Go sit on the couch."

Jay stormed into the bedroom. He shook his hand, which blazed like fire as the acidic juice seeped into the cut. The door shut so hard behind him that their framed wedding picture crashed to the floor. "Shit!" *Just calm down, Jay. Get it together.*

In the bathroom, he grabbed the first aid kit from under the sink then turned on the water and shoved his bleeding hand under the faucet. He needed to find exactly where he'd cut himself.

"*I said wrap it tighter!*" his dad's voice screamed.

In the mirror, his dad stood behind a twelve-year-old Jay in the bathroom. His father had finished beating Jay then broken and bloodied his own hand by punching the wall. His parents had been fighting like usual, but that time, after his dad punched her in the gut, his mom had screamed, "I'm leaving you, Walter! I'm taking the boys and leaving."

Walter's face had grown beet red. He lunged at his wife, wrapping his hands around her neck. "I'll kill you first."

Jay had believed he would, so he punched his dad in the head. Screaming, Jay yelled for him to get off his mom. Though it had worked and gotten his dad to leave his mom alone for the remainder of that night, Jay's punishment had been the worst beating he'd ever gotten. After his dad had punched the wall, he'd had the nerve to tell Jay to wrap his hand with an ACE bandage.

The bathroom door opened, and his mom walked in. "Jay?"

"Don't you dare come in here!" he screamed.

Tiana took a step back. "I'm sorry."

Realizing Tiana faced him, he reached for her. "Tiana—"

Without a word, she retreated.

Jay finished bandaging his cut then left the bathroom. Tiana sat on the edge of their bed, staring at their worn carpet. "I'm sorry, Jay. I shouldn't have gone to Devon's or made that comment about Ronnie."

How many times is Tiana going to run to Devon then apologize? No matter how much he loved her, he wouldn't sit around, looking like an idiot. "I'm gonna take Marcus to the community center like I said before." He waited for a reaction. Though he feared she would go back to Devon as soon as he left the apartment, Jay couldn't stop her if she wanted to be with him.

Tiana nodded. "I'll be here."

"I might not come straight home." He looked at the broken picture frame on the floor then stepped over it and out the door. Tiana had a visual representation of what would happen to their marriage if she continued down the path she'd been on.

Jay picked Marcus up and carried him out of the apartment. No media were around, and he figured the news must have moved to a bigger story. Unfortunately, it wouldn't be so easy for Jay to move on if Tiana did decide she wanted Devon in her life. He vowed to do everything in his power to prevent that, but he couldn't take much more.

CHAPTER FORTY-THREE

Tiana swept up the broken glass in their bedroom. She rested their wedding portrait on the dresser then carried the dustpan to the kitchen and threw away the shards. Though she resented Jay's attitude, she couldn't exactly blame him. If only the mess between her and Jay could disappear also.

What should I do? Never in one million years would she have thought Devon would be back in her life. She completely understood Jay's position. He didn't deserve for her to treat him this way. But at the same time, what Jay had done hadn't been fair to her either. It had ruined their lives. She would have given anything for her life to be less complicated.

Her phone rang. Her body couldn't move. She couldn't take any more drama. Still, she couldn't miss new information, so she answered.

"Mrs. Williams, it's Detective Kent McDaniel. We would like for you to come down to the police station. We have a lot to discuss with you."

"Sure, I'll head right down." She sent Jay a quick text telling him she was going to the police station. She wanted to make sure to give her exact location so he wouldn't worry she ran to see Devon again. Ready for progress in the search for her daughter, Tiana rushed out the door.

IN A SMALL OFFICE IN the police station, Tiana shifted in her chair as she waited for Detective McDaniel. She blew on the coffee they'd offered her then sipped the bitter liquid. The mood in the station had shifted dramatically as she'd transitioned from being a random person to a possible suspect to the victim's mother.

McDaniel entered the room. "Mrs. Williams, hello. I'm sorry to keep you waiting."

Tiana dismissed the wait with a wave. "Please, tell me what's going on with Zoe."

"We have a suspect, Ronnie Coleman. As you know, he went by the name Travis with your husband."

She tried to act surprised, not wanting to give Harker away. "Are there any leads about where he might be?"

"We have a couple, but nothing concrete. Your husband is a friend of Ronnie Coleman, correct?" McDaniel sat in the chair and rested his elbows on the table.

Tiana didn't like the way he asked the question. "No, not anymore. They were acquaintances." She took another sip of coffee.

McDaniel cracked his knuckles with his hand. "Did you know that Ronnie Coleman is a convicted child molester?"

Tiana choked on the coffee. "Excuse me?"

"I'll take that as a no?" He studied her face intently.

"Of course not." Her head spun as nausea settled in her stomach.

McDaniel opened a black portfolio book. "He was convicted of molesting his girlfriend's nine-year-old daughter fifteen years ago. Served several years in prison. Was their shared experience of prison something your husband and Ronnie Coleman talked about?"

Tiana shifted through her memories of what Jay had said about Ronnie. "I had no idea Ronnie had ever been in prison. Like I said before, other than the two of them playing basketball, my husband doesn't know anything about Ronnie."

"You said that you've been receiving notes from someone. That the notes contain personal information about you and your family. Where was your husband when you discovered these notes?"

Tiana stared at McDaniel. "Is my husband a suspect?"

"Mrs. Williams, I'm the one asking the questions. Where was your husband when you received the notes?"

Tiana fanned her hands out and searched her memory to recall exactly where Jay had been. "He's usually at home. One time, we were here at the police station. So there's no way he's involved."

McDaniel didn't look convinced. "What makes you so certain?"

"He's my husband," Tiana whispered, unwilling to admit that alone didn't mean much.

"He's also a convicted felon that had a relationship with a child molester who is the prime suspect. Your husband was at the location Zoe was last seen. There's a possibility he could have been acting as a lookout while Ronnie kidnapped Zoe. He could be an accomplice."

The words stung, and she hung her head. She wiped away the tears that dripped from her eyes. "Don't call him that. You're wrong about my husband."

"There are some questions we want you to ask him. We'll call him back in. Then a colleague and I will watch the interaction through the two-way window."

"What kinds of questions?" The proposition turned her stomach. But if Jay had worked with Ronnie to kidnap Zoe, she needed to know.

McDaniel pulled out a sheet of paper. "We'll go over these together. Are you willing to do this?"

She swallowed her fear. "Yes. I'll do anything to find my daughter."

CHAPTER FORTY-FOUR

J ay sat at a table in the community center with Marcus, who proudly held the painting he'd made of their family. Though just three colorful blobs, each representing one of them, Jay still thought Marcus had done a great job and was grinning at his son when his phone vibrated with a call from Tiana. She'd texted him an hour before, saying she was headed to the police station. Maybe she had news about Zoe. "Tiana?"

"Jay, I'm going to be at the police station for a while. Do you think you can come down now? They want to ask you a few more questions. You know, since you're my husband." Her voice sounded strained.

Jay didn't want to go anywhere near the police station. "I have Marcus, so I can't right now."

"You can bring him with you. Don't worry. It's fine."

He couldn't exactly say no. "All... right."

"Ask for Detective McDaniel when you arrive. He'll bring you back."

Jay had no desire to rush over to the police station. Though he'd done nothing wrong, the police still treated him like a criminal, and he cherished the moments he had with his son. *I'll be damned if anybody tries to take him away from me.* Jay reluctantly put Marcus in the stroller and headed to the car, hopeful that the detective wouldn't keep him long. He had absolutely nothing to add to what he'd already told them.

He drove slowly. He didn't feel right about taking Marcus with him, but not going would make him look suspicious. Once they arrived, he took his time unbuckling Marcus from his car seat and carried him inside. After checking in with the attendant, Jay sat with his son on his lap, expecting another long wait.

"Jaylen Williams?" McDaniel called at the door.

Jay stood, a layer of cold sweat coating his body. He held Marcus's hand and walked to the door. "I'm here."

The officer held out his hand, which Jay shook. "Follow me back. Your wife's waiting in one of our rooms."

Jay followed the officer down a hall.

"Is that my Marky?" Wanda hurried toward them.

"Gamma!" Marcus's face lit up as he reached for his grandmother.

"Wanda, what are you doing here?" Jay handed Marcus off. Based on how Tiana felt about her, Jay hadn't expected to see Wanda for a good while.

"The police want to speak with me since I'm Zoe's grandmother. I guess they want the whole family here. I'm expecting Martin will show up soon." A worry line creased Wanda's forehead. "I'm stretching my legs for a few minutes. My nerves are bad from all of this."

Jay interpreted Wanda's look as worrying about running into Josephine with Martin. Wanda probably didn't know about Josephine's cancer. The reality that Martin's mistress only had months to live introduced another level of drama into the situation. Jay couldn't imagine Martin leaving his dying lover to go back to Wanda. But then again, a week before, Jay wouldn't have believed Martin to be capable of most of the things he'd done.

"Jaylen, since Mrs. Moore is taking a break right now, why don't you leave Marcus with her while we talk?" The way McDaniel said it didn't seem like a question but an order.

Jay nodded, and McDaniel led him down the hall and opened the door to an empty medium-sized room similar to the ones he'd been in before.

When Jay entered, Tiana pushed back her metal chair and stood. Instead of a hug, she patted his shoulder and sat back down after he did. "Thanks for coming, Jay. Where's Marcus?"

McDaniel stepped in. "Your mother's watching him."

"My mother?" A sour expression crossed Tiana's face. "How long has she been here?"

McDaniel checked his watch. "About an hour. We're trying to get everyone on the same page. I have a couple matters to attend to briefly. I'll be back in ten or so." He exited through the door and closed it behind him.

Jay hadn't expected alone time with Tiana. "How are you?"

"I'm better now that you're here. I think they're gonna keep me for a while. I just"—she pressed her palms against the table—"it's nice to have company."

Jay still seethed with anger at the whole Devon situation, but he tried to push it aside and focus on supporting his wife. She needed him, and he liked that. "Do they have any leads to find Zoe?"

Worry lines creased Tiana's forehead. "They have a suspect. Your friend Ronnie." Her voice sounded unnaturally high.

"He's not my friend." Jay wished he'd never met Ronnie. He'd been so careful to stay far away from anything even remotely close to trouble. He never fathomed it finding him at the park a couple blocks from home.

Tiana sucked in a breath. "How'd you say that you met Ronnie again?"

He frowned. He cursed that day. "Playing ball, remember?"

"Right. I guess it all seems like a blur now. How long ago was that?" Instead of focusing on Jay, Tiana kept her eyes focused on her hands, which rested on the table.

Jay's gaze flashed to the fluorescent lights as he tried to remember. "Probably three or four months. It wasn't too long after I got out. Why?"

"It's just that Ronnie has been IDed as the person who kidnapped Zoe from Walmart. You were friends with him. You were even there at the Walmart. It's just"—Tiana's voice wavered—"a lot of coincidences."

"Tiana, what are you trying to say?" He glared at her.

She looked him dead in the eye. "Did you have something to do with Ronnie taking Zoe? Are you the one sending me the letters?"

He stood so fast his chair fell to the ground. "You think I have something to do with this?"

Tiana didn't answer.

"How you gonna think that 'bout me?"

"Did you and Ronnie bond over the fact you'd both been in prison?" she continued without answering his question.

Jay couldn't let on that Harker had told him that. "He was?"

"Yes, actually." Tiana used a cold and unfamiliar tone.

He sat and placed both hands on the table. "He never said nothing 'bout that to me."

"For molesting a young girl." Tiana stared him dead in the eye.

Jay's eyes grew wide. He shook his head. "No."

Tiana bit her lip. "Yes, Jay."

Jay slammed his fist on the table. "I'll kill him!" He immediately wanted to walk back his threat—he shouldn't have said that in a police station.

Tiana folded her hands. "You know what? I need to be alone right now."

He reached to grab her hands. "I'm so sorry. I didn't know. I would never—"

Tiana removed her hands from his grasp and placed them on her lap. "Please. Just leave. And leave Marcus here. I'll take him home with me."

Jay opened his mouth to speak but didn't. He opened the door and left without another glance at Tiana. Never in his life would he have imagined his own wife treating him like that. Everything he'd thought about their marriage shattered. If she could even think he had conspired to kidnap Zoe, she clearly didn't know him at all.

Outside the room, McDaniel approached him. "Jaylen, can I get you anything?"

"Where's my son? I got nothing else to say to you or nobody else. So I'll take him and be leaving." He couldn't even hide his contempt for the police department any longer.

"I actually had planned on touching base with you."

"Unless I'm under arrest, I'm going home." He stared McDaniel down, daring him to handcuff him.

McDaniel shrugged. "You're free to go. I'll show you to your son."

He needed to get as far away from the police station—and Tiana—as he could. He'd used all of his restraint to keep his head cool and had none left. The sooner he got home, the better. He was on the verge of doing something he would regret.

CHAPTER FORTY-FIVE

Tiana folded her arms on the table and buried her head in them. She wished she could erase the pure agony she'd just seen on Jay's face. She hated herself for what she'd done.

The door opened again, and Detective McDaniel walked in. "Your husband and son just left. How are you holding up?"

She closed her eyes and let the tears wet her arms. She had no words left.

"I know that was hard. You did well. I know you love your husband, but my job is to find your daughter. Why don't you go home? That's all we need for now. We'll keep you updated with any new developments. You have my card with my phone number. Call if you need anything in the meantime."

She sat up, wiping the tears from her eyes. "I won't do that again. I won't put my husband through anything like that ever again."

His gaze remained steady. "I'm focused on finding your daughter. Your husband served time for killing someone."

"Manslaughter. You don't know what happened." Tiana hated that the man could hold Jay's conviction over their heads.

"He just threatened to kill Ronnie." McDaniel arched an accusatory eyebrow.

"Oh, come on. He is rightfully disgusted at Ronnie. He wouldn't actually hurt him." At least she hoped not.

"Mrs. Williams, all I'm saying is that it will look really bad for you if it ends up that your husband has anything to do with Zoe's kidnapping. Like I said before, we're investigating Jay as Ronnie's accomplice. If that proves to be true, or if Jay has any involvement whatsoever, charges can be brought against you as well. You've already lost one child. Would you want to risk the chance of losing your son too?"

His wide-eyed stare intimidated her. "You're threatening me?" She couldn't believe it. She'd done absolutely nothing wrong. "I mean, what do you want me to do?"

McDaniel pressed his hands downward. "Easy, now. I just want you to be completely aware of what's at stake. Now, do you have a friend or family member you and your boy can stay with?"

Jay would hate that, but she couldn't risk losing Marcus. "Yeah, I do." Ava would be more than willing to take her in.

"Keep your phone close. I'll be in touch." McDaniel held the door open for her.

Tiana trembled as she stood. She'd surely aged several years in a few days. It took all the effort she had to make it through the police station and to her car. Outside, the afternoon heat threatened to swallow her whole. She covered her nose and mouth with the crook of her arm to keep out the smoke. Hurrying to her car, she wanted the nightmare to be over with. Once inside, she dialed Ava.

"Ava, I'm leaving the police station now. Can Marcus and I stay with you for the night? I need some space to think everything over."

"Yeah, girl. You're always welcome. I'll put fresh sheets on the bed in the spare room."

"I'm going home to pick up Marcus and pack a bag. We'll be over after."

"And Jay's okay with it?"

"Jay doesn't have a choice." They said their goodbyes.

Tiana dreaded facing her husband at home. Like a lot of hard situations in her life, she would just have to do it. After a short drive, Tiana pulled into their carport. She released a breath, dreading what would come next.

"JAY?" TIANA WALKED through the empty living room.

No answer.

"Jay? Marcus?" She hurried through the dark apartment to the bedrooms. But she couldn't find either of them. Jay had seemed absolutely crushed when he left the police station. She figured he would have come straight home. But apparently, she'd been wrong. She feared just how wrong she could have been about her husband. She dialed his number, but it went straight to voicemail. Her heart pounded in her chest. She sat on the couch, racking her brain, but she knew Jay didn't have plans. *Could he have taken Marcus and disappeared?*

No, he wouldn't have done that. *But where are they?*

Just then, the door opened, and Marcus ran through it. "Mama!"

Tiana breathed a sigh of relief. She embraced her son in a tight hug. "There you are. Jay, where were you two?"

Jay held up two brown bags. "Getting something for dinner. Where else would we be?"

"Right." She should have known better than to think Jay would do something like run away with Marcus. She carried her son to the kitchen table, strapped him into his high chair, then headed to her room to pack an overnight bag. Once done, she crossed the hallway to Marcus's room.

Jay met her in there. He watched her collect Marcus's belongings. "Whatcha doing?"

"Detective McDaniel said it would be a good idea for me to stay somewhere else. Marcus and I will spend the night at Ava's." She couldn't meet his eyes. Instead, she focused on the clothes she shoved into the bag.

Jay grabbed the bag and unpacked its contents. "Hell nah. You ain't taking my son nowhere."

Tiana tugged on the bag. "I'm not arguing with you about this."

Jay ripped the bag out of Tiana's hand and threw it to the ground. "I'm not the bad guy, Tiana. I haven't done nothing wrong. I'll be damned if you take my son away from me."

"I don't want to do this. But McDaniel said I could lose Marcus if I don't play my cards right. I can't take that chance." Tiana stared into his eyes, pleading with him to understand. "Would you want Marcus ending up in foster care?"

Jay threw his hands up. "What will it take for you to believe that I'm innocent? Someone's clearly setting me up. You know I'd never kidnap anyone. They can't take Marcus away from us if we haven't done nothing wrong. Come on! Listen to me!"

Tiana picked the bag up from the ground. "I've stood by your side and been there for you through all your stuff for the past three years. I know you don't like it, but I'm asking you to let me go to Ava's and take Marcus. Just for a few days until the smoke clears. Jay, this is the least you can do for me. For us. I can't risk anything happening to Marcus."

A tear streaked down his face. "We're a family. We need to stick together. Please don't do this to me. Stay."

She summoned her strength. "I can't. If anybody took Marcus from me, I wouldn't be able to handle it."

"Then how do you think I feel right now?" he yelled.

Tiana stuffed Marcus's clothes back into the bag. "I have to go." She walked out of the bedroom and to the kitchen with Jay close behind her. She picked Marcus up out of his high chair. "Say bye to Dada."

"Where going, Mama?" Marcus raised his small, chubby arms.

"We're going bye-bye for the night." She couldn't bring herself to look at Jay.

Marcus lunged for his father. "Stay with Dada."

"No, Marky." She struggled to hold Marcus, who tried to wiggle out of her grip.

"Dada! No leave. Stay with Dada!" Marcus yelled.

"Tell him bye, Jay." Tiana instructed.

With tears rolling down his face, Jay kissed Marcus then turned and walked down the hall.

Marcus screamed after him.

Tiana held him tightly, carried him out the door, and locked it behind her, unsure when or if she would be back.

CHAPTER FORTY-SIX

J ay sat on his bed, unable to stop the tears streaming down his face. His worst fear had come to pass. Tiana had left him and taken Marcus. He wanted to shrivel up and die, but he couldn't. The only way to get his family back would be to prove his innocence. He had to find the person responsible for kidnapping Zoe. He dialed Harker, the only person who could possibly help him.

"Jay," Harker answered. "How's everything?"

"Terrible. Can you meet for a drink? I'd like to talk and try to figure out how to get my life back together. Tiana just left with Marcus after the detective at the police station threatened her." It took everything he had not to go back down to the police station and cuss Mc-Daniel out or worse.

"Shit." Harker ruffled papers in the background. "I'm finishing something up, but I could probably meet you in half an hour. Do you want me to come over to your place?"

Jay didn't want to be alone in his empty apartment for another minute. He needed to go back to the bar and see if Danny had more useful information about Ronnie. Anything. "Nah, Danny's Dive Bar in South San Jose. I'll text you the address. My treat."

"If you're treating, I'll definitely see you there."

Jay grabbed his wallet and keys and hurried to his car. At five o'clock, the late-afternoon heat had begun to retreat from its assault for the day. Jay sped to the bar, eager to get some alcohol in his system.

When he arrived, he took a seat on a stool and flagged Danny down.

Danny smiled and slid a napkin in front of Jay. "Good to see you. What will it be?"

"I'll take a Guinness. I have a friend who's joining me." Jay handed the owner his credit card. "Run a tab."

"Is it that the friend you asked me about the other night?" Danny asked. "Ronnie, is it?"

"Nah, man. That dude is trouble. Have you seen him recently?" He was relieved that Danny had brought it up first.

"Not since that night I told you about. Haven't seen his friend he usually meets in here either." Danny walked to the Guinness tap then poured the rich, dark beer into a cold glass. He topped it with a light froth then handed it to Jay.

Jay took a few long gulps. "What friend is that?"

"I'm not sure of his name. He's rich, supposedly. Word is he's a venture capitalist." Danny rolled his eyes. "Lousy tipper, though. It's a shame how Silicon Valley has some of the richest people on the planet, yet people like you and me can't catch a break to save our lives. They have millions and billions of dollars. I'm just tryin' to pay my bills as a small business owner."

Alarm bells rang in Jay's mind. "Is Ronnie's friend Black also?"

"Yes. Tall too. About your height." Danny tapped the bar. "Let me know when you need another one. I have some accounting to do before the evening crowd comes. Counting all the pennies." Danny gave a wry smile.

Jay chugged the remainder of the beer. "That was so good, I need another one just like it." Jay pulled out his phone and googled Devon's name. A picture of him popped up.

Danny laughed. "Sure thing." He poured an identical beer and placed it in front of Jay.

"Wait one second." Jay held out the phone to Danny. "Is this Ronnie's friend?"

Danny peered into the phone. "Yep. That's him."

Well, I'll be damned. Devon knows Ronnie too.

The door to the bar opened, and Harker strode in. He patted Jay on the back then slid into the stool next to him. "Tough break with your wife and kid."

Jay hung his head, the fresh pain hitting him again. "Worst-case scenario. But you won't guess what I just found out."

Harker arched his eyebrows. "What's that?"

Jay gestured toward Danny, who sat at the end of the bar, typing on a laptop. "He just told me he's seen Ronnie in here with his friend. Guess who he said his friend is?"

"No idea. But I would like him to get me a beer." Harker drummed his fingers on the bar top.

"Devon is Ronnie's friend. He's seen them here together. Just like I thought, Devon must have set me up." Jay seethed with anger thinking about it. "Danny?" Jay waved down the owner. "My friend will have Jack Daniel's on the rocks."

Danny poured the drink and placed it in front of Harker. "Let me know if you need anything else."

Harker held up an index finger. "We were just talking about our friend, Ronnie. Jay mentioned you know his other friend, Devon, the VC. Now, don't get me wrong. You got a great gig going for you here. But I would imagine Silicon Valley money mixing in places like Palo Alto, Los Altos, Menlo Park. Why would they be at a dive bar in the middle of San Jose? I mean, this is a top-notch place. I'm just saying..."

Danny smirked. "I've been told we have the best beer in the 4-0-8 area code. But in all seriousness, we're a good spot for a private business transaction, if you know what I mean. I don't like getting in my customers' business. So forget I even told you about the two of 'em, would you?" He wiped the counter with a towel then sat back down at his laptop.

Jay turned and looked at Harker. "Should I go back to the police with this information?"

Harker took a long sip of his beer. "Not just yet. We need to verify they know each other with something we can bring to the police, not just Danny's recollection."

"I want to nail Devon's ass. Somehow, someway, he's behind all of this. I know it." Jay finished his beer. Though he wanted another one, he still had to pay for Harker's drink. He couldn't run the tab too high. If Tiana didn't come back, he would no longer have any source of income. He could end up on the streets.

"The more we find out, the more I think that too. But like I said, now we have to prove it. That's the hard part." Harker finished his whiskey then held up the empty glass. "Danny, I'm ready for another."

Danny refilled Harker's drink. "Cheers, friend."

Harker pointed up to the corner of the ceiling. "Do those security cameras actually work?"

Jay's gaze ventured in the direction where Harker pointed. An almost-impossible-to-see half-dome security camera was hidden in plain sight. *Damn, Harker is good.*

Danny smirked. "You're the first person who has ever asked me about those. Yeah, they work. They stream straight to my laptop, so I can keep an eye on things here. You know, some people who work for me like to put the profits straight in their pockets, not the cash register."

After sipping his drink, Harker smiled. "What are the chances you have video of Ronnie and his friend? For a price, of course."

Jay tried to contain his excitement.

Squinting, Danny sized Harker up. "It just streams to my laptop. It doesn't record. Sorry, but I can't help you." He walked back to his laptop and put his glasses on, looking at Harker out of the corner of his eye.

Jay's shoulders slumped. "I'm screwed. There's no other way I could possibly prove Devon knows Ronnie."

"Don't give up yet, Jay. We'll keep working on it." Harker gulped the rest of the Jack Daniel's.

"I've run out of time. Tiana's gone. There's nothing I can do to bring her back." He cradled his forehead with his palm. Everything hurt.

"I'm going to head home and do some more research on Devon. I bet there's some way to link him and Ronnie."

Jay signaled Danny. "We're ready to settle our tab."

Harker took out his wallet. He fanned out five hundred-dollar bills, waiting for Danny to print them their bill. When Jay looked at him, Harker winked.

Danny turned back to them, his gaze focused on the cash. He laid their tab down with Jay's credit card.

Jay shooed Harker's money away. "I told you. I got this. Run the card, Danny."

Harker slowly returned the money to his wallet. "Danny, thank you for the drinks." He let out a loud belch.

Jay rose, disappointment heavy like a wet blanket on his shoulders. He would willingly go down to the police station and tell them that Devon knew Ronnie, but they wouldn't believe him. Even if he tried to convince Tiana that Devon was behind it all, he doubted it would sway her. She probably wouldn't even take his call. Danny confirming Jay's worst suspicions about Devon just made it that much harder. He hung his head and left the bar. *There ain't nothing I can do.*

CHAPTER FORTY-SEVEN

"Will he just stop calling?" Tiana rolled her eyes, declining another call from Devon. He'd called her at least ten times in a row. She'd rejected each.

With Marcus resting comfortably on her lap, replaying the song "Baby Shark" over and over on her phone, Ava raised an eyebrow. "After that crap he pulled at your apartment, I wouldn't answer his calls either. He put you in a really bad situation. I mean, following you to your house just to pick a fight with Jay? Hell no."

"Right? He was completely out of pocket. I'm already under so much pressure. After everything Detective McDaniel told me about Ronnie, the last thing I need is Devon fomenting more trouble." Tiana shoved her phone in her purse and took a closer look at Ava's new apartment.

Ava had moved into her boyfriend's place the month before, after two years of dating. With San Jose Sharks paraphernalia, shot glasses, computer screens, and whiskey bottles filling much of the living room, their home seemed more like a college dorm than an apartment. "When will Brad arrive? I hope he won't mind us staying over." It broke Tiana's heart that she had to stay there and not with Jay. She couldn't forget his tears when she'd left. But she had to protect herself and Marcus, whether from police suspicion or her husband.

"Brad's totally fine with you two staying over. He's having a gaming marathon at a friend's house, and that can last awhile." Ava chuckled. "I'll have to slowly start redecorating this room. Let me

215

show you where you and Marcus will stay." Ava hoisted Marcus onto a hip and carried him with her. "Wanna see something?"

Marcus's eyes lit up. "See Dada?"

"No, Dada's home, Marky." Tiana's voice broke.

"Go home? See Dada," Marcus whined.

Ava patted Marcus's back then led them through the apartment and to a room in the back. A framed painting of the Golden Gate Bridge hung front and center. Floating vases with green plants lined the walls. Ava rested Marcus on a bed covered with a beautiful em-broidered beige-and-rouge comforter. She pulled a basket filled with toys from under the bed. Marcus squealed in delight. "So, this is gonna be the baby's room. You know, whenever we're ready to take that step."

Tiana appreciated Ava so much, so she didn't voice her thought that, based on the decorations and video game marathons, she doubted Brad would be ready to start a family anytime soon. "This room is lovely." She sat in the wooden rocking chair, and the swaying calmed her a bit. With her phone continuing to vibrate, Tiana finally pulled it out to see Detective McDaniel's number. "I need to take this."

Ava titled her head. "Go ahead. Marcus and I will play in here."

Tiana stepped into the hall. "Yes?" She skipped the formalities after the way McDaniel had threatened her earlier.

"Mrs. Williams, I wanted to provide you another update. Devon Price showed up at the police station. Since he is not listed on Zoe's birth certificate, we conducted a Rapid DNA test and confirmed he's Zoe's biological dad. We've briefed him on all our efforts thus far. He also provided information about your husband's threatening call to him and an assault at your apartment earlier today. Devon said he does not want to press charges at this time. But I am reminding you to heed my earlier warning. Our plan is to bring Zoe home safely and for you to meet your daughter. That won't happen if you and Mr. Williams end up behind bars."

She couldn't believe her ears. Devon had some nerve. "I'm staying at a friend's. There won't be any problems."

"I'm glad to hear that. I'd like you and Mr. Price to come to the station tomorrow at nine a.m."

"I'll be there." Fuming, Tiana dialed Devon. "What is your problem?"

"Excuse me? After everything the police just told me about your husband's connection to the suspect who kidnapped Zoe, you have some nerve. You were hiding the truth from me."

Tiana's heart thudded. She couldn't admit it. "Someone set Jay up."

"Oh, come on, really? That's the oldest line in the book. You're completely oblivious to the truth right in front of your eyes. Jay and Ronnie both did time in prison. They're friends. Video captured them both at the Walmart where Zoe disappeared. How can you possibly defend him after all the evidence? How can you not do anything?"

Tiana sucked in a breath. The way Devon laid everything out, it looked terrible. "I did do something. I'm staying at a friend's until Jay's name is completely cleared." Tiana didn't have to justify her behavior to Devon. She did it anyway.

"A friend's house? Why don't you come stay with me? I have plenty of room."

"No, that's not right." Staying with Devon would be the worst move she could possibly make, regardless of Jay's guilt or innocence. "I'll be at the police station tomorrow morning."

Without answering, Devon hung up on her. His rage unsettled her, but she understood it. She returned to the room, where Marcus had fallen asleep with Ava rocking him in the chair. "Devon's furious," she whispered.

Ava stroked Marcus's curls. "I can only imagine."

"Am I a complete idiot for still believing Jay's innocent? He's my husband. I can't believe he'd do anything at all to help Ronnie kidnap Zoe." With her heart and head in conflict, Tiana needed Ava's perspective.

"Even with Jay's conviction, there's more than what meets the eye. I understand where you're coming from. I've known Jay your whole relationship too. I agree with you that I don't see him involved in this. But the evidence piling up against him is glaring. You're making the right choice by following the detective's advice. If Jay's exonerated, you go back home. If he's guilty, you made the right decision by leaving."

Everything in Tiana wanted Jay's name cleared. But even if that happened, after the hurt she had caused him, she didn't know how willingly he would welcome her back home.

CHAPTER FORTY-EIGHT

Sitting before the Virgin Mary statue outside in the heat, Jay wiped the sweat from his face. It was Sunday, so more visitors than usual milled about between the church services. What would usually have been a beautiful blue summer sky was tainted with a thick yellow film. He could have been transplanted to Mars. It took everything he had not to contact Tiana and beg for her to come home. But he still had pride, even if nothing else.

A middle-aged Latino priest with black hair approached Jay, extending his hand. "I've noticed you up here several times the past few months. Ever think of venturing into the church? We have perpetual adoration twenty-four hours a day. It means the church is always open with a parishioner praying in there. I'm sure it's cooler inside than out here. There's definitely better air. Public health officials are advising people to stay indoors due to the wildfire smoke hovering in the valley."

Jay shook the priest's hand. "To be honest, I'm not Catholic. I don't even know what perpetual adoration is."

The priest chuckled. "We believe that Jesus is present in the communion host after a priest consecrates it. So when mass isn't taking place, we have the host on display in the church. People take turns spending an hour or so in the church around the clock. Why don't we walk there? I'll show you."

Jay wiped the sweat from his forehead. He couldn't remember the last time he'd stepped foot in a church. "You know, I don't think I should go in there. I've done something..."

"There's nothing anyone can do that, if confessed, won't be for-given by God. Nothing. You can speak directly to God from your heart and say you're sorry for whatever you've done. Come on. We'll take a peek. The door is always open to you." The priest started walk-ing toward the church. When he didn't budge, the priest stopped and gestured Jay toward him. "Come."

He shrugged and followed the priest. They walked down the steps, across the parking lot, and up to the church. After dipping his finger in holy water and crossing himself, the priest passed through the atrium and held the door to the church open for Jay. Inside, with the lights low and a handful of people praying throughout it, he be-came surrounded by a peaceful stillness.

The priest patted him on the back. "Stay as long as you'd like." He walked out of the church, leaving Jay to himself.

Unsure exactly what to do, Jay sat in the very last pew in the back, grateful for a reprieve from the heat and smoke. He took in the mod-estly adorned church: A bunch of candles burning in the back, stat-ues and Catholic-looking paintings in the front surrounding a large crucifix. A pair of angels framed the altar. *God, all I'm asking is that you bring my family back home. Tiana and Marcus are my everything. I just wanna have my life again. Help us get out of this mess.*

Jay sat in silence. *Why does life have to be so hard?* From his child-hood until now, he'd dealt with absolutely horrible circumstances. It felt so unfair. He'd tried as an adult to right the wrongs he'd experi-enced while growing up. But one day had ruined all of that for him.

Jay wiped his face and rose from the pew. God wouldn't listen to his prayers. He walked out of the church and headed to where he had parked.

Fearing his empty apartment, he got in his car and drove to Xavier's. Though his brother might have popped into Google to do some work, Jay would wait for him in his car. He had nothing else to do. Nobody at home. When he got to the condominium, he knocked on the door.

Xavier opened the door. The smell of fried fish wafted outside. "Jay. What are you doing here?" He shifted uncomfortably, shooting a quick look over his shoulder.

Jay assumed he had female company. "Sorry. I can leave if it's a bad time. I've just had the worst day. Tiana left me. She took Marcus with her."

With no warning, Janice appeared behind Xavier. "Son. Hello."

Jay's pulse spiked. He stumbled backward.

Xavier opened the door wider. "Why don't you come in? Mom cooked dinner."

Janice took a couple steps toward him. "Jay, please, will you forgive me? I want nothing more than to repair our relationship." She reached toward him.

He glared at his mother, anger scorching him. "You're the reason I was torn away from my family and locked up in prison. I was defending you! I'll never forgive you for ruining my life!"

Tears streaked her face. "I'm so sorry. It was all a terrible mistake."

Jay spit on the ground. "The only mistake was me trying to help you. I shoulda known better. Even on the day I die, I won't forgive you." He stormed back to his car.

Xavier ran after him. "Jay, I'm sorry. I didn't know you were coming over."

Jay climbed into his car, but his hands shook so badly that he couldn't get the key into the ignition. "Nah, I shoulda called first."

With pain etched on his face, Xavier put his hand on the roof of Jay's car and leaned toward Jay. "I'll come over after Mom leaves so we can talk about what happened with Tiana."

"Forget it. I wanna be alone." He finally got the car started then sped off.

He wanted nothing more than to go back in time and do that fateful day over.

Janice had called Jay, hysterical and begging him to pick her up after another drag-out fight with Walter. She swore she would take the step and leave her abusive husband for good.

When Jay had knocked on his parents' front door, Janice opened it. Her face was bruised and bloodied, like usual. "Jay, please leave. Everything's okay now. Dad and I worked everything out."

"Look at yourself, Ma. It's ain't okay now. It won't never be. You said you leavin' him. Come home with me. He ain't worth it." Jay's heart broke at his mother's state.

Walter barged through the house, confronted Jay on the porch, and pointed a gun directly in Jay's face. "I'll kick your ass if you don't get off my porch right this second."

All the hate and rage pent up in Jay over decades of abuse exploded. He swung at his dad. Jay's fist delivered a blow clear across his dad's face. Blood spurted out of his dad's nose. The gun flew into the air before landing on the ground.

"I'll kill you, boy!" His dad growled and punched Jay in the jaw.

He and Jay both dove on the ground for the gun. After a brief wrestling match, the gun went off, and his dad slumped to the ground. Blood painted his white T-shirt bright red. A pool of ever-expanding red soaked the ground below him.

The prosecution argued that California's Castle doctrine gave Walter every right to protect himself at his home. They refuted Jay's self-defense claims since he'd been the one to go over to his parents' home and had swung first. Forensics experts determined both men's fingerprints had been on the trigger. With Tiana's dad's intervention, the district attorney overseeing the case finally offered a plea deal. Jay pled to manslaughter and served eighteen months in jail. Had he known how his life would crumble after his prison stint, he would have let the trial play out and continue to fight for his name to be completely cleared.

Jay still couldn't recall who had fired the gun.

As he sped home, guilt still plagued him like a chronic illness. *Did I kill him?* Regardless of what the priest had said, God surely wouldn't forgive him. He certainly couldn't forgive himself. His dad would still be alive if Jay hadn't tried to help his mom. Not only that, but he'd ruined his life, his marriage, and his son's future. Nothing he could ever do would erase his felony conviction. Nothing.

CHAPTER FORTY-NINE

After Marcus's nap, he'd spent the rest of the evening grouchy and whining for Jay. When Tiana had finally gotten him back to sleep, she had nothing but time to mull over every detail from the past few days. Her life played in her mind like a bad movie.

Light rays from the hallway pierced the darkness, and Ava stood in the doorway. "Tiana?" Ava whispered. "Are you awake?"

"Yeah." Tiana eased her arm from under Marcus. *Please stay asleep.*

"Come out. You've got to see something on the news." Ava gestured Tiana toward the hall.

Tiana tucked the blanket around Marcus and tiptoed out of the room. She left the door open a crack behind her. "What's going on?"

Ava grabbed Tiana's hand and led her down the hall to the living room. "You'll see." They sat on the couch, and Ava played the paused television.

"In a new twist in the case of Zoe Miller, the missing Oakland girl, an additional seventy-five-thousand-dollar reward has been offered for a credible tip that leads to finding her. This brings the total reward to one hundred thousand dollars for any tip that helps the police bring Zoe home."

The TV zoomed in on Devon at a podium outside the police station earlier in the day. "I'll do anything to ensure my daughter's returned home safely. Please. If you know where she is, do the right thing and call the police."

Tiana's jaw dropped. "Devon?"

Ava squeezed Tiana's shoulder. "This is good. Even more people are going to be looking for her now."

Tiana didn't know what to think. "I can't remember any cases my dad worked where a family member had enough money to offer a hundred thousand dollars. With that kind of reward, maybe people involved will turn on the kidnapper just to get the reward money. I'm surprised Devon didn't mention to me that he planned to a make a statement. But then again, he's furious with me."

"Maybe he was also worried you'd talk him out of it, since you didn't think a reward was a good idea before. But I agree—he could've at least given you a heads-up."

Devon's public plea seemed disingenuous. "I want to be happy that Devon offered the reward, but my gut feels like there's something more to it."

"Let's have a drink." In the small kitchen, Ava pulled out two glasses and a bottle of vodka. After filling the glasses with ice, she mixed vodka with cranberry and handed a glass to Tiana. "Tell me what's going through your mind."

After her hangover yesterday morning, Tiana cradled the drink in her hand but had no intention to drink it. She needed complete sobriety in case anything came up. "At one point, I thought Devon and I would marry, have a baby, and be the perfect family. In a flash, he and my baby girl were both gone. Some days got so dark, I didn't think I would make it." Tiana winced, the pain from her past seeping from her psyche.

Ava sighed. "I can't even imagine how horrible that must have been. I'm so sorry you endured that."

"I never thought I'd love again. That changed after I met Jay. He was real and down-to-earth. He made me laugh. Our wedding was absolutely perfect. I remember thinking, with this beginning, we will have such a great life. When I became pregnant with Marcus, we were so happy. Everything fell into place." Tears streamed down her face. "When I found out that Jay's dad was killed, it was a nightmare. But I couldn't leave Jay the way Devon had left me. During Jay's criminal trial, I heard him, his brother, and his mom testify against his dad. I couldn't believe the things they had survived. I still can't. I couldn't leave him then. He'd gone through so much. But now there's this. It's just awful. If he does have something to do with Zoe's kidnapping, it's the end of us." The heavy burden of sorrow pressed on her shoulders, threatening to bury her.

Ava sat next to Tiana. "I have absolutely no idea what's going on with any of it. I wish we could just know, one way or another, who to believe."

Tiana gasped. "I just remembered something." She dug through her purse and pulled out the psychic's card. "I'm going to call a woman from the command center set up for Zoe. She might help." Tiana typed in the number and dialed.

Ava shook her head. "I don't think—"

"Hello?" Tiana read the name off the card. "Is this Clementina?"

"Why, yes. It is. How can I help you?" The woman's singsong voice on the other end of the phone put Tiana at ease.

"You gave me your card, and I'm interested in talking with you about my missing daughter." Tiana's heartbeat pounded in her ears.

"Sure. Your daughter's missing after the fire?" Clementina asked.

"No. Remember, I met you in Oakland?" Tiana needed Clementina to recall their conversation.

"Oh, yes, Oakland. Was that at the church or the farmer's market?"

Tiana couldn't believe the woman. She apparently made a living preying on families searching for missing loved ones. "Never mind." She hung up the phone, cradled her head in her hands, and sobbed.

Ava rubbed Tiana's back. "We'll get through this together. You just gotta keep your eyes open. I only want what's best for you, Marcus, and Zoe. I just don't know if that's Jay or not."

"I know." Tiana sat up, trying to pull herself together. "That's my exact problem. I believe him, but that's not enough for me to risk losing Marcus. I'm sorry. I'm such a mess right now. I know you have to get up early for work tomorrow. I'm going to call in. I have to be at the police station at nine. Plus, I can't face everyone at work."

"I'm here for you. We can stay up and talk."

"Thanks, but I want to be alone. Just to think. Do you mind?"

"Of course not. I'll be right down the hall if you need anything at all. Feel free to either stay out here and watch TV or go back in the room with Marcus. If you're up before me tomorrow, help yourself to whatever is in the kitchen and stay as long as you need. My home is your home." Ava handed Tiana the remote.

After Ava left the room, Tiana checked her phone. She had missed calls from her mom and Devon but none from Jay. She hated to think about him home alone. Since she had to meet Detective Mc-Daniel, she took a breath and dialed.

"Tiana?" her mom answered.

"Yes, it's me." She sighed, partly relieved to hear her mom's familiar voice.

"How are you? I started to fear you'd never speak to me again."

"I'm doing terribly, Mom. Everything is horrible. I didn't call to chat. I need to ask if you can watch Marcus for me tomorrow. We're staying at Ava's, and I'm planning to go to the police station first thing in the morning. I'd prefer not to take Marcus."

"Yes, of course I'll watch Marcus. Tiana, I understand why you're upset with me. I want to let you be the first to know something. I've told your father there's no going back for us. Not just because of the affair, but because of what he did to you. All I wish is that I would have done it years sooner."

Tiana had definitely not expected that. "Oh, Mom. I don't know what to say. It's going to be really hard for you. I mean, you don't even work."

"Well, your father told me something that was a hell of a shock. We're bankrupt. He's been paying for cancer treatment for Josephine. Even if I stayed with him, which I won't, I would have to start working. It's not going to be easy, but I'm only forty-five. I have a lot of life left. I refuse to spend it with a dishonest cheater."

"So is Josephine going to be okay?" Tiana had nothing but contempt for the woman, but she wouldn't wish cancer on anyone.

"Your dad said she only has months to live, if that. He's made it clear he's spending the rest of her life with her." She sighed. "It's late, and I'll have to get some good rest if I am watching Marcus tomorrow. What time should I expect him?"

"Will seven or eight work?"

"Yes, that's fine. I'll see you then. Thank you for calling me. It's so good to have you speaking to me again. When Zoe comes home, I want both my grandchildren in my life. Good night. I love you."

After Tiana hung up, she turned off the TV and put her glass in the kitchen. The new information about her dad's bankruptcy and Josephine's health only further complicated the matter. Her mom had made the right decision. The more she learned about her dad, the more she realized she didn't know him at all. If he so easily lied to her, took her baby, and raised Zoe for ten years, he could definitely have had something to do with her kidnapping as well. Devon had just put up a seventy-five-thousand-dollar reward, money her dad clearly needed if he'd gone bankrupt. She would have to make sure the police knew every single detail. Her daughter's life was on the line.

CHAPTER FIFTY

Jay paced his living room and clutched his phone, willing Tiana to call. Over the past days, he had mulled over every single person involved and what motive they could possibly have for kidnapping Zoe. Now everything pointed to Devon. The police could figure out all the details. Jay just needed something concrete to take the focus off of him.

With nothing else to lose, he picked up his phone and called Martin. He doubted the man would answer, but he had to try.

"Jaylen, it's after midnight. Why the hell are you calling me?" Martin said by way of a greeting.

"The police told Tiana to leave me and take Marcus. Martin, I need answers, and dammit, I know you got them." Jay had never spoken to Martin like that before, but the time had come.

Martin scoffed. "What exactly do you want from me?"

"I think you know why Devon is on surveillance video having drinks with Ronnie months ago, before Zoe was kidnapped. I have the proof. I'm going to the police with it." Jay hoped Martin couldn't sense his bluff.

"What on earth are you talking about?"

Martin sounded genuinely surprised, so Jay had the advantage. "Exactly what I said. Devon knows the guy who kidnapped Zoe. He must have been the one to set up the whole thing. Now, Devon has a ridiculous amount of money—something you don't have, since you're bankrupt. I know all of this is going to be real important to the police. So tell me what you know, Martin. Zoe's life is at stake. So is your reputation. If you haven't learned yet, all your sins will come out. It's just a matter of time."

"I've already told you—"

"Cut the bullshit!" Jay couldn't calm himself down. "Haven't you done enough damage? Look at all the lives you've ruined with your lying and scheming. Tiana's and Wanda's lives are torn apart. Your granddaughter has been kidnapped. If you know anything, you better come clean."

Martin sighed into the phone. "You know what? I'm tired. All I've ever done is try to provide the best life for everyone. My wife, Tiana, Zoe, Josephine. I honestly thought I was doing that. I swear to you I have nothing to do with Zoe's kidnapping."

"I don't buy it. What do you know about Devon?"

"I gave him the hundred thousand dollars to break up with Tiana and disappear when they were seniors in high school before Zoe was born. That's it. I told him to go far away and not come back until after she graduated from college. I told him I'd make sure they were well taken care of, and when the time presented itself, he could have them back. I didn't know he'd invest the money and literally come back. I figured it was puppy love. That he'd move on and find someone else. But Devon contacted me the summer after Tiana graduated and said he wanted his family. But guess who Tiana had fallen in love with?"

Jay sucked in a breath. That was the summer he'd met Tiana. "You gave Devon one hundred thousand dollars to leave Tiana?"

"Oh, come on. Don't say it like that. I love my daughter and have always wanted the best for her. Getting married and having a baby at eighteen wasn't it. If there's anyone who ruined the plan, it was you. You've never had anything to offer Tiana. You were a loser from the start. Now, after your conviction, you're only bringing her down. Yes, I gave Devon the money. But look what he's done with it." He cleared his throat. "Just face it. Even if he did know Ronnie, there's no way Devon would agree to him kidnapping his own daughter. You're an idiot, Jaylen. Devon could provide Tiana with a life you couldn't even imagine. If you love Tiana like you say you do, let her go. You don't deserve her. You'll only hold her and Marcus back."

After Martin hung up, Jay father's voice continued the conversation. *You'll never amount to nothing, Jay. The worst mistake I ever made was allowing your mother to have you instead of an abortion like I wanted. So many resources and so much time have gone to you, a worthless piece of shit. You're completely and utterly useless, just like your mom. Everything you do fails. You are a failure. With you around, Tiana and Marcus will fail too.*

Jay flinched, anticipating his father's fist in his ribs. He bent down, cradling his head between his hands. *They're right. I'm nothing.* He'd fought so hard to keep his family together. He had to face the truth. He'd become a liability for Tiana and Marcus. He'd failed them. Promising he would get a job and get his life back together meant absolutely nothing if he couldn't do it.

Jay made a decision: he would simply disappear. No other option would suffice. He stood to survey the apartment. He needed to imprint every detail of their life in his mind to take with him. Though Tiana hated the apartment, Jay loved how close the three of them had grown in the small space. He would never forget all the mornings he'd spent sitting on the living room floor with Marcus, building Legos, running Thomas the Train around the wooden track, or singing television-show songs with him. The kitchen held memories of giggles over dessert and tantrum standoffs over pureed vegetables.

Jay paused in front of the family pictures hanging in the hall. He stared at each photo capturing good moments and much simpler times. Stopping himself from taking the photos out of their frames to pack them, he took a mental snapshot of each memory instead. He needed Marcus to have the pictures to remember him.

He dwelled in the doorway of Marcus's room, inhaling the familiar scent of his son. Jay had never imagined a tiny human could enlarge his heart so much. Walking away from him would be the hardest thing he'd ever do. *I'll never finish Kenny's story.* But if Jay couldn't provide for Marcus, he had nothing to offer his son. Marcus deserved nothing but the best the world had to offer. But to ensure that Marcus had a chance, Jay had to leave.

After crossing the hall, Jay entered the room he shared with Tiana. He would never forget all the love they had made and the tender moments he'd shared with his wife. From the moment Jay had met her, he'd known he didn't deserve her. After their wedding, Jay's dad had pulled him aside and smugly said, "The countdown's on for you screwing this up." Jay had walked on eggshells, trying not to mess it up somehow. And then he'd done it—he'd ruined their lives. Now, to prove he loved Tiana, he would have to leave her alone for good.

Jay grabbed his suitcase and duffel bag then spread them open on the bed. One by one, he placed the few items of clothing he owned into them. It took him back to when he'd packed up on his last day in San Quentin. He'd been so eager to get out of prison and back home to his wife and son. At the time, the possibilities seemed endless. He had anticipated getting his life back on track and picking up where he'd left off.

Without a decent job, he didn't have a future. So, wherever he ended up going, he would just have to lie. He would need to get a fake ID and social security number. Of all his problems, that would be the easiest. He'd call Harker on his drive tomorrow and ask him for the fake identity information. Even if Jay's name could somehow be exonerated from Zoe's kidnapping, it wouldn't change anything about his circumstances.

He tried not to think about what would happen if he got caught. Violating parole and using a different identity would land him back in prison. But he didn't care anymore. His main goal was to leave so

Tiana would have the freedom to move on with her life. And without Tiana and Marcus, Jay might as well die.

After packing all his belongings in his suitcase and duffel bag, he carried them and a blanket and pillow to the living room and parked them next to the front door. The urge to pick up and go overwhelmed him. But he wouldn't dare leave at that time and risk drawing attention to himself on the roads. Instead of fleeing, he opened the door and stepped outside.

The cool midnight air nipped at his exposed skin. The wildfire smoke clogged the night sky, hiding the stars. Jay walked through the sleepy apartment complex. He would leave first thing in the morning and drive out of state. He didn't know where he would end up. It didn't matter. Jay only cared about Tiana and Marcus, and him getting as far away as possible was best for them.

After walking back to his apartment, Jay crashed on the couch. He needed sleep, so he shut his eyes tightly. Tears leaked down his face. He brushed them away. His dad had always said real men didn't cry. The only way Jay could redeem his manhood would be leaving for good and never looking back.

CHAPTER FIFTY-ONE

Tiana had plenty of time to drop Marcus with her mom and head to the police station. "Marky, time to get up." She glanced at the clock on the dresser. It was only seven.

"Where Dada?" Marcus opened his eyes and searched the room.

Tiana drew a breath, unsure how to answer. "He's not here, Marky. Let's get up and get ready. I'm going to take you to Grandma's house." Tiana tried to add enthusiasm to her voice but failed.

"No see Gamma. See Dada." Marcus slid off the bed and walked to the door. He opened it and called, "Dada!"

Tiana wished the separation from Jay didn't have to be so hard on Marcus. She picked him up and kissed both his chubby cheeks. "Daddy's not here, Marky." She wished she could call Jay, but surely, Detective McDaniel would frown upon any communication with him. "Let's get dressed and ready to go."

Ava came down the hall. "Morning. I thought I heard Marcus's voice. How'd you two sleep?"

Though Tiana had tossed and turned all night, she said, "Good. I'm going to get us ready then take Marcus to my mom's."

"I'll make breakfast before heading off to work. Marky, do you want to help me stir the eggs while Mommy gets dressed?" Ava reached out to Marcus. "I'll turn on Mickey Mouse."

Marcus leaned toward Ava for her to carry him. "Yay. Mickey."

Ava winked at Tiana. "We'll be in the living room. Take your time."

Tiana closed the bedroom door. Her phone buzzed. She antici-pated Jay, but instead, Devon's number lit up her phone screen. She hesitated to answer after their argument. But she would have to see him in a couple hours, so they might as well try to reconcile. "Good morning, Devon."

"Tiana, did you see I offered a larger reward to anyone who finds Zoe? I'm sure that's going to help us bring our daughter home."

"Yeah, I saw that on the news last night. What made you decide to do that?"

"Whatever the police are doing hasn't led to a credible tip. But money talks. I anticipate a hundred thousand dollars will make peo-ple who know Zoe's whereabouts start turning on each other. If someone's following you, there's more than one person conspiring together. Probably with your husband."

Devon's words landed like a punch to the gut. She didn't need to put up with his bullshit. "I'll see you at nine." She hung up. With time ticking by, every second counted.

AFTER DROPPING MARCUS at her mom's house, she parked at the police station. Though only nine, the smoke-filled sky shielding the sun made it seem much later in the day. To her dismay, her dad and Josephine sat in the waiting area. She resisted the urge to retreat. She took a breath and headed to the attendant's window. "I'm Tiana Williams. I'm here to see Detective McDaniel."

The police attendant picked up the phone and said a few words. "Have a seat. He'll be with you shortly."

Tiana remained standing and glanced around the waiting area.

With his hands shoved in the pockets of his suit pants, her dad approached. "How are you?"

Tiana recoiled at the sound of his voice. He'd only told her lies, and she had no desire to speak to him ever again. "I'm terrible."

He nodded. "Everything's so complicated right now. I can't fix it. I don't know how to even start. But I need to apologize. I need you to know I'm sincere."

Tiana scowled. "Your sincerity means nothing to me."

Detective McDaniel walked through the door, interrupting their terse exchange. He gestured them in. "Come on back."

They made a right turn into a large conference room, where Devon already had a seat at the table. She found an available chair a safe distance from him. Her dad and Josephine made themselves comfortable on the opposite side of the table.

McDaniel sat at the head. "The phone hasn't stopped ringing since Mr. Price offered the additional reward. We're working all the leads that seem credible."

"Where might Zoe be? Do you have any idea?" Josephine asked.

"We can't say right now. But the car registered to Ronnie Coleman was abandoned in Napa. We have DNA evidence in the car that matches Zoe's."

Tiana sucked in a breath. She didn't want to imagine Zoe in a car with a convicted child molester. "I've heard the Yountville fire has spread to parts of Napa. This is awful."

"Napa's only about an hour and a half away from here," Devon said.

"If they were that close, how have you guys not located her yet?" Tiana's dad yelled.

Josephine placed her hand on his arm. Wanda always did that when his temper flared. Tiana couldn't get used to another woman taking her mother's place.

McDaniel didn't seem fazed by the outburst. "We're doing the best—"

"Your best isn't good enough!" Martin yelled.

Tiana couldn't stop the anger from rising. Her dad had basically stolen Zoe from her and still had the gall to get upset. "None of this would have happened if you hadn't taken Zoe and lied about it all these years. You have some nerve, sitting here after you kidnapped her from me."

Devon cleared his voice. "Detective McDaniel, Tiana and I are Zoe's biological parents. I don't think that Martin's presence is helping the situation."

Martin turned red and pointed at Devon. "Look, you piece of shit. You think you can just waltz in here and act like you care about Tiana or Zoe? Not a chance in hell!"

"I've always cared about Tiana. You're the one who threatened me and forced me to break up with her. You're sick, Martin!"

"You know that's not what happened." Tiana's dad lunged across the table at Devon. McDaniel grabbed his arm. "Okay, okay. We all need a time-out. Mr. Moore, Mr. Price—both of you need to step outside."

"Martin, you have got to calm down," Josephine interjected, sounding frail.

Without another word, he stormed out of the room.

Devon followed Officer McDaniel out.

The room fell silent with only Josephine and Tiana remaining. Josephine cleared her throat. "Tiana?"

She glared at the other woman, who had exchanged her wig for a scarf covering her bald head. "What?"

"I love Zoe." Josephine's voice was barely a whisper.

Tiana scoffed. "She's *my* daughter."

Josephine folded her hands on the table. "She's my daughter too."

Tiana stood, shaking her head. "How dare you. She is not your daughter. You've been playing house with a married man and my baby girl. You're pathetic. You should be ashamed of yourself. Why didn't you have your own life and family instead of stealing mine? Once Zoe's found, I'm going to make sure you never see her again. You and my dad will pay for what you've done." Tiana left the room, unable to stay a minute longer in Josephine's presence. She bit her lip, wishing she'd kept her cool, but she meant every word. Regardless of Josephine's health, neither she nor her dad deserved Zoe in their lives.

CHAPTER FIFTY-TWO

Someone pounding loudly on the front door jarred Jay awake from sleep. He didn't even have time to think about what he would do if the police stood on the other side. With nowhere to run or hide, he had no choice but to go with them. He stretched his legs, which were cramped from sleeping on the couch. Wiping the sleep from his eyes, he trudged to the door and opened it.

"Jay, I have great news." Harker stood outside, his eyes dancing with excitement. He waved a USB stick in the air. "Danny sold me the surveillance video for five hundred dollars. You need to go straight to the police with it."

Suddenly fully awake, Jay motioned Harker in. "I thought he didn't have video."

Harker entered the apartment. His gaze ventured to Jay's pile of belongings by the door. "I didn't want to get your hopes up because I wasn't sure. When we were at the bar, I had a pretty strong hunch that Danny did in fact have video recordings of the past surveillance. He just didn't seem like he wanted to get involved in whatever you might have going on that would require the footage. I hung back after you left and told him that if he produced the video, he'd have an extra five hundred dollars. He called me first thing this morning and told me to come pick it up. So you owe me five hundred dollars and a big thank-you."

Suddenly, a glimmer of light shone in the darkness. With the video, the police would at least have to interrogate Devon about his relationship with Ronnie. "Harker, you don't know how much this means to me." He grabbed his wallet off the table. *Finally, a break.* After pulling out five hundred-dollar bills, Jay handed them to his friend.

Harker glanced at Jay's belongings again. "Don't tell me you were planning to run. I know you wouldn't leave your wife and baby boy like that."

Jay's shoulders slumped. "You have no idea what it feels like to wake up every morning and feel like a failure."

Harker held up his hand like a stop sign. "Listen to me. You're a hard worker. You're loyal. You're a great husband and father. Don't you dare let insecurity run you out of your own home. Your family needs you. Your wife especially needs you right now. We're both facing an uphill battle. I won't take that from you and act like you're overreacting. But you can't give up. Ever. This is the twenty-first century. There are so many different ways to make money now. Legal ways. If someone won't give you a job, build your own company. Become your own boss. I'm doing it, Jay. It's not easy, but giving up is not an option. You can't walk out on your son. Or your marriage. You need to believe in yourself." He held out the USB drive.

Jay'd felt paralyzed by fear his whole life. Everything he'd done growing up had disappointed his dad. And since he'd been home, Martin couldn't even stand to lay eyes on him. But Harker's words broke through that. He took the USB drive. "You're right. But I need to ask one more favor of you."

Harker arched an eyebrow. "What's up?"

"Come to the police station with me. If things go south and they take me into custody or something, I need you to let Tiana know what went down. You gotta convince her that you heard, with your own ears, Danny confirm that Devon and Ronnie met multiple times. Even if the police won't listen to me, I need Tiana to know Devon's not who she thinks he is. She can't trust him."

"Sure thing."

"Let's go, then. It's time I fight for my family and my future." Jay stood as terror and determination rose in him.

CHAPTER FIFTY-THREE

Tiana sat in a makeshift waiting area surrounded by boxes, away from everyone. With only two chairs and a small table tucked deep within the police station, she probably shouldn't even technically have been sitting there. But with her emotions running rampant, she had to be careful not to do or say something she would regret later. The high stakes called for her to act in a calculated manner. She needed to calm down and regain control of herself.

Devon turned the corner and threw up his hands. "There you are. I was looking everywhere for you. You didn't answer my phone calls."

She had no excuse. She wouldn't try to offer one. "You found me."

"I'm sorry about my temper earlier. I shouldn't have talked to your dad like that." He took a seat next to her.

"I can't really say anything after what I said to Josephine." She cringed with regret for her cruelty toward a woman with stage four cancer. It didn't matter how she felt about Josephine. Tiana hadn't been raised to be disrespectful.

Devon chuckled. "It's a mess of a situation that we're in, huh?"

She nodded. "You could say that."

"I know it must be really tough that your husband was friends with the kidnapper. That he is most likely an accomplice." He took her hand. "I want you to know that I'm here for you. Zoe's our daughter. We're in this together. We're family."

Tiana wanted to defend Jay, but she had nothing to say. "I'm focused on finding Zoe. That's all that matters right now."

"I know your husband hasn't had a job in a while. But if you need any help financially, let me know. I got you." Devon squeezed Tiana's hand.

She freed her hand from his grip. Awkward silence filled the space between them. After Devon had left her senior year, Tiana wanted nothing more than for him to come back so they could be a family. But then her heart moved on to Jay. Jay and Marcus were her family now.

Devon's phone rang. He held it up. "I should get this. My phone's been ringing with possible leads all morning." He took a couple of steps away and answered the phone. He turned suddenly and rushed back to Tiana, his index finger to his lips. Devon pressed speakerphone.

The same ominous voice that had called her over the past couple days spoke through the line. "I have your girl. You speak a word of this to anyone—especially the police—and you'll never see her again. Give me the money, and you get your girl back."

A chill ran down Tiana's spine. "That's him," she mouthed.

Devon's eyes focused on the phone. "I've gotten calls like this all morning. If you give me proof that you have Zoe and she's okay, then the money's yours." He spoke forcefully into the phone.

"Proof's coming." The caller hung up the phone.

Tiana jumped to her feet then grabbed Devon's hand and yanked it to get him to start walking. "That's who's been calling me. We need to tell Detective McDaniel."

Devon didn't budge. "Wait. He said not to speak a word of it to the police. I don't want to ruin our only chance of finding Zoe and bringing her home."

Devon's lost his mind. It's too risky. Tiana placed her hands on her hips and narrowed her eyes at him. "What do you want to do?"

He held up his phone and tapped it. "I want proof that Zoe's alive. Then I'll bring her back."

"How on earth will we find her? It's not like the person who kidnapped her will simply hand her over to us." Surely Devon couldn't think it would be that easy. Tiana had heard horror stories from her dad of kidnappings. Never once did they end with the kidnapper simply giving the child back.

Devon glanced around the police station then stood. "Let's go outside."

Tiana hesitated. Two individuals definitely didn't have the same capacity as a police force. Devon apparently had no idea what they faced. "Let's talk it over with Detective McDaniel."

"I'm not saying we have to make a decision right now. Let's just go outside so we can talk privately." Devon grabbed her hand and hurried through the police station. Once they were outside, he stopped in a shaded corner. His phone rang again. "It's a FaceTime call." He held out his phone so Tiana could see it.

The man's voice came through the black screen. "Say hi, Zoe."

The phone displayed a blindfolded girl sitting in a chair. Tears streaked down her face. Tangled black hair sat atop her head. Silver duct tape covered her mouth. "What's your name?" the man asked. "Oh, right." He ripped the duct tape off her mouth. "Go ahead?"

"Z-Zoe... Miller. Mama—"

Blackness blanketed the phone.

Tiana gasped. Her heart ached like a dagger had pierced it. Her daughter needed her. Zoe's young life depended on her. The possibility of ever meeting her daughter rested on whether they found her or not. "We need to go inside now and tell McDaniel."

Devon clenched the phone. "McDaniel hasn't done anything. It's up to us to find our daughter."

Tiana would do anything to find Zoe, but she wanted to make the right decision. "How?"

"The car was ditched in Napa. I say we head in that direction. It won't take long. Maybe an hour and a half. By the time we get there, I'm sure we'll hear from that punk again. All he wants is the money. You know the police won't allow us to just give it to him. They'll want to apprehend him instead. That could end very badly for Zoe." He must have sensed Tiana's reluctance because he embraced her in a tight hug and whispered in her ear, "I know there's a lot on the line. Please, trust me on this."

Though his comforting and familiar embrace almost put Tiana at ease, she couldn't simply give Devon her trust. She suspected everyone. She flung his arms off her. "You want us to just pick up and go? Not even tell Detective McDaniel where we're going?"

"Yes, exactly." Devon leaned in close and lowered his voice. "We'll stop by the bank. Get the money. Then go."

Tiana's stomach somersaulted. She wanted to run and vomit at the same time. It seemed too reckless and dangerous to take matters into their own hands. "The fire has spread to Napa. It could be dangerous going there. I'm sure roads are blocked off. I don't think—"

"You want to leave our daughter up there with a crazed man? Yeah, it might be dangerous. But it's the only way. He could leave her there to burn for all we know. We can't let another second go by." Devon's voice had a razor-sharp edge to it. "Do you want Zoe back or not?"

Tiana upturned her palms. "Of course—"

"We have to go. Now. Worst-case scenario, we drive out there and don't find the guy. Or the roads are blocked. If so, we come back. But I have to try. I can't sit here waiting for the police to do something one minute longer. They've failed us. The only reason the guy called today is because I offered the reward. I'm the only one actually doing anything. Not the police." Though his tone had softened, Devon obviously wasn't going to back down.

Zoe had looked absolutely terrified. She could have been tortured for all Tiana knew. She didn't like Devon's idea, but he was right. They had to do something. All McDaniel had done so far was threaten Tiana and try to blame Jay. He seemed more focused on tying Jay to Zoe's kidnapping then actually bringing Zoe home. "All right."

Devon's arched eyebrows relaxed. "Great. Let's go."

They ran to the parking lot. Her stomach continued somersaulting. She said a silent prayer that this wouldn't be the worst mistake of her life. Then she climbed into his sports car.

CHAPTER FIFTY-FOUR

Jay parked at the police station but couldn't get out of the car. Not only would he have to convince the police to watch the surveillance video, but he would most likely come face-to-face with Tiana. They hadn't spoken since she'd left him. He didn't want to fall apart at the sight of her and plead with her to return home with Marcus.

After a couple minutes, Harker spoke up. "I know this is hard, but it's necessary, Jay. Let's go in."

Grateful his friend had come with him, Jay mustered all the courage he had and willed himself to open the car door. "Now or never, right?"

Once inside, Harker sat on a metal bench while Jay headed to the police attendant's window. After a short line, Jay's turn had come. "I need to see Detective McDaniel. He's working closely with my wife, Tiana Williams. I have new and really important information for him about Zoe Miller's kidnapping. Tell him it's urgent I see him."

The police attendant told Jay to sit and wait. Instead, he paced back and forth in the lobby. He shoved his hand in his pocket and gripped the USB drive. Showing the surveillance footage had the possibility of changing the whole course of the investigation into Zoe's kidnapping. But only if the police took him seriously.

He glanced at Harker, who scrolled through his phone. Jay had lucked out by meeting Harker in prison. If things went badly for Jay, at least Harker would tell Tiana Jay had tried.

The door opened, and McDaniel appeared. "Jaylen Williams?"

Jay hurried to McDaniel, holding held up the USB drive. "I have a surveillance video you got to watch. It's connected to Zoe's kidnapping."

Though McDaniel didn't look particularly interested, he opened the door wider for Jay to walk through it. "Come on back."

Jay followed him to a conference room then sat in a chair and held out the USB drive. "You need to watch this."

McDaniel took the drive. "What exactly is *this*?"

"It's surveillance video showing Devon Price at a place called Danny's Dive Bar in San Jose with Ronnie Coleman about six months ago. This proves not only that Devon knows Ronnie but also that he set me up. Devon orchestrated Zoe's kidnapping." It was a stretch, but Jay had to sell the video to get McDaniel's interest. He tried not to let his contempt for Devon seep out. He had to seem impartial and not like he had a grudge to settle.

McDaniel turned the drive through his fingers. "Where exactly did you get this?"

"From the bar owner, Danny. You can call him to verify. He'll tell you it's real. Look, Ronnie took me to the exact same bar where he'd met up with Devon. Apparently, Ronnie does his business there. They probably set up the whole kidnapping in that bar." Though it made sense to him, Jay admitted it sounded crazy.

"I'll be right back." McDaniel rose and left with the USB drive.

Jay patted the sweat on his forehead. Everything rested on what McDaniel did next.

AFTER TWENTY MINUTES, McDaniel came back into the room. "I watched the video and had a quick conversation with Danny. We're going to investigate this further."

"What do you mean 'investigate'? You should arrest Devon. Drag him in for questioning like you did me. Or is he here now?"

Fury swelled up in him. The police had never once given him the benefit of the doubt. Devon didn't deserve special treatment, no matter how much money he made.

McDaniel's gaze fell to his hands. "No, Devon's not here. Neither is Tiana." He looked at Jay. "Have you heard from your wife?"

He glared at McDaniel. "No. As a matter of fact, I haven't talked to her since you told her to take my son and leave me."

McDaniel's eyes darkened. "Why don't you try to contact her? If she's with Devon, it would be good for her to know Devon's wanted for questioning. A text is probably better than a call in case they are in fact together."

"When's the last time you saw Tiana?" Jay's anger morphed into dread. If Devon had taken Tiana somewhere, Jay feared what could happen to her.

"They were both here earlier this morning. But neither have been seen since about nine thirty. Go ahead and text her now. We'll see if she responds."

"Oh, so now you want to tell me to talk to my wife? You tried to tell her I was an accomplice to kidnapping Zoe." Jay scoffed. "You threatened to take our son away from us."

McDaniel's shoulders stiffened. He spoke through clenched teeth. "Do you want to contact your wife or not?"

Jay wouldn't let his anger at McDaniel interfere with finding Tiana. He took out his phone. *What's the best way to get a response from her?*

He quickly composed a text: *Ti, I'm at the police station. Where are you?*

Jay placed the phone on the table then glanced up at McDaniel. "It's sent."

McDaniel focused on the phone, avoiding eye contact with Jay.

The phone buzzed. Jay grabbed it. "She said, 'What's up, Jay?'"

McDaniel blew out a loud breath. "Okay, good. We made contact."

"What should I say?" Jay needed the perfect words to make Tiana believe she needed to stay away from Devon.

"Ask her where she is." McDaniel paused. "Tell her I need to talk with her and Devon about developments in the case. Ask if she knows where he is."

McDaniel needs to talk to you and Devon. Where you at?

After Tiana didn't respond for a couple minutes, Jay wrote another text: *Are you with Devon?*

Yes.

Jay read the texts to McDaniel. "She doesn't want to tell me where they are."

McDaniel chewed his cheek. "It's risky because Devon might read the text. But she has to know we want to question Devon specifically. Let her know about the surveillance video."

The police got video of Devon with Ronnie months ago. They need to question him NOW. Ti, tell me where you are.

After a minute, Tiana texted back: *No. You knew Ronnie. Not Devon.*

Believe me. I'm your husband. Trust me.

The phone sat silently for minutes. Jay stood and paced the room. "She doesn't believe me, thanks to you. Devon could do anything to her."

McDaniel took out his phone and typed a text. "I've sent her one, as well, asking her to contact me. I also sent out an APB to track Devon's car. They can't be that far."

Jay slammed his hands on the table. "This is all your fault! My wife's in danger, but she won't even listen to me because of the lies you planted in her mind." He itched to hop into his car and try to chase down Devon.

"I understand your frustration. I've done what was appropriate based on the information I had. You've presented new evidence. I'm adjusting." That would probably be the closest to an apology Jay would get.

Jay wouldn't accept it. He had to do something. "I'm outta here."

McDaniel stood. "Look, I need you around in case Tiana answers. I'll show you to the break room. Get a coffee and relax here."

Jay mulled over the offer. Alone, he didn't have the slightest idea of where to find Tiana. If he ventured outside of the fifty-mile radius, he would have a one-way ticket to jail. He found himself stuck in a lose-lose situation. *Story of my life.* "I have a friend waiting for me in the lobby. Is it cool if he comes back to wait with me? It seems like I could be here for a while."

"Sure. We'll go get him." McDaniel led the way down the hall to the front of the station. He held the door open while Jay walked out.

Greeting Harker with a nod, Jay approached his friend and explained what happened. "Do you want to come back and wait? Or I could pay for a ride for you to get your car at my place."

Harker wrung his hands together. "I've never been back on that side without being in trouble." He let out a nervous chuckle.

"They got coffee." Jay wouldn't beg, but the prospect of waiting for hours without a friendly face didn't exactly appeal to him.

"I hope they have donuts." Rising from the chair with a smirk, Harker elbowed Jay in his side.

Jay and Harker followed McDaniel back through the station. Jay needed them to find Tiana unharmed and soon. If anything happened to her, Jay wouldn't be able to live with himself.

CHAPTER FIFTY-FIVE

Tiana's heart raced as she stared at her phone. She had deleted Jay's texts out of fear that Devon could somehow read them. But now she held her phone tightly, anticipating more accusatory texts would come through. After she had left the police station with Devon, he had stopped home and switched cars. When Tiana questioned him about it, Devon had said he needed a full tank of gas. Now Tiana second-guessed his answer. *Could Jay be telling the truth about Devon? Could Devon be in on Zoe's kidnapping somehow?*

Devon glanced at Tiana. "Who texted you? You got quiet all of a sudden."

Tiana couldn't tell him the truth. She searched for a good response. "Oh, it's my mom. She said she thinks Marcus might be coming down with a fever. I hope he's okay." She glanced at Devon to read his expression for a sign he believed her.

"Poor kid. I'm sure he's in good hands with Grandma." Devon smiled, apparently appeased.

"She said Marcus is asking for me. She wants to know when I'll be back to pick him up. Devon, do you have an actual plan? Or are we just kinda winging it right now?" She had a gnawing pain in her gut. She'd made a huge mistake.

Devon scowled. "How exactly do you want me to answer that question? I already told you, we're heading to Napa. Once that kidnapper calls back, we'll take it from there. Don't get cold feet now. You should know by now that you can trust me. I'd never do anything to hurt you. I just want to bring our daughter home."

Tiana glanced out the window. The closer they'd gotten to Napa, the darker the sky had grown with thick smoke. Now half an hour away, it almost completely blackened the sky like a plague spreading across the Bay Area. She was woozy, stuck between day and a bizarre night. Similarly, she felt torn between Jay and Devon. At times, she'd loved them both immensely. But now she didn't know who to trust.

Devon softened his tone. "Once we find Zoe and bring her home, it will all be worth it. Believe me."

Tiana shifted closer to the passenger-side window. She longed to be out of Devon's car. To breathe freely.

They fell into an uncomfortable silence. Tiana checked her phone. She had a text from McDaniel's number. He, too, said he wanted to talk to her and know her whereabouts. *Jay must have been telling the truth.*

A loud ringing startled Tiana.

"Hello?" Devon answered the call through his Bluetooth.

"Do you have the money?" the same man's voice asked.

Tiana's heart thudded in her chest.

"Yes. Tell me where to meet you and get Zoe. Once I have my daughter, you'll have one hundred thousand dollars." Devon dug into his glove compartment. He pulled out a pistol and placed it on his lap.

Tiana's eyes were glued to the gun. Her heart threatened to gallop out of her chest. She couldn't get out of the mess. Someone might not make it out alive.

"Listen very carefully. I'm going to give you an address. You are to put the money in the mailbox. After the money's in the mailbox, Zoe will come out of the house. If I see any police or another car anywhere near yours, Zoe dies."

Tiana gasped then covered her mouth. Having Zoe's life in their hands was far too dangerous. Any misstep could lead to her daughter's death.

Devon tightened his grip on the steering wheel. He stomped on the gas, and the car sped forward. "If I do what you say, how will I know my daughter's in the house and safe? I'm not an idiot. You could take the money but not live up to your end of the bargain."

"Put the money in the mailbox, and you'll get Zoe. Otherwise, you'll never see your daughter again."

The man hung up. Devon's phone beeped. A text message with an address popped up on the car display.

Tiana took out her phone. "I'm calling the police now."

Devon grabbed the phone from Tiana. "Hell no. Didn't you just hear him? We're so close to bringing Zoe home. There's no way I'm going to mess our chances up." Devon typed the address into his GPS. "It's only thirty minutes from here. We'll be there in no time. We give him the money. He'll give us Zoe back."

Tiana eyed her phone in Devon's hand, worried Jay or McDaniel would text her again. "Devon, we can't just show up at some random house and expect him to hand Zoe over to us. That's crazy! He kidnapped Zoe and has been stalking me. I don't know what else he's capable of. I don't plan on finding out." Tiana gripped the door handle, trapped in Devon's car.

"You heard him. If we involve the police, they're going to take over and storm the house. Whoever this is might panic and do something drastic. I can't take that chance. I'll put the money in the mailbox. If anything seems off, I'll signal for you to call the police then." Devon pressed the pedal harder, and the car lurched forward.

Her stomach was twisted in knots and her forehead lined with sweat. Tiana needed a way out. The faster Devon drove and the closer they got to the location, the crazier Devon's plan became. Trusting him had turned into the worst decision she'd ever made. "Give me my phone back. I'll only use it to call the police if you tell me."

Devon tossed Tiana the phone. "I want what's best for our daughter. This bastard clearly just wants money. I've done a lot of thinking about this. The mastermind behind this whole kidnapping is Jay. He teamed up with that loser, Ronnie, who did time in prison, and now neither of them can get a job. They just want my money. Once I give Ronnie the cash, we'll have Zoe back. We'll be a family. And Jay will be locked up for good."

Tiana couldn't fathom how Devon could actually think what he planned to do made any sense. But if he had actually met with Ronnie like Jay said, then Devon could actually have been the one behind Zoe's kidnapping the whole time. She opened her message with Jay then shared her location with him. After, she sent a quick text with the address the man had texted Jay. She shoved the phone back into her purse. "I texted my mom to keep Marcus overnight."

Devon sped faster down the freeway. "It's all going to work out."

Tiana examined Devon's face. His forehead was wrinkled, and he squinted at the road. The apocalyptic sky loomed overhead. "How are you so sure?"

Devon shrugged. "Money's the only thing that makes sense. We give it to him. We get Zoe back."

The faster Devon drove, the more convinced Tiana became that Devon knew exactly where he planned to go. If Devon had staged a kidnapping, Tiana feared what else he could be capable of doing. She hoped Jay could somehow help her. Jay had become her last resort.

CHAPTER FIFTY-SIX

After drinking a couple cups of coffee, Jay circled the police station's break room. Harker typed away on his laptop. Jay would have given anything to have had work to do—anything to keep his mind from imagining every worst-case scenario. His phone dinged. "Tiana just shared her location with me. I need to show McDaniel this." Jay ran down the hall to McDaniel's office with Harker trailing him. Jay stopped abruptly in the doorway. Martin and Josephine both sat in his office.

McDaniel stood when Jay stepped in. "Did you hear from Tiana?"

Jay shoved the phone into McDaniel's hand. "She shared her location with me. They're near Napa. She sent another location. Maybe it's where they're headed."

"I'll be right back." McDaniel darted out the door. "I'll send police down there."

"Wait." Harker, who'd kept quiet around McDaniel, spoke to him for the first time. "We have no idea what's going on. If Devon's acting on a lead, a bunch of cops showing up could ruin the whole plan. Ronnie or whoever could freak out and do something drastic. I'm not going to sit here and tell you how to do your job. But I strongly caution you to be discreet. If Ronnie thinks he's cornered, he might take the only way out and take that little girl, Tiana, and everyone else with him."

Jay couldn't have that happen. McDaniel had to listen to Harker.

"Absolutely. I'm not going to do anything to hurt Zoe. The plan is to bring her home safely. Sit tight." McDaniel hurried down the hall with Jay's phone.

As Jay turned to leave, Martin approached him. "Tiana told you where they are?"

"Yeah." Jay had no desire to converse with Martin ever again. He'd almost caused Jay to run out on Tiana and Marcus for good. "No thanks to you."

"Tiana chose you, Jay. All those years ago, she chose you. After you did time, she chose you. And now she did again. I should have accepted that a long time ago. You're a good guy who's seen some hard times. I'm sorry for the way I've treated you and what I said last night." Martin patted Jay on the back. "I hope you'll accept my apology."

Jay scoffed. "All I care about right now is helping bring Tiana and Zoe home." Tiana had trusted him with her life, and he couldn't let her down.

"I checked the news an hour ago," Josephine said weakly. "The fire's rapidly spreading throughout Napa. They're running out of time to save Zoe. Whatever that address is, I'd give anything for Zoe to be there. Unharmed."

McDaniel returned to the room. "We have a state trooper trailing them. Devon's driving a different car. That's why we couldn't locate his plates earlier. We'll have the neighborhood surrounded." McDaniel turned to Harker. "A SWAT team will be on standby to approach the house on foot. We don't want Devon to suspect Tiana tipped us off."

"What can I do to help?" Jay couldn't sit idly by with his wife in a precarious situation.

"You've done good. I know it took a lot for you to bring that surveillance video down here. Now we wait. They should be approaching the location within minutes. Our guys are trained for this."

Jay's whole life had felt out of his control. He'd never known what would trigger his dad's wrath and lead to a beating. He'd helplessly been sent to prison. Ever since his release, every day presented new obstacles. Regardless of the risk, he had to go to Tiana. Now. He left McDaniel's office.

Harker followed him out. "Where are you going, Jay?"

"I have to go out there. I can't just sit by and wait." Jay sped through the police station, through the lobby, and out the door with Harker right behind him.

Harker planted his hand on Jay's shoulder. "You know you can't. You just have to trust the process. Remember what a mess I was when I first came to San Quentin? I thought I would lose my mind there. I'd never faced that type of environment before. Less than a week in, remember what you did?"

"It doesn't matter, Harker—"

"You stepped in when a gang of big Black dudes cornered me after I'd run my mouth. You didn't know me other than a short conversation in the kitchen. But you stuck your neck out to tell them to leave me alone. They beat your ass for it. Bad. But you fought back. They never crossed me again after that. I'm stepping in for you right now. You've done everything you can. Don't risk it all by going down there. It will violate your parole."

Jay appreciated his friend trying to talk reason to him. But it wouldn't work this time. "I have no choice. Tiana needs me." He couldn't stay and risk God-knew-what happening to Tiana. She'd reached out to him and trusted him to help her. He had to do just that. He loved Tiana too much not to act. He knew it would land him in hot water, but he had no choice. He opened his car door and slid into his seat.

"Jay, wait," a man called.

He turned to see Martin and Detective McDaniel running toward his car. His first instinct was to slam the door and speed away, but instead, he got out and stood there. "Wassup?"

Martin caught his breath. "I know you want to go help Tiana. I talked to McDaniel, and he's willing to talk with your probation officer to clear the trip. You'd have to go to the police station in St. Helena. It's too dangerous for you to meet Tiana at the location she sent you. We have no idea what's there other than a raging fire."

Jay eyed McDaniel. "You think my PO will agree to let me go? If not, I still gotta go unless you arrest me now."

McDaniel nodded. "I'm sure he'll let you go, because I'll tell him I'm going with you. Just come back into the station to finalize the details. I can't have you, Tiana, and Devon all disappear on me."

Harker patted Jay's back. "This is the best offer you'll get."

"Let's go, then. Time's running out." Jay led the four men back to the station.

CHAPTER FIFTY-SEVEN

Tiana gripped the handle above her seat as Devon zoomed down the freeway. Thick smoke clogged the view like fog, hampering visibility. In the distance, fire blazed around them. All the traffic travelled in the opposite direction, a pileup of cars evacuating the area. A blinking traffic sign said to exit and take a detour back the other way on the freeway. "Devon, we have to go back."

"There's no way we're turning around." He crossed two lanes to get off the freeway. Instead of getting back on and heading in the opposite direction, he turned onto a back road. His navigation rerouted. "We'll still get there." Devon pushed forward, closer to the raging fire.

"We can't drive into the flames. Turn around." Sweat dripped down Tiana's face. *He's going to kill us.*

"We also can't leave our daughter to die. We have to get her out." Like a crazed man, he wouldn't stop. He had a singular focus. Nothing Tiana had said deterred him from the plan.

Tiana scanned the neighborhood. She wanted to imprint street names in her memory in case she needed to flee on foot. But the thick smoke prevented her from reading the street signs. Devon recklessly drove them into the belly of the fire.

The car slowed. Devon leaned forward, scouring the abandoned streets that must have been under evacuation orders. "The house has to be around here somewhere." His navigation announced they'd arrived at their destination. Devon slammed on the brakes in front of a dilapidated two-story house. A sagging fence partially lined the yard. He pointed past Tiana to a pole holding a triangle-shaped box. "There it is."

His phone rang. "Leave the money in the mailbox," the man said.

"Zoe better be okay." Devon parked then grabbed his gun and bag of money. "I'm going to get her."

"Wait, what does that mean? Are you gonna leave the money in the mailbox?"

"I'll leave the money. Then I'm going to get Zoe." Devon opened the door and strutted to the mailbox. He covered his mouth and nose with the crook of his arm.

Tiana opened the car door and stood outside. "Devon, come on. You can't go in there." She coughed as smoke filled her lungs. Ash floated in the sky.

Devon jammed the bag into the rickety box then ran to the front door. He turned the doorknob then slammed his body against the door. It didn't budge. He ran across the lawn then disappeared around the corner.

What do I do now? Anything could happen to Devon inside the house, and they weren't even certain Zoe was actually inside. Devon had taken his electronic key, so Tiana couldn't even drive to safety if someone tried to attack her.

She fumbled around for her phone, which she'd dropped, dialed 911, and had a brief conversation with the operator, who said she'd send police immediately. She opened the car door, figuring she would be safer inside, when a gunshot rang from inside the house. Before she could dive inside the car, a girl's frail scream pierced the air. It sounded like it came from behind the house.

"Zoe?" Racing to the house, she cursed herself for allowing Devon to come here without the police. If anything happened to Zoe, she would never be able to forgive herself.

Her maternal instinct kicked in, and she ran toward the scream. She passed the side of the house and rounded the corner. Wild grass and weeds up to her ankles filled the backyard. Metal car parts were strewn around the space, and she tripped over an old bumper but didn't fall. A wooden shack with a broken window sat a few yards back.

"Help," a soft voiced call from the shack.

Tiana sprinted across the uneven terrain, her eyes burning from the smoke. "Zoe?" She didn't have time to think of what or who else could be in the shack. She just needed to help her daughter.

"Tiana, be careful!" Devon yelled. He walked out the back door of the house, his shirt covered with bright-red blood.

She pushed open the door to the shack and shone her phone's flashlight into the dark. Zoe sat on the dirty wood floor, her hands bound behind her back, but got up and ran to Tiana, tears streaming down her face.

Devon barged into the shack and picked up Zoe. "You're safe now, Zoe."

"What happened in the house, Devon? You're bleeding."

"We need to get out of here." Carrying Zoe, Devon hurried out of the shack.

Tiana ran behind them, unsure what had happened or if they were still in danger. She felt so relieved they'd found Zoe, but she didn't trust Devon and didn't know what he'd done or what he was capable of.

As they turned the corner of the house, red and blue lights swirled down the street. Tires screeched to a halt. People dressed in black appeared from the shadows and surrounded the house.

A loud voice blared through a speaker. "Put your hands up and turn around."

Tiana froze and raised her arms. With the bright lights shining in her face, she couldn't see Devon or Zoe anymore. She turned and shut her eyes to shield them from the blinding lights illuminating the dark street. A semicircle of police had their guns pointed directly at Tiana. "Don't shoot!"

"Put your hands behind your head and drop to your knees," the cop demanded over the speaker.

Tiana did as he said. Her knees slammed onto the concrete walkway.

The same bullhorn blared again. "Step away from the girl."

"I'm Devon Price. Zoe's my daughter. I saved her. The man in the house kidnapped my daughter and tried to kill me."

A police officer ran to Zoe, covered her with a blanket, then rushed her into a van waiting on the curb. Two of the officers surrounded Devon. "Devon Price, you're under arrest for conspiracy to kidnap a minor." They handcuffed him.

"What the hell? I'm Zoe's father. What are you talking about?" Devon screamed. The agents marched him past Tiana. "Tiana, did you call them on me? I haven't done anything! It's her husband, Jaylen Williams. He planned the whole thing."

Tiana coughed as smoke suffocated her. She turned her head as the agents forced Devon into the back of a squad car. She had no idea what he had or hadn't done and didn't care in that moment. Zoe was safe.

After patting Tiana down, the officer twisted her arms behind her back and clamped handcuffs on her wrists. "Tiana Williams, you're under arrest. Anything you say or do can be held against you in a court of law."

"I had nothing to do with Zoe's kidnapping. I'm her mother. I don't know anything." For the first time in her life, she had a glimpse into what Jay must have experienced.

The officer led her to a squad car and opened the back door. "Watch your head."

"I haven't done anything." She couldn't believe it. "I want to see my daughter."

"Get in the car." The officer glared at her.

Tiana ducked her head and sat down. She jumped when the officer slammed the door. Never in her life had she imagined being arrested and suspected of a crime. She had to make them believe that she hadn't done anything wrong. She'd spent days agonizing over whether she would ever see Zoe alive, but her own actions had gotten in the way of being able to meet her daughter. *What if they lock me up like they did Jay?*

Tiana choked on her tears as they drove to the police station. Terrified, she wanted to believe her name would easily be cleared. But she'd witnessed Jay sentenced to prison for an accident. After suffering decades of brutal abuse, he'd had to face prison for the death of a man who had pointed a gun at him. She'd blamed Jay for how hard their lives had become, but she suddenly empathized with Jay in a new way. If she was allowed to go home to him and Marcus, Tiana had to impart her regret for the way she had treated him.

CHAPTER FIFTY-EIGHT

Jay focused on the road, itching to step on the pedal and accelerate to a hundred miles per hour. He glanced in the rearview mirror, eyeing McDaniel's car trailing him. Jay despised the guy but just a little bit less since McDaniel had gotten approval from Jay's probation officer for the trip to St. Helena. He played over the events from the last days over and over again, wondering if he could have done anything differently that wouldn't have ended with Tiana in danger.

His phone rang with McDaniel's number. Jay's heart pounded. *He must have news.* "Hello?"

"Tiana, Devon, and Zoe have been located."

"Are Tiana and Zoe a'ight? Was Devon arrested?"

"It's more complicated than that. Both Tiana and Devon were taken into police custody. Zoe's under observation at the nearby children's hospital."

"Wait, why Tiana? She ain't done nothing wrong."

"She and Devon are being held under suspicion for staging the kidnapping. A lot of taxpayers' resources have gone into this investigation, and if it turns out they conspired to defraud the public and the police for whatever reason, they'll be facing serious civil penalties as well as criminal charges."

Jay's hatred of McDaniel resurfaced. "You know Tiana didn't do that. She's been working with you the whole time. Even when you told her to leave me. You can't sit back and let them try to frame Tiana for this."

"We'll speak with the St. Helena police when we get there. I have no further information at this time," he said before hanging up.

Jay glared at McDaniel through the rearview mirror. He clenched the steering wheel, trying to force himself to breathe. Though he hadn't spoken to Xavier since the encounter with his mom, Jay dialed him, needing to hear a voice other than his own.

"Jay, how you doin', man?"

Jay filled his brother in on everything that happened and the update McDaniel had provided. "If Tiana goes to jail, it'll be all my fault. I should have stopped her from going with Devon."

"None of this is your fault. You gotta let go of thinking you can save Tiana. You've done everything in your power to protect her and Marcus and clear your name. But she made her choice to take off with Devon. It's on her."

"No, I should've—"

"Stop. Don't you see it's the same situation that happened with Mom? You can support people, but you can't feel responsible for the decisions someone else makes, especially if they choose self-destruction. It wasn't on you to save Mom from Dad, just like you couldn't stop Tiana from risking everything to find Zoe."

Jay focused on the road ahead and the plumes of smoke lining the night sky. "Mom always made excuses for Dad's abuse. She'd say that's all he knew because he'd grown up in a house where Grandpa did the same thing. That it was common for men to be physical back in the day. Or that life in America already beat a Black man down hard enough, so she just wanted to love Dad like no one else did. I felt completely helpless whenever he hurt her. I just couldn't act like it wasn't happening. How could I have loved Mom if I didn't try to protect her?"

"You can't make someone love themself. Dad had beaten her down to the point that she didn't think she had a self left to love. I'm mad at what Mom tolerated and allowed us to go through. But I can understand how she felt because I loved Dad, too, in spite of how he treated us. I have a lot of memories of the good times with him, not just the bad.

"Remember how whenever Dad would hit Mom, the next day, he'd bring her flowers and dinner from her favorite Italian restaurant so she wouldn't have to cook? It was playbook abusive behavior. I've made peace with the fact that you can love someone and hate them at the same time. I wish Mom'd just left Dad and you hadn't gone to prison. I miss him no matter how crazy that sounds. But we're all free now. I hope Dad's free from his demons too. Tiana's innocent. Her dad will make sure that's proven."

"You can't be so sure. It didn't make no difference in my case." The indignation from the time Jay served for an accident threatened to overcome him.

"I know, man. But thank God your name is cleared in Zoe's kidnapping. You got your freedom and your future. Marcus and Tiana both need you to stay strong. But that starts with you not beating yourself up over her mistake. You hear me?"

As the oldest son in a dysfunctional family, Jay had always felt an overwhelming responsibility to help Xavier and his mom and try to keep them safe. He exhaled, trying to let it go. "You're right. My only job is to be there for Tiana like she was there for me. Look, I'm almost at the police station. I'll call you back when I have news."

"You do that. Peace."

Jay hung up the phone and exited the freeway, McDaniel following close behind. He couldn't wait another minute to see Tiana. He just hoped he'd be able to.

CHAPTER FIFTY-NINE

Due to the fire, the nearby Napa police station had been evacuated, and it took longer to arrive at the St. Helena Police Department, a town over. Tiana had been dumped in an interrogation room over an hour ago. Her attempts to stop herself from crying failed. Tears steadily streamed down her face. She wanted to meet Zoe so badly, to wrap her arms around her daughter and tell Zoe how loved she was. *What if I won't be allowed to for a long time? Or ever?*

A tall brunette with broad shoulders finally entered the room. "I'm Detective Samantha Collins. I'm Kent McDaniel's counterpart here in St. Helena." She unlocked Tiana's handcuffs.

Tiana rubbed her wrists, wiped the tears from her eyes, and straightened in the chair. "Thank you."

"So take me through today. Kent said you and Devon were at the police station in San Jose. Then you two disappeared. Next thing you know, you two are on your way to Napa." Collins opened a notebook and took out a pen. "What happened?"

Tiana recounted everything that had happened with Devon. As she talked, she couldn't believe her stupidity. "I never should have agreed to his plan. But I swear, I had no idea what was going on. I only wanted to rescue my daughter."

Collins put her pen down and leaned toward Tiana. "Did you know where Zoe was being held?"

"Absolutely not." Tiana's eyes pleaded with the woman.

After writing in her notebook, Collins stared intently at Tiana. "Did you know that Devon had met with Ronnie Coleman?"

She rested her cheek on her palm. "No. I had no idea. I mean, Jay texted me that. Is it true?"

Collins didn't answer. She wrote more in her notebook. "Last question. Did you have anything to do with Zoe's kidnapping?"

Tiana threw her hands up. "No. Why would I? I knew nothing about my daughter's whereabouts before all this. I had no idea she was living with Josephine in Oakland. I certainly couldn't have planned to kidnap her."

"That's all the questions I have for now. Sit tight." Collins stood and left the room.

Tiana's heart raced. Since the detective had worn absolutely no hint of expression on her face during the questioning, Tiana couldn't tell whether she believed a single word she'd said or not. She clasped her hands and closed her eyes. *Please, God. Help me get out of this.*

CHAPTER SIXTY

Jay knocked on the door then opened it. Tiana sat at the table, her head buried in her arms. He tapped her shoulder. "Tiana."

Her eyes met his. She jumped up and wrapped her arms around him. "Oh my God! What are you doing here? I'm so happy to see you. I'm sorry for everything."

Jay squeezed her and kissed her forehead. He'd feared he would never have the opportunity to embrace her again. Now he didn't want to ever let her go. "Don't apologize. You were in an impossible situation."

She gasped. "How'd you get here? It's too far for you."

"It's okay. I drove him here with permission from his PO." McDaniel walked into the room and stood next to the table. "Leaving like that was not only reckless but extremely dangerous, Mrs. Williams. You're lucky you and Zoe are alive."

"It was a terrible mistake. I have no idea why I was so stupid." Several tears slipped down her cheek.

Jay brushed the tears away. "What matters is you're safe. And Zoe's found."

McDaniel pulled out a chair. "Let's sit?"

Jay sat, wary of McDaniel's tone. He'd overheard McDaniel speaking with another officer, who'd considered Tiana a possible suspect before they'd left San Jose. Once they arrived at the St. Helena Police Department, McDaniel had spoken with a female detective for at least half an hour while Jay waited. He hoped they didn't plan to press charges against her. "When is Tiana free to go?"

Tiana sat next to Jay and held his hand. "I've told Detective Collins that I had absolutely nothing to do with Zoe's kidnapping. I made a mistake going with Devon. I swear, I had no idea where we were going. I thought it was the best thing to do to find Zoe. I was desperate."

"What happened to Devon? I'm sure he'll tell you Tiana had nothing to do with any of it. Have you questioned him? You sure spent a lot of time questioning me." Jay still couldn't believe he hadn't gotten so much as an apology after the way he'd been treated.

"We have questioned Devon. And Ronnie Coleman and—"

Tiana squeezed Jay's hand. "What happened to Ronnie? I saw the blood on Devon's shirt, so..."

"Devon shot Ronnie Coleman. But Coleman survived and confessed to kidnapping Zoe. He said Devon paid him one hundred twenty-five thousand dollars to kidnap Zoe and promised to pay him another hundred twenty-five thousand when he returned Zoe to him, untouched and unharmed. Apparently, Coleman had someone who works for him follow you around and make the calls and leave the notes." McDaniel briefly glanced at Jay.

"What did Devon say?" Jay wished he could have witnessed Devon's interrogation.

"Look, this is an ongoing investigation, so what I say needs to stay in this room. Tiana, since you're Zoe's mom, you have a right to know the truth. Devon's still livid with Martin. After Devon relocated to the Bay Area, he ran across Martin, Josephine, and Zoe in Oakland. Devon had hired a private investigator to look into them under the table. That private investigator was Ronnie. Ronnie discovered Zoe's birthdate was the same as the daughter who had been given up for adoption. Devon swears he had no idea of Ronnie's past and claims he had nothing to do with Ronnie kidnapping Zoe."

"Can Devon get away with this? I'm sure he'll hire the best lawyers." Tiana's cheeks turned bright red.

McDaniel shook his head. "I believe Devon when he says he didn't know who Ronnie really was or anything about his criminal past. But Ronnie's confession will hold. My theory is that when I told Devon about Ronnie's past—especially that he is a convicted child molester—and with the fire out of control near the house, Devon must have decided to end the charade. I've become convinced he knew exactly where Zoe was the whole time. I'm sure a jury will believe that too."

Jay clenched his fists, trying to contain his wrath. "That sick bastard did it. All that money got to his head. He thought he could just buy his way back into Tiana's and Zoe's lives while trying to put me behind bars."

"Look, both Ronnie and Devon said Tiana had nothing to do with it. We're not going to press charges against you, Tiana. When the doctor and social worker are finished with Zoe, you'll be able to see her. She's at the children's hospital." McDaniel tapped the table. "I'll have Detective Collins brief you on Zoe's condition."

Tiana's eyes lit up. "How is she?"

McDaniel stood. "As you can imagine, Zoe's been through a lot. Not to mention, she's about to learn that her mom and dad aren't who she thinks they are."

Jay sucked in a breath. He'd been so relieved that Tiana and Zoe were safe, but the only life Zoe had known for the past ten years was about to be turned upside down. "Poor girl."

Tiana's forehead wrinkled with worry. "Are my dad and Josephine at the hospital?"

"No. They're here at the police station. You're Zoe's legal guardian, so it's your call whether you inform them of her location at the hospital. They're aware of that. Not happy, but aware. Detective Collins will be in shortly." McDaniel left the room.

Jay rubbed Tiana's back. "How are you holding up?"

"I just can't believe any of it. I want to see Zoe and have her come home with us. But it will be even more devastating to rip her from the only parents she's known. Josephine doesn't have much longer to live. In spite of how I feel about them, I think she has to be there when I meet Zoe. I have my lifetime ahead of me to establish a relationship with Zoe as her mother. I don't want to cause her any more trauma right now."

Jay kissed Tiana on the cheek. Her generous heart and spirit never ceased to amaze him. "You're absolutely right. I'm behind whatever you wanna do."

"I'm going to call my dad. I'll tell him and Josephine to meet us at the hospital." Tiana took out her phone and dialed.

Jay texted quick updates to Xavier and Harker. He owed so much to Harker for helping him through the day. If Harker hadn't shown up at Jay's apartment that morning, Jay would be halfway to another state, with a one-way ticket back to prison if caught. When he got back to Silicon Valley, Jay would find the courage to walk back into the church and thank God.

CHAPTER SIXTY-ONE

Tiana's heart raced as she and Jay sat in the children's hospital's waiting room. When her dad and Josephine walked through the automatic door, Tiana stood and met them. "The doctors are ready for us."

Josephine grabbed both of Tiana's hands. "God bless you, Tiana. Thank you for calling us." Tears pooled in her eyes.

Tiana suppressed her anger. It wouldn't serve her anymore. "I want to do what's best for Zoe. We'll say I'm a relative who hasn't seen her since she was a baby, but I love her very much and will be in her life from now on. We can explain the truth when we think she's ready to handle it."

"You're doing the right thing, Tiana." Her dad patted her on the back.

Tiana shrugged off his hand. "I don't need your approval."

Josephine seemed to sense Tiana's discomfort. "There are two guest rooms at my house. "Both of you"—she nodded to Jay—"and Marcus are welcome to stay there any time until Zoe's ready to spend time at your place."

"I'll let them know we're all here and ready to see Zoe." Jay headed to the nurse's station.

Tiana followed him there. "This is so hard after everything my dad's done."

He pulled her into a tight hug. "You're being the bigger person. That's never easy. It'll all straighten itself out. We'll get through this."

A doctor with Winne the Pooh cartoon characters on her coat came to speak with them. "Tiana Williams?"

"Yes, that's me." Tiana gestured for Josephine and her dad to join them.

"I'm Dr. Patricia Walsh. Let's have a quick talk." The doctor opened the doors, and they all walked into the hospital's main area. Dr. Walsh stopped and addressed the group. "Zoe's checked out very well. It does not appear that she was physically or sexually abused, but she's definitely in shock. The child psychiatrist is going to talk to you about the best way to approach her psychological trauma. We'll keep her overnight for evaluation. But Zoe just really wants to see her mom right now. I've been briefed on the situation. But Mrs. Williams, it's your call."

Tiana grabbed Josephine's hand. "We're both here. We'll go in."

"Great. Gentlemen, there's a waiting room with a couple vending machines and coffee down the hall to the right. Why don't you wait there?" Dr. Walsh had a pleasant but firm smile on her face.

Tiana's dad opened his mouth as if to speak then closed it. He squeezed Josephine's shoulder. "Tell Zoe I'm here and I love her." He marched down the hall.

Jay rolled his eyes. "I'll be waiting, Ti." He strolled away like a huge weight had been lifted off his shoulders, freeing him to walk easier.

Too many emotions swirled inside of Tiana in anticipation of meeting Zoe. Dr. Walsh knocked before opening the door and popping her head in. "Hi, Zoe. Look who's here to see you."

Zoe sat on a hospital bed, wearing a white gown with animal characters on it. She seemed completely frazzled, as if she'd just watched a horror film. But up close, Zoe appeared even more beautiful in person than all the pictures Tiana had seen. The way Zoe favored Tiana made her seem so familiar.

Josephine ran to her, sobs racking her body. "My poor baby." She consumed Zoe in a tight hug, and Zoe cried along with her.

Tiana stood awkwardly in the corner. The maternal side of her wanted to reach out to Zoe, but she forced herself not to, acknowledging herself as a complete stranger to her daughter.

When Josephine let go of Zoe, she glanced at Tiana. "Zoe, I want you to meet Tiana. She's..."

Zoe's gaze travelled to Tiana. "My mom." Her small palm waved at Tiana. "The news was on the TV the whole time I was kidnapped."

Tiana stopped the tears rising in her. She didn't want Zoe to link tears and sadness with their first time they officially met. "Can I give you a hug?"

Zoe looked at Josephine then back at Tiana. She nodded.

Tiana walked to Zoe and embraced her thin frame. A tear slipped down Tiana's face. She wiped it away quickly. "I know everything probably feels scary and confusing. But I want you to know that we're only going to do what makes you comfortable, okay?"

Zoe looked at Josephine, her eyebrows raised in a question.

Tiana tapped Zoe's hand. "When you leave, you'll still go home. But I'm going to stay there, too, for a while. And I have a really nice husband, Jay. And you have a little brother named Marky."

A tiny smile crept onto Zoe's face. "A baby brother?"

Tiana smiled back at her. "What do you think about that?"

Zoe shrugged her bony shoulders. "Good."

Josephine kissed her face. "We love you so much, Zoe. I'm so sorry for all you went through. But I promise you're safe now." Tears crawled down her face.

"Don't cry, Mommy." Zoe briefly closed her eyes.

Josephine wiped her face. "Everybody at church and I prayed so hard for you to come back home."

"I prayed too, Mommy," Zoe whispered.

Tiana couldn't stop the tears. Zoe's faith and love for Josephine touched Tiana's heart. "I can't wait for us to get to know each other, Zoe. You look tired, sweetie. Why don't you sleep? We'll be here the whole time."

"'Kay." Zoe closed her eyes again.

"I'll be right back. I'm going to tell Jay he should probably head home to pick up Marcus," Tiana whispered to Josephine.

"Go ahead. I'm staying put." Josephine pulled a chair over to Zoe's bed then sat and held Zoe's hand.

Tiana left the room and found Jay.

Exhaustion was etched on his face. "How'd it go? How is Zoe?"

Tiana's heart had melted. It amazed her she could love Zoe so immensely, though they'd only spent minutes together. "She's tired and scared. But she said the news was on the whole time where Ronnie held her captive, so she knows I'm her mom. I told her about you and Marcus. I can't wait for you and him to meet her. I was just remembering our conversation the night we learned Zoe had been kidnapped."

Jay raised his eyebrows. "So much has gone down since then. Remind me what we talked about?"

Tiana smiled. "You said maybe Marcus needs a brother or sister."

Jay hugged Tiana and whispered in her ear. "I couldn't ask for a better family. I'm so blessed to have you, Tiana. I already love Zoe like she was mine."

Tiana pulled back and looked into his eyes. "I'm sorry for how I've treated you. You've endured so much in your life. I never fully understood that. I'll never take you for granted again. I love you."

Jay held her in his arms and spoke into her ear. "That means a lot. I know we can get through anything together. It's a crazy life, but I wouldn't want to share it with anyone else. When Zoe's ready, I want all of us to go to that church in Santa Clara. I prayed to God that everything would be straightened out. For the first time, I feel God heard and answered me."

Tiana agreed completely. Though it'd taken a hell of a struggle, the missing pieces of her heart had come together. With Jay, Marcus, and Zoe, Tiana's life had become complete.

Acknowledgments

I would like to thank God for the blessing it has been to write and publish three novels. To my husband, Israel, thank you for always supporting me and all my endeavors. Alex, Gabrielle, Derrick, and BJ, you four are the best kids a mom could ask for. Thank you for keeping me on my toes. And thank you to my entire extended family who will probably never read this.

A special thank-you to Armando DePina, who shared his invaluable experiences as a person who was formerly incarcerated and later became a Parent Advocate who helped others with a history of incarceration and/or addiction navigate reentry and parenting their children. You are an inspiration, and many lives have been transformed because of your work and witness.

Many writer friends in various critique groups have provided their input on this book, and I'm thankful for their time and helpful critiques.

Thank you to Red Adept Publishing for allowing me to tell my stories, my editors, Jessica Anderegg and Kate Birdsall, and my mentor, Erica Lucke Dean.

About the Author

Alessandra Harris doesn't shy away from controversial topics, and writes novels that reflect the diversity of her world. She loves stories that break your heart but leave you smiling at the end, so that's exactly what she writes: made-up stories about almost-real people. She lives in the San Francisco Bay Area with her husband and four children, and is the organizer of San Jose Novel Writers, a group of eclectic writers offering fellowship, support and tips on all forms of writing. Alessandra's debut novel, Blaming the Wind, was published by Red Adept Publishing in 2016, followed by Everything She Lost in 2018, and Last Place Seen in 2022. Visit Alessandra at alessandraharris.net/ or Twitter @AlessandraH17.

Read more at alessandraharris.net.

About the Publisher

Dear Reader,

We hope you enjoyed this book. Please consider leaving a review on your favorite book site.

Visit https://RedAdeptPublishing.com to see our entire catalogue.

Check out our app for short stories, articles, and interviews. You'll also be notified of future releases and special sales.

Made in United States
Troutdale, OR
03/05/2024